I0542465

BOOK THREE
OF THE
ST. EDMUNDSBURY
MYSTERIES

BISHOP'S PRIDE

ANNE-MARIE AMIEL

HEADLIGHT FLUID PRESS

Editing: Elizabeth Patrick, Headlight Fluid Press

Cover: Cathy Helms, Avalon Graphics LLC

Formatting: Victoria Ellis, Cruel Ink Editing + Design

FIRST EDITION

Printed in the United States of America

ISBN: 978-1-956992-11-3

www.annemarieamiel.com

Dedicated to Agnes Irene Winterman, whose immortal words on the gracefulness of cows have helped make her memory one of smiles

ACKNOWLEDGMENTS

First of all, I wish to acknowledge the amazing work done by the embroiderers of Alderney, one of the Channel Islands of England. To commemorate the 950th anniversary of the Norman Conquest, they determined to embroider a panel faithful to what is thought to be the original ending of the Bayeux Tapestry. Their outstanding work inspired this book, and to them many thanks are due.

I cannot, of course, fail to acknowledge my editor Libby Patrick, who tirelessly attempts to keep me up to date with the latest changes in grammatical styling.

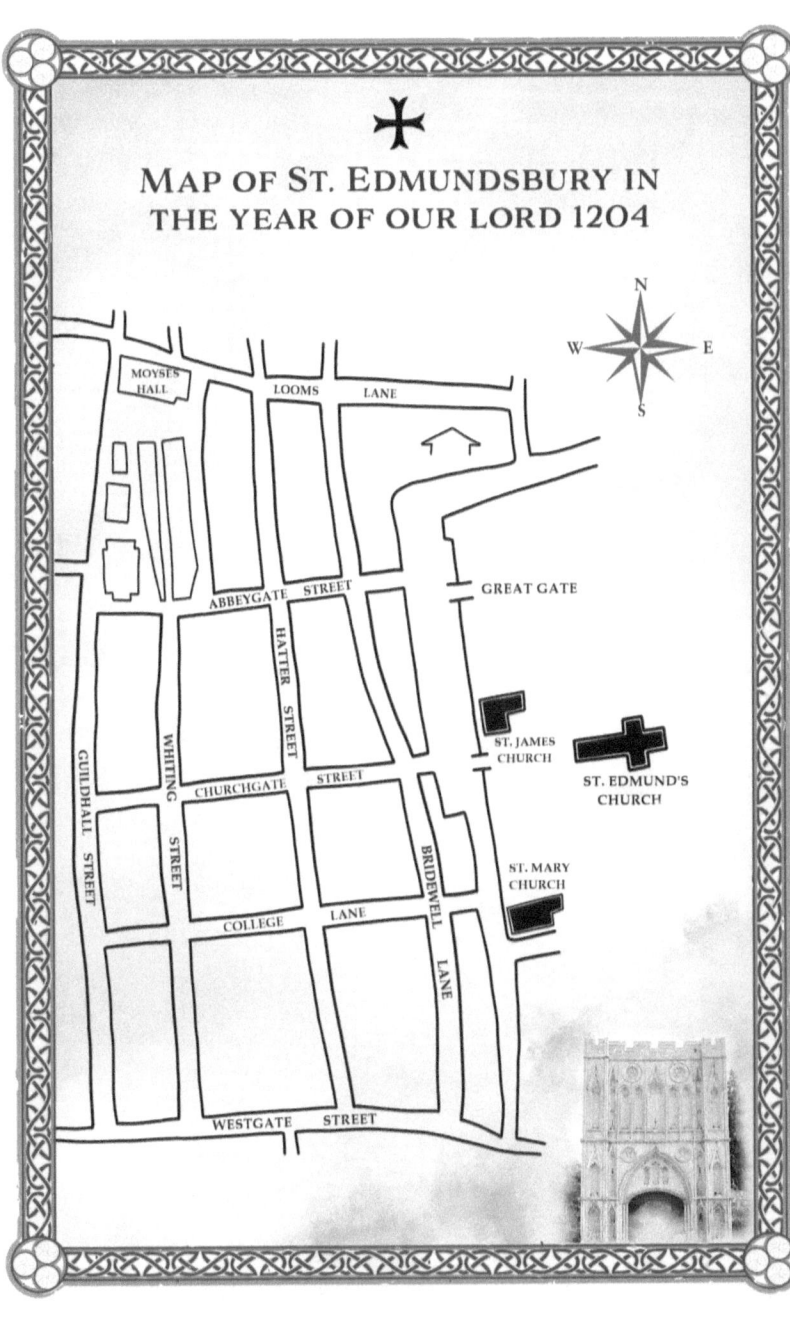

MAP OF ST. EDMUNDSBURY IN THE YEAR OF OUR LORD 1204

THE ABBEY OF ST. EDMUNDSBURY
1204

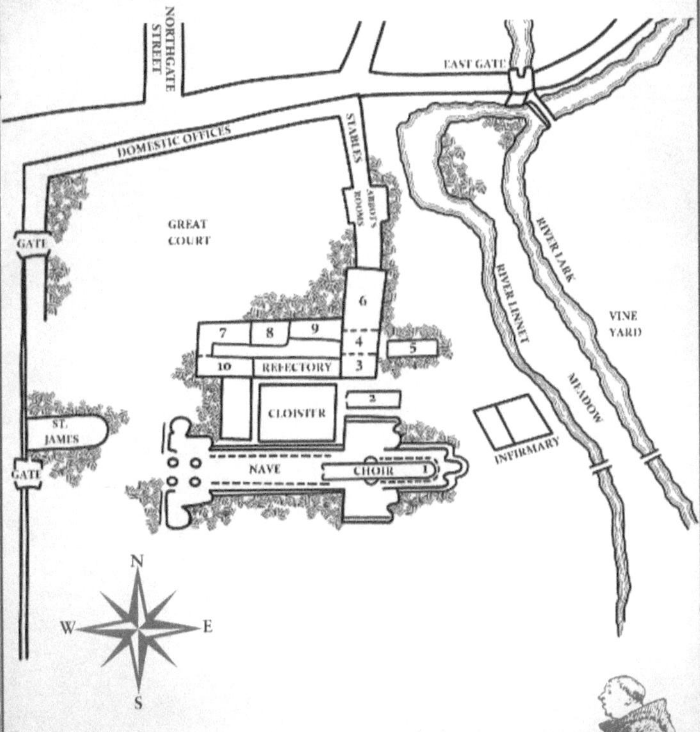

NORTHGATE STREET

EAST GATE

DOMESTIC OFFICES

STABLES

ABBOT'S ROOMS

GATE

GREAT COURT

RIVER LARK

RIVER LINNET

VINE YARD

6

7 8 9

4

5

MEADOW

10 REFECTORY

3

ST. JAMES

2

CLOISTER

GATE

NAVE CHOIR 1

INFIRMARY

N
W   E
S

1. ST. EDMUND'S SHRINE   6. CHAMBERLANE'S DEPT.
2. CHAPTER HOUSE   7. CELLARER
3. WARMING-HOUSE   8. KITCHEN
4. PITTANCERY   9. LARDER
5. LAVATORIES   10. GUEST MASTER

HISTORICAL NOTE

The Abbey and town of Bury St. Edmunds are real, and Abbot Samson, Brother Jocelin, and the reeve really lived. Bury St. Edmunds was founded about 600 years before the time of this story and was originally called Beodericsworth.

Bury is still a market town. The abbey, which Abbot Samson thought would stand forever, was destroyed in the time of King Henry VIII. Little remains today except for ruins. You can see the ruins if you pay a visit to the Abbey Gardens, which lie behind the only gate of the abbey still standing. The streets along which the characters in this book walk are also still there, as is the market square (which still functions as an open-air market on certain days of the week).

Much of what we know about Bury St. Edmunds at the beginning of the 13th century comes from the journal of a monk named Jocelin of Brakelond, who recorded the daily events in the area from 1173-1202. Brother Jocelin was the Guest Master of the abbey for periods of time during his life, and I have made him so in this story, although we do not know anything of his history after the end of his chronicle in 1202.

The abbey itself survived until the time of Henry VIII. The Dissolution of the Monasteries was a policy enacted by Henry VIII in 1536, after he separated from the Roman Catholic church, to confiscate the lands and wealth of all the monasteries and abbeys in England. St. Edmundsbury survived for another three years, but was destroyed in 1539. Today, the ruins of the abbey are a part of a public park in Bury St. Edmunds.

Bishop Odo was a half-brother to William the Conqueror. He was one of the most powerful men in the kingdom until his fall from grace in 1082 when he participated in a revolt against the king. He was responsible for the building of the cathedral at Bayeux and is thought to be the man who commissioned the Bayeux Tapestry. He was never deprived of his title of Bishop of Bayeux, and he died in Sicily in 1097 while on crusade.

The Bayeux Tapestry technically is an embroidery, not a tapestry since it does not utilize tapestry weave stitches. It is worked in wools on linen cloth and is believed to have been made in England. Most scholars believe it to have been made by women embroiderers, probably in the Canterbury area. Some modern writers have suggested that the knowledge of warfare, ship-building, and construction is so evident that the work must have been carried out by a team of men, some of whom may have been warriors, but all of whom were probably not monks. This is not as strange as it may seem, because there are examples of secular men illuminating manuscripts of the period, perhaps the most famous being the *Bury Bible of St. Edmunds*, which was illustrated by a secular artist and metalworker employed by the abbey in the 1130s.

While it is not known for sure who embroidered the Bayeux Tapestry I have taken the liberty of including supervision of the embroidery team by a skilled woman artisan.

The end of the tapestry was lost at some unknown time in its history. In 2013, stitchers from the Island of Alderney in the Channel Islands completed a possible finale to the story of William's conquest of England. Most commentators on the original tapestry believe that the culmination of the story is the coronation of William at Westminster Abbey, and this is indeed what is depicted in the Alderney panel. My story incorporates details taken from this work.

The quotes at the beginning of each chapter are translations of the Latin captions found on the Bayeux Tapestry.

GLOSSARY OF
MEDIEVAL TERMS

Some words and descriptions that were in common use in the early 13th century may not be known to you. They include:

Addlepate: The concept of an addlepate comes from the Middle English "adel eye," which was an egg that had gone bad. Eventually a comparison was drawn between the lack of soundness of the egg and the lack of soundness of a bad head (or pate).

Bake Mete: For hundreds of years, the only container for cooking over a fire or in a fire oven was a thick crust made of flour and water. Using crusts several inches thick kept in meat juices but also preserved the contents by excluding air. The crusts were called coffins, and the dishes made using such crusts were often called Bake Metes.

Cockalorum: In medieval times, this was a word used to describe a boastful and self-important man.

Coffin: In the 12th century, a coffin was a thick, inedible pastry made from flour, water, and sometimes fat. It was used to keep the air away from the contents of the pie so that it would not go rancid as quickly. In the 13th century, edible pastry started to become more common.

Great Survey: When one of the characters in this story mentions the "great survey" carried out by William the Conqueror, he is referencing the Domesday Book, which was a survey of all towns, estates and assets held in England twenty years after the Norman conquest.

Jobbernowl: Instead of calling someone an idiot or a fool, people in medieval times would use the word jobbernowl.

Jongleur: The medieval name for a traveling entertainer, jongleurs earned their living juggling, singing, reciting tales and doing acrobatics.

Journeyman: Once a craftsman had completed his apprenticeship, he would either be employed as a worker by another or he would travel for up to three years, earning his living as he went. The increase in his knowledge base would most often then lead the artisan to open his own business.

Liberty: The Liberty of St. Edmund was the term for all the land under the control of the Abbot. He effectively stood in the king's shoes, levying taxes and acting as the judge in civil and criminal cases.

Mystery and Miracle Plays: Although these two terms are often used interchangeably there was a difference in these medieval art forms. Mystery plays presented Bible stories, often in tableau form, whereas miracle plays told of the lives and actions of saints.

Reeve: In most towns, the Reeve was the man who did the police work for the nobleman appointed Sheriff of the whole district. In Bury St. Edmunds though, there was no civilian sheriff, and the Reeve had less power. He reported directly to the officials at the Abbey.

Serf: Serfs were the poorest of the peasant classes in medieval times. They performed mostly agricultural labor and were considered a part of the land. If the land was sold, the serfs were passed along to the new owner.

Small Ale: This drink, which contained very little alcohol, was also known as small beer. Often more like porridge than pure liquid, it was commonly drunk in the Middle Ages, because the water supply was often polluted, and true beers and wines were too expensive for most people to drink on a daily basis.

South Sea: This was the name given to the English Channel in Anglo-Saxon times, and it remained so until later in the Middle Ages.

Treasure Trove: The ancient law of Treasure Trove in England was thought to date back to the time of Edward the Confessor. Under common law, any gold or silver which had been deliberately hidden, and which was later found, belonged to the person who had hidden it or their descendants as long as no other person could prove it was, in fact, theirs. To be considered treasure trove, however, the find had to consist of more than 50% gold or silver.

Villein: Medieval society was very hierarchical. Locally, the lord of the manor was top of the heap. Bottom of the heap was the serf. A villein was not exactly free, but he had more rights than did the serf. A villein was a tenant farmer who was subject to the lord's will. He owed dues and services in exchange for the land he was permitted to farm.

CHAPTER ONE

Where Harold, duke of the English, and his knights ride to Bosham Church

T*HUNK!*

The sound wrenched Bron out of his musings. "Stay," he instructed the oxen he was leading down the field. "Stay."

Obediently, the oxen halted, and Bron walked back to the plough. Bending down, he could see no damage to the plough itself. God be praised, he thought to himself. I don't need any more trouble than I already have. The habitually sour expression on his sallow face eased not at all as he resettled his cap over his lank black hair.

Walking around behind the plough he looked for the source of the sound. It was not hard to find.

Only a couple of feet behind the plough, Bron

spied a depression in the earth where the plough had disturbed the ground. A piece of wood poked out of the soil.

What idiot threw some wood into the middle of the field? Bron thought angrily, bending over to pick it up. If the plough had been damaged, Cuin would have made my life a misery. "Why were you not paying better attention?" Bron mimicked his brother. "Dreaming again, were you? Cannot you do anything properly?"

Snorting, Bron pulled on the piece of wood, but it refused to come out of the ground. Bron realized that it was attached to something. He got down on his hands and knees and dug around the old wood with his gnarled hands.

The shard of wood was attached to a piece of iron. As he dug his fingers into the earth, Bron slowly realized that what he had found was an old chest. The plough had pulled the nailheads out of a few of the planks in the side, but otherwise it seemed to be in fairly good condition.

Excited now, Bron frantically dug further and finally pulled the chest out of the soil. Placing it carefully on the ground, the serf knelt in front of it and dusted the worst of the dirt off the old box. Sitting back on his haunches, he inspected this unexpected find.

It is not very large, Bron thought. Scarce the length of my arm and less than that in width. It is heavy, but not so heavy I cannot carry it away. There is no lock on it either. Can there be anything worth saving if there be no lock?

Carefully, Bron reached out and gave a tentative pull on the latch of the chest. Long years underground had sealed the lid to the body of the cedar box, and it took some time and effort to open it without doing too much damage.

Finally, the lid groaned open and Bron peered into the interior of his discovery.

"All that work for nothing," he said out loud in a disgusted tone. All he could see was dirty fabric. No gold, no silver, no jewels.

Who buries a chest in a field without it having something valuable inside? he thought. His eyes shifting left and right to make sure he was not being watched, the serf put his hand in the chest and pulled at the cloth. Mayhap there is something more worth the effort wrapped within, he said to himself.

The cloth was linen; he could tell that much. But it seemed there was nothing wrapped up in the heavy folds. It seemed to be one long piece of fabric folded over on itself.

Angry at having wasted so much time on this thankless task, and only too aware that he had to finish ploughing the field before dusk, Bron tugged on the length of fabric and threw it onto the ground. As he did so, he saw a flash of color highlighted by the afternoon sun. Reaching out for the cloth, he looked at the edge that had been turned inside out by the force of his throw.

Gold wool. That was what had caught his eye. Eagerly, Bron turned over more of the cloth and saw that it was embroidered all down the length of the linen. The serf knew nothing of art and embroidery, but to his eyes it seemed that this was a particularly fine piece of work. Men and horses and battles told a tale of valor, but for the life of him, Bron could not understand why anyone would bury such a thing in a field.

For a moment, Bron just looked at the linen in his hands. Then, nodding his head decisively, he quickly folded the fabric back into the chest, closed the lid, and stood back up. He carried the chest to the edge of the field and then walked back to the oxen and returned to the ploughing that was his task for the day.

"You cannot keep hold of it," said Cuin that evening, staring at the cloth laid out on the table. "It was found on our master's land, and therefore it belongs to our master."

Cuin looked much like his brother, except for the fact that his face almost always bore the expression of a contented man. He was a short, stocky man with black hair and deep brown eyes.

"The master knows nothing of it," said Bron

sharply. "What will it hurt him if we get some pennies for it?"

"Bron, you cannot do that," gasped his sister-in-law. "That would make thieves of us."

Ardith was the same height as her husband but thin and wiry. All three of them had grown up in the same community, and both brothers had loved her from the time she was but five years old. Her light brown hair and hazel eyes, coupled with her musical laugh and bright energy, had attracted many admirers. That she had chosen Cuin over all others had disappointed Bron more acutely than he could ever say.

That the three of them had perforce to live in the same house was almost more than Bron could bear. He had asked their lord for a holding of his own, but Sir Roger FitzGilbert had said that Cuin, as the older brother, had a greater claim to work their father's holding after he died. There was no other landfor Bron.

"How are we thieves?" Bron asked angrily. "Was not our whole country stolen from its rightful owners by these Normans? For all we know, this chest was buried by the Saxon owner of this property. Why should the usurper profit from my uncovering it?"

"These are old arguments," Cuin said, sighing. "It is a long time since our ancestors fought the Normans and the world changed. We have never known anything other than the life we now have, and there is nothing to be gained by looking to the past."

"That is all very well for you to say," spat Bron, his

face turning dark and his fists pumping the air. "You have our father's holding from the lord and hopes of your son being granted it when you die."

Turning to Ardith, Bron continued: "Truth it is that you also won the wife every man in the village coveted."

Ardith blushed and put her hands to her face as if to cover the rosy flush. "Hush, Bron," she said. "So much anger is not good for you. Certain it is that you are loved and valued in this household."

Bron scowled so fiercely that Ardith took a step backward.

Seeing that Bron was working himself up into a fury, Cuin put a hand on his brother's arm. "Come," he said. "Sit with me and we will talk about it. Ardith will fetch us some ale to slake our thirst while we talk." Cuin cocked an eyebrow at Ardith who, nodding in response, moved away to fetch the drink.

Bron wrenched his arm out of Cuin's grasp. "What is there to talk about?" he shouted into his brother's face. "You have everything I ever wanted. I have nothing, and there is no hope of that changing in the future."

The jealousy was clear, even to a man such as Cuin who was plain-speaking but not a deep thinker.

Sitting down on a stool, he gestured to Bron to do the same. Bron glared at him for a moment and then, letting his breath out in a whoosh, he unclenched his fists and sat down.

"Now that be better," said Ardith, coming into the

room with a pitcher and two tankards. "You do frighten me so, Bron, when you become this angry. I am sure it is not good for you." She laid a quick hand on his shoulder, smiled at the two brothers, and left to see to the chickens.

"So Bron," his brother began, "I am sure you must see that we cannot keep this chest or what lies within. Sir Roger, as the lord of this manor, does own the land and all that is found there. We must take this to Sir Roger." Cuin smiled at his brother and took a long pull at his ale, confident that Bron would see the sense of what he said.

Bron's color began to rise again, and the tightness of his lips and blazing of his eyes expressed more clearly than any words the strength of his true opinion of this viewpoint. This time, however, he kept his own council and said nothing out loud.

If you believe so, he thought to himself, then I will say no more. What I do will be for myself alone. I have been alone almost my whole life. It is my fate to be so, at least for now. Mayhap things will change and then I can be a man of substance, not one without hope.

Cuin chatted on happily as Bron sat in silence, drinking and refilling his tankard with a steely expression on his face.

"And so," Cuin said after some minutes, "I do believe that we can take a short leave from our labors tomorrow and make our way to our master's manor. What think you, brother?"

"Your words are those of a wise man," Bron responded grumpily..

With that, the two men rose and went to their beds.

CHAPTER TWO

*Here Harold sailed by sea and with sails filled with
wind came to the land of Count Wido*

"**H**E IS GONE, AND SO IS THE CHEST!"
Cuin ran into the house waving his
arms, panting slightly from exertion.

Ardith, alarmed, looked up from her mending.
"Ow," she said and sucked the finger she had just
stabbed with the needle . "You startled me, Cuin."

"Your pardon," Cuin said contritely. "I was just so
shocked when I realized Bron was nowhere to be
found. He has run away, Ardith, and he has taken that
chest he found with him."

Ardith, ever one to look for the best solution to a
problem, thought for a moment.

"Mayhap he has taken it to Lord Roger already,"
she suggested.

"I thought of that," said Cuin, sitting down on a

stool to regain his breath and his composure. "I started to walk in the direction of the manor, but I met John the barrel maker as I crossed the stream and he asked me where Bron was going in such a hurry."

Cuin took a deep breath before continuing. "I asked him where he had seen Bron, and he said he had seen him in the distance going across the fields to the north."

"But Lord Roger's manor is to the east," said Ardith, becoming a little worried herself.

"Yes," said Cuin. "I know not whether to go after Bron and persuade him that what he is doing is dangerous and can only lead to his ruin or whether I should keep silent and hope he comes to his senses."

Cuin looked miserably at his feet. Ardith reached out and put her hand on his shoulder.

"You are a good man, husband," she said. "You care not only for me but for your brother. That is one reason I love you." She smiled at Cuin, who looked up and smiled in return.

"And I love you," he said. "Yet I fear that the lord may be unhappy with us as with Bron if we do not tell him what has passed, but I do not wish to bring down upon my brother the punishment that may be meted out to a thief and runaway."

"I share your concern," she said quietly. "What shall we do?"

Cuin thought for a moment longer and then stood, determination written all over his face. "I do not see that we have any choice," he said. "I must go to

Lord Roger and make the best explanation I can for Bron's behavior. Mayhap if I say that Bron drank too much ale last night and his senses have left him for a brief moment, the master will not be as angry."

"It would be truth," said Ardith. "He was very much in his cups afore the end of the night."

Cuin nodded quickly, laid his hand on his wife's cheek and kissed her gently. "I will go now," he said, suiting his actions to his words.

Cuin had gone but a short distance when he saw a cloud of dust coming toward him and heard the sound of hoofs.

"Too late," he breathed. "Lord Roger has heard of the theft and is coming to demand answers."

He stopped and waited for the rider, hanging his head and trying desperately to think of what he could say to avoid suffering any punishment for his brother's betrayal.

As the rider drew closer, he slowed, coming to a stop in front of the serf.

"Good morrow, Cuin," a deep voice intoned.

Cuin looked up and saw Lord Roger FitzGilbert regarding him with a stern yet not unfriendly expression. Even were he not astride a horse, the knight would have towered over the small serf, being nigh on six-and-a-half feet tall, and his strong build added to the general impression of authority that he carried with him. Now his stormy grey eyes looked hard at the man before him.

"Good morrow, my lord," said Cuin faintly.

"I see you are on the road to my manor," said the rider. "Mayhap you were coming to see me?"

"I was, my lord." Cuin was wringing his cap as though it had fallen into the river and become sopping wet.

Sir Roger FitzGilbert smiled thinly. "Perhaps you were coming to tell me of your brother's latest transgression?"

Cuin swallowed and squirmed a little. "Yes, my lord."

"Well?" The knight asked after a pause. "I am waiting."

Cuin looked up at his lord, squinting to see something other than the bright sun which dazzled his eyes.

"My lord," he began tentatively. Taking a deep breath, he began again. "My lord, I know not how you came to know of my brother's discovery and his flight, but I do take my oath that I am on this road now because I was coming to tell you about it."

Sir Roger looked at his serf. This is a man who has faithfully served me, as did his father, thought the knight. When he asked permission to take over his father's holding after the old man's death, I was glad to grant it. Had Bron been the elder son, I would not have been so ready to do so.

"I know you to be an honest man, Cuin," he said finally. He dismounted and, letting his horse nibble at the grass verge, stood in front of the serf. "Speak," he commanded.

So Cuin told Sir Roger how his brother had come

home last night after ploughing a field, and how Bron had shown them a cedar wood chest he had dug up out of the field. Out of filial loyalty, he omitted the more intemperate remarks made by his brother, but his account of the chest and its contents made an impression on the knight.

"This cloth," he said after Cuin had ground to a halt. "Was it richly embroidered with silks of gold?"

Cuin's brow furrowed, and his nose crinkled. "No, my lord," he said after deep thought. "I would not say the design was richly worked. It looked to me as though it was simple linen worked with wools. The cloth was narrow, and it seemed to me it told a tale."

"A tale, say you?" Sir Roger's interest was caught. "Do you know what tale?"

"No, my lord," responded Cuin. "There were men and horses and swords, I do think, but they did not look like anything I have seen afore. We did lay out but half the cloth, and that seemed old to me as well. It were dirty, of course, through having been in the ground. Dirt sifts through even the best wood, as you will know well."

"Of course," said the knight distractedly. "So it was linen worked in wools," he mused.

Turning once again to Cuin, he stated. "The chest was old as well."

"Yes, my lord," Cuin said. "It was good cedar, but the iron clasps were rusted."

Sir Roger, concluding that he had learned all the peasant was able to tell him of Bron's find, returned to the more immediate problem. "I am certain sure you did not encourage your brother to run away with this discovery," he said sternly, his eyes boring into Cuin's. "Your brother has ever been a stubborn, rebellious man, but I have never had cause to doubt you."

Cuin was torn between a desire to protect his brother and his inherent truthfulness.

"No, my lord," he said. "I did not. Last night I thought it was his intention to bring the chest to you today."

"And yet here we are," said Sir Roger. "You and I on the road, talking about how your brother has run away and taken with him a treasure that belongs to me."

Cuin could contain himself no longer. Ignoring the grim countenance of the man before him, he burst out: "My lord," he said. "True it is that my brother has ever had a spirit that seeks adventures beyond this land. But I cannot—I will not—believe that Bron intends harm by his actions."

The knight looked skeptical at this version of the runaway serf's character but said nothing.

"He was in his cups last night, my lord," Cuin went on. "I am sure that, when the drink wears off, he will be as horrified at what he has done as are we."

"Think you he will return?"

"Yes, my lord. That is my hope," Cuin said. Indeed, he thought to himself, I dearly hope that it be the truth. Yet in my heart, I fear Bron may have taken leave of the few senses he has.

Almost as though Sir Roger could read Cuin's mind, he half-laughed. "Cuin," he said. "You are a loyal brother and a good man. In this case, however, I think your assessment of your brother's character is a little too generous. Bron is a man of little sense and great discontent. I fear he has gone too far this time."

"My lord," said Cuin weakly. "What are you going to do?"

"I am going to go after my serf to bring him and his find back. Those who rebel against my authority must be brought to understand that such actions will not be allowed to go unpunished. I will stand on the law of the land and thus will Bron be judged."

The knight's words, spoken with force, betrayed the first sign of anger he had shown in his conversation with Cuin.

"Yes, my lord," was all that the serf could say in response.

"Go back to your work, Cuin," said Sir Roger. "I have no more to say on the matter."

I must be grateful, Cuin thought to himself as he trudged back to his fields, that Sir Roger has not punished my wife and I for Bron's actions. At least, he has not done so yet, he added. Pray God that Bron sees what a mistake he has made and returns to take his punishment before Sir Roger can find him and bring him back in chains. My brother is a foolish man, but I would not like to see him maimed or hanged for that foolishness.

CHAPTER THREE

Here Wido seized Harold and led him to Beaurain and held him there where Harold and Wido confer

"MOTHER, THERE IS A MAN HERE who wishes to speak to you."

"Thank you, Aileen," Anne said as she came to the door, dusting her hands on her apron.

"Good morrow, sir," she said to the small, brown man in front of her. He seemed nervous but returned her greeting courteously.

"Good morrow, mistress. I pray that I am not disturbing your peace."

The man had the dust of long travel on his face and his clothes. He was dressed in the garb of a peasant but in his arms he held a chest that, although obviously old, was just as clearly made by a skilled artisan.

"No, sir. Indeed you are not," she said politely. "We have risen from our noonday table only a few minutes since and there is nothing pressing for me to do. How may I help you today?"

"I have but today arrived in this town," he said. "I did ask some of the merchants who it was I should see to look at an embroidered cloth. Each man that I asked told me I should come to see you, if you be Mistress Arundel. They said you know all that there is to be known about embroidery."

Blushing with pleasure, Anne murmured that people were very kind. "I am she whom you seek," she said.

Aileen smiled to herself. Her mother was a modest woman who would never talk of herself or her skills to anyone, but the townsfolk had the right of it. It was because of her mother's reputation as a skilled needle-woman that Aileen had become proficient enough with her needle to be employed by the abbey.

"I hope that I may not disappoint you, sir," Anne added, standing aside to allow the man in.

"May I know your name, sir?" Anne asked as she led the way to her workroom. Aileen trailed behind them, curiosity overcoming the fact that she had not been invited to join them. Anne, knowing her daughter well, hid a smile behind her hand.

"Your pardon, Mistress," said the peasant. "My name is Bron . . . nart, My name is Bronnart."

"You are welcome, Master Bronnart," said his hostess, thinking that that may be his name, but she rather doubted it.

I doubt that is his name, thought Aileen to herself,

unconsciously echoing her mother's sentiment. The hesitation gave him away.

Her mother, ever the gracious hostess, turned to her daughter.

"Aileen," she said. "We forget our duties as host. Master Bronnart has come a long way and must be tired. I am sure he would be glad of a tankard of ale."

Bron's face lit up. "Indeed I would, Mistress Arundel, and I thank 'ee for the offer."

Aileen ran and fetched the tankard for the man, hoping that nothing much would happen before she could return.

As she re-entered her mother's workroom, she could see that the cedar chest the man had been carrying was now open and Anne was reaching in to take out the fabric within. Gently, her mother lay the folded cloth upon the table and began to unroll it. Aileen, giving the tankard to the grateful man, went over and stood beside her mother, eager to see what had brought this man to their door.

Before them appeared a design worked in wools on fine linen. It seemed to be a tale of soldiers and kings. The story was bordered top and bottom by figures of men and beasts, and there were some words inscribed upon the work.

Aileen could see that one end of the piece was ragged while the other was neatly finished. It would appear that we do not have the first part of this knightly tale, she thought. The stitching on the piece before them appeared to be of good quality, however.

"It is fine work, is it not, mother?" asked Aileen.

Receiving no answer, Aileen looked at her mother and was surprised to see a look of deep concentration on Anne's face. Anne was bent over the part of the design near the end of the fabric and was peering closely at it, a frown upon her face.

Standing up straight again, Anne turned to the stranger, looking at him with an intense gaze. Bron squirmed a little bit under her inspection but said nothing.

"Master Bronnart," she said. "May I ask you how this piece of embroidery came into your possession?" As though she thought herself too forward, she flushed a little and then added, "Please know that I am not simply being curious, but it would help me a great deal if I knew something of the history of this linen."

"I cannot tell you much about it," said Bron carefully. Aileen thought he did not seem offended by the question her mother asked, but rather uncomfortable with the idea of parting with what knowledge he had.

"Is there nothing you can tell me?" asked Anne gently.

"I had it of a trader who had me do some work for him," said Bron, his face set but his eyes darting from side to side as though he feared being overheard. "He said he did not have the coin to pay me but that this had value greater than the amount that was owed."

Bron looked up into Anne's eyes, his face creased into a gap-toothed smile. His smile makes his face look more like a rat grimacing, thought Aileen to herself, raising her hands to cover the giggle that almost escaped from her mouth.

"There is nothing more?" Anne persisted.

"Nay," said Bron, his confidence growing. "I know nothing of its history before that day."

"I see," said Aileen's mother slowly. "Well, I know not for sure how much I can tell you about it. May I ask if that is why you came to my door. Do you wish to know more about the work itself?"

A wheedling expression came over the small man's face. "Aye, Mistress," he said. "I am certain sure it would be good to know."

Bron hesitated a moment, hands wrapped around the now-empty tankard of ale as though white knuckles could help find the words he needed.

"There is more?" Anne asked, smiling at the man.

"Well, Mistress, you see as how this cloth was payment for my work," said Bron in a rush. "I have no use for such a fine piece of work, and I would sell it to get bread and shelter. I came to you to see if you could tell me where I might find someone who would buy it and how much coin I can get."

"I understand," said Anne. "Man cannot live on beauty alone. Our bodies demand more." If Bron did not get the gentle humor in Anne's comment, Aileen certainly did. She looked down, hiding her smile.

"Aye, Mistress," said Bron. "That be the truth." He paused a moment. "So can you tell me what this is worth in coin?"

"Alas, Master Bronnart," said the embroiderer. "I

would need to clean this fabric carefully before I could hazard a guess."

Bron's face fell.

"But all is not lost," declared Anne.

The serf's frown cleared.

"If this embroidery be as fine as I believe it may be, it would be a great gift for the abbey."

"A gift," Bron said in horror. "I said nought about it being a gift. I must needs sell it."

"Calm yourself, Master Bronnart," said Anne, putting out her hand in a conciliatory gesture. "I did not mean to say that you should gift it to the abbey. I meant only that such a piece of work does not present itself often and that the abbot may be interested in having it for the abbey."

"Oh," said Bron, letting his breath out in a whoosh. "Say you I should take this to the abbot?"

"I think that would be the best thing to do," responded Anne. She took up one end of the fabric and examined it closely. "I doubt not that he will tell you he cannot give you a price until he can see the design in better order. Pray tell him that I would be glad to clean this work if he so wishes, for I believe the work to be fine and thus it may be of value."

Bron smiled. "I will do so, Mistress," he said. "I hope to be allowed to stay in the abbey guest hall, so I will be close by to ask for an audience with the abbot."

"Just so," said Anne.

Bron gathered up the fabric reverently and placed it once again in the chest.

"I thank 'ee, Mistress Arundel," he said. "I will take my leave of you now. Mayhap I will see you again."

"It may be so," Anne responded. "Aileen, please open the door for Master Bronnart. He has his hands full."

"Yes, mother," said Aileen in an unusually demure manner. I do hope that Abbot Samson will ask that the embroidery be cleaned, she thought as she led the man to the street door. The work looks very interesting, and I would know more of it.

"Fare thee well, Master Bronnart," she said as the man passed her in the doorway.

"Fare thee well," said Bron. Shifting the chest in his arms, the man turned and strode down the street in the direction of the abbey.

I would that I could be a fly on the wall when Abbot Samson sees the embroidery, Aileen thought to herself. Mother seemed very interested in it. And if that be the case, then I am certain sure the abbot will wish to know more of the history of both man and chest.

CHAPTER FOUR

Where the messengers of Duke William came to Wido

T HE DAY WAS GREY AND CHILLY, AND Abbot Samson was glad to be seated beside his cheerful fire, warming his hands on a tankard of mulled wine. The small, bald monk drew the fur rug which lay over his knees further up.

I know not how the cold can make its way through such substantial walls as those of our great abbey, the monk thought to himself. Yet there are others who must labor in the cold even as I sit here warming myself. Praise be to God who has called me to this life.

As he sat there gazing into the fire and musing over the twists and turns of life, there was a knock at the door. "That must be Prior Herbert." The abbot smiled to himself. "No one else has a knock that speaks of such a mix of authority and uncertainty.

"Enter," Abbot Samson called. The door opened and indeed it was Prior Herbert who walked in.

"I pray that I do not disturb you, Father Abbot," said the prior.

Samson regarded the small man with the ring of clipped grey hair around his tonsure and anxious grey eyes. Prior Herbert was a patient, kind man, well loved by the community. He did not hesitate in carrying out his duties, but even in his discipline of wayward monks he was fair. The abbot was always grateful for such a second-in-command. Many another abbot had cause to be concerned about the ambition of their prior. Samson believed that there was ambition beating within the heart of the man before him, but Herbert would always put his current duty before his future expectations.

"Brother Prior," said Samson, forcing his wandering mind back to the present, "You do not disturb me in the slightest. Please come in.Be seated and join me in a tankard of mulled wine."

The prior looked tempted but remained standing. "I thank you, Father Abbot, but I have come to tell you that there is a man outside who craves an audience with you."

The abbot was a little surprised. Most of the Liberty knew that the abbot was available for pleas or business during certain hours of the day. The hours between Sext and Nones were more usually set aside for abbey business and prayerful contemplation.

Mayhap this man is a stranger to our town, Samson thought to himself.

Looking at his prior, the abbot realized the monk appeared more than usually perturbed. "There is something unusual about this man?" he asked.

"Father Abbot, as soon as Brother Jocelin informed me that there was a man in the guest hall asking for an audience, I went straightway to talk to him." Samson knew that the prior was ever jealous of his abbot's time and would most often respond to whatever request was made without troubling Samson at all.

"Your care for the needs of the abbey and its inhabitants is not unappreciated," said the abbot. Prior Herbert's usually rosy cheeks turned a darker shade of pink, his pleasure in the compliment clear.

"Tell me about this man," said the abbot, his bland tone calculated to ease the other monk's embarrassment.

Prior Herbert cleared his throat. "Father Abbot," he said, "I found a man of low estate within the walls of the guest hall. When I entered, he mistook me for your worthy self, an error I swiftly corrected."

He sounded so indignant that the man should have thought the prior to be the abbot that Samson had difficulty keeping a straight face.

Apparently unaware of the abbot's amusement, Prior Herbert continued with his account.

"The man told me his name was Bronnart and that he is a journeyman carpenter," said Herbert. "He was holding tight to a small chest that looked as though it was about to fall apart."

"Hardly a good indication of his skill," said Samson, smiling.

"My thought exactly, Father Abbot," Herbert said eagerly. "To me, the man did seem a little too careful in his speech, as though he hoped I would not ask him too many questions."

Samson was intrigued. Herbert was a cheerful man, known by all to be open and unassuming. Rarely did he comment on anything that was not good and honest.

"You doubted his tale?" said the abbot.

"I do not know," admitted the prior. "I cannot say with certainty that what Master Bronnart told me was not the truth, but I confess I did wonder about the history he presented."

"Pray tell me more," Samson said.

"This man asked audience with you, Father Abbot," Herbert went on. "He told me that he had received the chest and its contents in exchange for labor and did wish to sell it."

"Did he show you what those contents were?" asked Samson.

"He did open the chest and show me a roll of cloth within," said the prior. "He turned back one corner of the cloth to reveal linen with some sort of embroidery on it."

"This does not sound like a matter that would be of interest to the abbey," the abbot said, puzzled not only by the reason for the man to seek him out but also by the prior's seeming willingness to accede to the request.

"I was about to tell him so," the prior responded. "But then he told me that Mistress Arundel had sent him to speak to you."

Samson's brow cleared. Mistress Arundel was a renowned embroideress within the Liberty. She came from a long line of women skilled with the needle and would not have sent any man to him without good cause.

"I understand why you have come to speak with me, brother prior," he said. "Is the man without?"

"Yes, Father Abbot," said Herbert.

"Then pray bring him before me," Samson said.

Herbert bowed to the abbot and then turned and went out of the room.

Before the prior could return, there was another knock on the door. That is not Prior Herbert returning, thought Samson. The knock is much more demanding, as if the hand were one of a man sure of his right to be admitted.

Samson smiled to himself, amused at his sudden interest in the style of a man's plea for access to his chambers.

"Enter," he called.

The man who walked into the room was unknown to the abbot. He was tall with a commanding air. Startlingly blue eyes looked out from a pale face topped with light brown hair.

Rare it is for a stranger to demand entry with no introduction, thought Samson, rising to greet the stranger.

"You are welcome, sir," he said. "I am Abbot Samson. Methinks you are a guest of our abbey?" he said, his tone rising in question.

"Indeed I am, my lord abbot," replied the man. "I arrived but this morning. My name is Lanfranc, and I am from the chapter of the great cathedral at Bayeux." The man stood taller as he spoke, his words almost a pronouncement of the greatness of his native land.

Samson's bushy eyebrows rose as he studied the face of the man before him, but he said nothing other than to offer the man a seat and some mulled wine.

"Thank you," said Lanfranc. "I came but to present my compliments. I am come on pilgrimage to the shrine of the blessed St. Edmund and have sworn to touch no wine until I have knelt before the shrine itself."

"Our abbey is honored to offer you our hospitality," said the abbot, the pride in his voice an echo of that which had touched the words of Lanfranc. "I trust that brother hospitaller has provided you with all that you need."

"He has been most helpful," replied Lanfranc. "Now, if you will forgive me, Father Abbot, I would like to attend upon the blessed shrine before the evening prayers."

"Of course," said Samson, wondering at his visitor's abrupt behavior. "God go with you, my son," he raised his hand to make the sign of the cross as he intoned the words of the blessing.

Lanfranc made his obeisance and turned to go. As he exited through the door, he met Prior Herbert returning with a scruffy-looking man cradling a small chest hard to himself. Lanfranc looked curiously at the pair: The monk walking with the assurance of a man who knows his position in life, followed by the shuffling steps of the small black-haired man with filthy clothes, dirt-ingrained fingers, and the air of a terrified weasel.

Herbert paused as he saw Lanfranc coming out of the abbot's chambers. Mayhap he should not trouble the abbot now. Yet Samson had said to bring the peasant to him.

"Good morrow," he said to the tall man before him. "I pray we have not caused you to shorten your audience with Father Abbot."

"Be assured my audience was neither lengthened nor shortened by any man," said Lanfranc and walked on past the pair.

What a proud, severe man, the prior mused as he looked after the retreating visitor. Bron, standing behind the monk, was cowering close by the Prior Herbert.

"Come, man," Herbert said. "Father Abbot has granted you your request. This is no time to be afeared."

Knocking on the door of the abbot's chambers,

Prior Herbert heard the familiar "Enter," and led the other man into the room.

"Father Abbot," he said once Samson turned his attention to the pair. "As you have asked, I have brought Master Bronnart." He gave Bron a slight push toward the abbot. "Master Bronnart is a journeyman carpenter, as I have told you, and he has an interesting artifact that he wishes to sell."

Giving Bron another small nudge, Herbert continued. "Master Bronnart, this is Father Abbot, the head of our great abbey. He it is whom you must convince of the value of your offering."

"Offering?" squeaked Bron, brought to life by the prior's introduction. "I cannot afford to make such a valuable offering to any abbey, however great."

Abbot Samson smiled. "Be still, my son," he said. "Brother Prior did not say so."

Bron's face, which had become alarmingly red, gradually regained its former sallow tone. He stood awkwardly in front of the abbot, saying nothing.

Sighing, the abbot sat down and waved his hand to indicate that the prior should sit also. Prior Herbert added some logs to the glowing fire before sitting down opposite the abbot and folding his hands in the sleeves of his habit.

"Tell me, my son," Samson said to Bron, hoping that the man might be less intimated by the sight of the two monks being seated. "What is it that you have brought for me to see?"

Screwing up his face in concentration, Bron hesitated for a moment. Then, seeming to come to a decision, he placed the small chest he carried on the floor between the two monks and lifted the lid.

Abbot Samson smelled the musty odor of a box and its contents long buried in the earth. His nose crinkled a little, but Bron did not notice, so intent was he on drawing out a length of the cloth inside the chest.

"Father abbot," he said. "I was plough . . . doing some work for a trader in a town not far from St. Edmundsbury. He was well satisfied but could not pay me in coin. This chest and its contents, so he told me, was worth more the sum I was owed."

Neither the abbot nor the prior had failed to notice Bron's slip of the tongue. The abbot's bushy eyebrows rose, and the prior looked sharply at the peasant. Neither man chose to interrupt the narrative.

"I did bring my treasure to your town," Bron went on, oblivious to the doubts he had raised in the two men's minds. "I was told that there was a woman within its walls who had a reputation for being a good embroiderer, so I took it to her."

"Mistress Arundel," said the abbot, his expression quickening into a greater degree of interest. "She is indeed renowned for her craft."

Bron nodded, pleased that he had drawn the attention of this great man.

"She did tell me to bring it to you," the peasant said simply.

"You interest me, Master Bronnart," said Abbot

Samson. "May I see what it is that has brought you to our abbey?"

Bron had been clutching the cloth in his hands. Now he unfolded one end of the fabric and handed it to the abbot. Samson took it somewhat gingerly in his fingers thinking that this old cloth did not seem to be of any great value and that it was going to take some time for the fusty old smell to dissipate.

The light from the fire illuminated a dull gold color in the cloth. Abbot Samson, surprised, looked more closely at the fabric in his hands. This is an embroidered cloth, he thought. Spreading it out further, he realized that, dulled though the thread was by the passage of time, it looked to be fine work.

"I see now why Mistress Arundel thought to send you to me," the abbot told the peasant. "Come, let us lay it out on the table."

The three men moved over to the long table upon which wine and fruit stood. Prior Herbert moved both and brought over a candlestick to provide more light to view the fabric. Bron carefully placed the length of the linen on the table and unfolded it.

The two monks peered at the work before them. With a shock, Abbot Samson realized that this was not simply a piece of embroidery on old linen. One end of the fabric was frayed as though it had been torn from a larger piece, but it seemed as though the whole had been a tale of soldiers and battles.

"Hold the candle closer, brother prior," said the

abbot, bending over the table. "It seems that there is some writing within the design."

Prior Herbert brought the candle as close to the fabric as he dared.

"Can you tell what that says?" asked the abbot, pointing to a particular area of the piece.

"It certainly seems to be writing," said the prior, his brow creased as he stared intently at the dark splodge to which the abbot was pointing.

Samson waited. Bron shuffled uneasily as the silence stretched out.

"Could it be a name," mused the prior.

"It did seem so to me," affirmed the abbot. "I may be mistaken, but I think it may possibly be 'Williem D.' I can decipher no more."

"You have the right of it," exclaimed the prior. "Even though the linen is almost as dark as the thread, I can trace the lines of the letters."

"Who be Williem D?" asked Bron, curious in spite of himself.

The abbot paused for a moment, his hand stroking his chin, a habit his colleague recognized as a sign of deep thought.

"We cannot know for sure," said the abbot. "At least, not yet. And I would be loathe to suggest who it may be until this embroidery be cleaned."

Bron did not look too happy at the abbot's words. "If I wash this cloth, it may be ruined," he said. "Then it will be useless, and all of this will be for nought!"

The man sounded so distraught that the abbot hastened to reassure him.

"I do not ask that you clean it," he said. "Such an artifact will need the care that only an expert can provide."

The abbot paused. "I will ask that the same Mistress Arundel who sent you to me clean and repair this fabric," he said decisively.

Bron's expression was calculating. "And will you also pay Mistress Arundel for this work?" he said.

The abbot's bark of laughter took the peasant by surprise.

"Yes," Samson said. "I will pay her, Master Bronnart. And, if this work is shown to be of value, then I will consider buying it from you."

Bron was pleased. Mayhap this treasure would bring him even more than he had hoped. But then he had another thought, not so pleasant. "If I leave it with you how can I be sure you will not keep it without payment?"

Abbot Samson drew himself up as tall as his short stature would allow.

"Dare say you so to a man of God?" he thundered. "Would you call the abbot who rules over the Liberty of St. Edmundsbury a thief?"

Bron cowered before the ferocity of the abbot's anger. "Your pardon, Father Abbot," he sniveled. "I spoke without thinking. I am faint with hunger and thirst, for it has been a long, hard journey."

He drew his hand across his forehead in an

exhausted fashion, swallowing as though his mouth was dry as sand. Peering up at the abbot from under his drooping eyelids, Bron allowed his knees to buckle so that he ended up on his knees in front of Samson, whimpering softly behind the filthy, work-worn hands that now covered his face.

What a performance, thought the prior, immediately ashamed of his lack of charity towards the peasant before him.

What a performance, thought the abbot, not the least bit ashamed but finding his mood improved in spite of himself. Such a ridiculous display was almost comical.

"Stand up, man," Samson commanded. "We will say no more of this insult."

Bron rose from the floor, his knees creaking. The peasant's expression was uncertain.

"Take yourself to the guest hall, Master Bronnart," said the abbot. "Brother Jocelin will no doubt find you bread and ale. I will send for Mistress Arundel, and in due time we shall discuss the matter of this cloth and its value again."

Bron knew dismissal when he heard it. Bobbing his head in a small obeisance, he backed out of the room, closed the door carefully behind him, and made good speed to the guest hall and the hospitality it offered.

Abbot Samson and Prior Herbert stood quietly for a moment, looking at the door as though to see the man on its other side.

Shaking himself slightly, the abbot turned to the

prior. "See you to the matter of Mistress Arundel?" he said.

"I will, Father Abbot," responded the prior.

He hesitated a moment.

"What do you think of Master Bronnart's tale?" he queried.

"I am not certain," said the abbot. "Something does not ring quite true, and yet it all may be as he says."

The abbot returned to his chair, picking up his mulled wine and taking a sip. "It will be no easy task to clean this fabric," he said. "Time a'plenty to test the truth of Master Bronnart's tale and find out more of the history of this work."

The prior smiled at the wisdom of the abbot, bowed to receive the customary blessing, and took his leave.

CHAPTER FIVE

Here the messenger comes to Duke William and here
Wido led Harold to William Duke of the Normans

As Aileen left the abbey to return home Thursday evening, she was glad to see Robert steering his father's good-tempered cart horse through the throng.

"Robert," she called, waving her arm.

Robert smiled and pulled the cart over to the side of the street. "Aileen," he said, happy to see her. Bella flicked her creamy white tail and nuzzled Aileen's hands hoping for a treat, neighing softly when she found nothing there.

Rubbing the horse's chestnut head fondly, Aileen looked up at Robert. "I have seen little of you these past days," she said. "Your father must be keeping you very busy."

"Always," laughed Robert. "My mother has told him not to give me so much leeway that I can get into any more trouble finding villains and relics and such like."

"My parents have said much the same thing," Aileen said ruefully. "But I think secretly they are quite proud of us."

"Yes," said Robert. "Although it is perhaps not that easy to tell so from the way they talk." Robert laughed as he spoke.

Aileen nodded and softly joined in the laughter.

Bella tossed her head and whinnied, always glad to be in the midst of human merriment.

"Are you on the way home?" Aileen asked.

"I am," affirmed Robert. He had always been tall for his age, with limbs that did not seem to coordinate with his body too well, piercing blue eyes, and a face made for laughter.

He grows taller every month, thought Aileen to herself, noting that his wrists seemed determined to put as much space between them and his sleeves as possible. Why, even his chest has grown in breadth, Aileen realized.

Mother says I am grown into a young woman now, but it is certain sure that my friend is become a man almost without my noticing it. Aileen's eyes opened wide, and she all but gasped with surprise.

"What is it?" asked Robert, looking over his shoulder. "What do you see that surprises you so?"

Aileen's cheeks burned with embarrassment. "Oh, nothing," she said unconvincingly. "I merely remembered that I had promised mother to bring home some comfrey oil from Brother Infirmarer."

"Do you need to go back to fetch it?" asked her friend, noting the becoming color in her cheeks but oblivious to the cause. "I can wait here if you wish."

Now I'm in a fine pickle, thought Aileen. Mother did mention she would like some this week, but it seems I had better go back and ask Brother Infirmarer for the comfrey oil today, else Robert will wonder what is wrong with me.

As she opened her mouth to thank Robert, she had another thought. "I would not wish to keep you from your tasks, Robert," she said. "It is not so very late. I am sure visiting Brother Infirmarer can wait a few minutes more."

Happy to know that speaking with him took precedence over her mother's errand, Robert stroked the horse's nose and smiled at Aileen. "So what is it that you have to tell me?"

"Have you heard about the cloth brought to the abbey by the journeyman Bronnart?" she said.

"I would have had to have had my head in Bella's feed bag not to have heard about it," laughed Robert. Bella whinnied again and butted her head against Robert's shoulder.

Aileen laughed with them. "That paints a pretty picture in my mind," she said. "But I really wanted to talk to you to see what you thought about it."

Robert thought for a moment. "There are some

strange tales going around about what this can be," he said. "I often think that people make up stories when they do not know any facts. No one knows much beyond the fact that this man has an old piece of fabric with embroidery on it, so they pass the time making up tales about it."

Aileen was impressed. "I think you are right, Robert," she said. "It is like tales told to children; a little piece of truth at the heart of a ball of fantasy. Mayhap it is hard to leave the stories behind when you are grown."

Robert nodded but said nothing.

"So, tell me what tales you have heard," Aileen continued. "I have heard none of the gossip, and I am curious to know what it is that the townsfolk believe."

"Well," Robert said slowly, rubbing the horse's velvety nose. "I have heard that this is a piece of the cloth in which our Savior was buried. I heard only this afternoon from Mistress Oliver that it was certain sure that the fabric is in fact part of a map that will lead its owner to a great treasure. She told me word was that the chalice of our Lord's last supper would be found if one could solve the clues in the embroidery."

Aileen's eyebrows disappeared into the curls on her forehead. "Those are tales indeed," she said. "Anything else?"

"The butcher's apprentice told me very seriously that though the cloth was dirty, it was in fact cloth of gold and the thread was silver shot with jewels."

Aileen smiled and shook her head.

Robert, warming to his account, continued: "And

then Hugh Short took me aside to tell me that he had heard rumor that this was a part of a great tapestry that showed the battle between good King Harold and the Conqueror. Of course," he went on, blithely unaware of the expression on Aileen's face, "Hugh is a student at the abbey school, but I still do not understand how he could have heard any tale so unlikely."

Laughing, Robert stopped rubbing Bella's nose and turned to look at Aileen. His smile froze on his face.

"What?" he said. "You look shocked. What was it that I said that was so astonishing?"

"I am not shocked," Aileen said primly. "Merely surprised."

Robert looked a question at his friend.

"Hugh may be very close to the truth," said Aileen.

It was Robert's turn to be surprised. "Indeed? Yet his tale did not seem so much different from any of the others except for the fact that Hugh is not one given to exaggerated speech."

"That is true," said Aileen. "We have both seen our friend agitated though, have we not?"

The pair smiled wryly at the memory of Hugh seeking their help for his family, and how their desire to solve that riddle had led to the solving of the murder of a pilgrim to the tomb of St. Edmund.

"Nevertheless," Aileen went on. "If my mother's belief is borne out, then Hugh may be closer to the truth than you might have thought."

"I know it was your mother who sent the journeyman to Abbot Samson," said Robert. "That is common talk around town. I hear also that your mother has been commissioned by the abbot to clean the fabric. I did not realize she was more involved with the embroidery than that."

"That is all she has been asked to do," agreed Aileen. "I do believe that the abbot will ask her also if she can tell him whether the cloth is valuable once she has done all she can."

"Will it take her long to finish her work?" Robert asked. "I do hear that the length of the design is not complete, but I have not heard the length of it."

"It is close to nine feet in length," said Aileen. "One end is ragged as though torn from a longer work. I did not have much chance to look at it when the journeyman brought it to our house, but I have seen more of it since the abbot ordered that it be brought to the linen room and laid out on a long table."

"Is your mother then doing her work there?" I don't know why I am so surprised at that, thought Robert to himself. It is the obvious place for Mistress Anne to work on a task for the abbot.

"Yes," said Aileen. "It is strange to have Mistress Taylor the robemaker calling out to us all to look to our own work instead of looking at another, more skilled embroiderer doing hers. Sometimes Mistress Taylor will tell them that if I can ignore my own mother and focus on my work, then there is no goodly reason why they cannot do so as well. Every time she says something like that, all the other women in the room turn and stare at me instead of mother. The first time, I know my face turned red, but now I just ignore it and try not to smile."

"How does your mother react?" asked Robert.

"I did not think she even heard the robemaker," Aileen responded. "That is, until she told me last night she hoped I was not embarrassed to have her so close while I was plying my own needle."

"Your mother is always calm," said Robert. "It is a quality I know my mother greatly admires. Often, she has said that Mistress Arundel is the first person she would call in any emergency."

"Truly?" said Aileen. "I suppose that I have never thought about it much, but now that I hear you say so, I can see that it is true. Mother rarely raises her voice, and she always seems to know what to do in any situation."

"The abbot certainly believes she knows what to do with this cloth," said Robert.

"She does," said Aileen simply. "And wait until I tell you what she said about the embroidery after the journeyman left our house."

Robert's eyes lit up, and his eyebrows danced. "What did she say?" he asked eagerly.

"Mother told me that the embroidery reminded her of an account that has been passed down in her family of a commission upon which her great-grandmother had worked."

"That is a long time ago," said Robert, a little startled by Aileen's pronouncement. "What was it that made your mother think so?"

"I think it was the design upon the linen," Aileen said. "Mother told me that it was a proud family tradition that our ancestor's great skill was called upon to teach and guide a group of men who were to stitch a great work in the time of the Conqueror."

"Men!" exclaimed Robert. "I know that many men are skilled in crafts such as illustrating manuscripts or weaving or the making of nets, but I have not heard of men being hired for their skill in embroidery."

"I think it was more common in times past," said Aileen. "It seems as though people these days learn skills that are thought seemly according to whether they be men or women. Mother told me that in the time of her great-grandmother, it was not so, for any man or woman might be called upon to perform any task necessary for the support of their community."

"That makes sense," said Robert. "So tell me more of what your mother said."

"It seems that a great Norman lord, the half-brother of the first King William, desired to commission a great work to celebrate the victory of his brother over poor King Harold." Aileen said. "It was to be an embroidery that told the story from beginning to end in one length of linen."

Aileen's gaze was fixed somewhere in the past. She did not see Robert leaning toward her in rapt attention or Bella snorting at the lack of attention she was receiving of a sudden.

"And your ancestor was one of those chosen for this task?" Robert prompted his friend. He was impressed. He had never heard of anything like this, but it sounded as though it was an important task. Surely only the best in their field would be selected for such a job.

"Not exactly," Aileen said. "My ancestress was a part of the team that worked on this assignment, but our family pride stems more from the fact that she was chosen to supervise those creating this work."

"Your mother's great-grandmother supervised male embroiderers?" Robert's eyes opened wide, and Aileen tried hard not to laugh. His astonishment really did make him look just like the 10-year-old boy she had played with all those years ago. A young man he may be now, and apprenticed to his goldsmith father, but this was still her best friend in the world. Somehow, that was comforting.

"Yes," she said. "Mabel, for that was her name, was as renowned in her time for her skill with the needle as is my mother in our time. She taught and guided many of those men who were responsible for carrying out the commission."

Robert's exhalation of breath was almost a whistle. He opened his mouth to say something but found himself unable to form a coherent sentence.

Aileen smiled and laid a hand on his arm. "I know 'tis a rare thing, but it was not unheard of in that time, I am sure," she said.

"Mayhap you are right," said Robert, pulling

himself together. "I am still trying to work it out in my mind. You know it takes me a while to get used to new ideas," he added, shrugging and looking a little abashed.

"I know that you always work your way through any puzzle," she said. "I know also that the result is always worth the wait."

A rosy color worked its way up Robert's neck, and he put up his hand to cover a cough.

"So." The word came out a little louder than Robert had intended. He stopped and cleared his throat again before continuing. "So what was it about the fabric Bronnart brought for your mother's inspection that made her think of the embroidery commissioned by the Norman king's half-brother?"

"The tale that has come down in the family is that Mabel could not resist putting her own mark on the work at the last. Apparently, the men put their knowledge of fighting and building and tending animals to good use with their needles, but Mabel found it hard to teach them how to draw the people well with thread."

"I can understand that," said Robert with feeling. "Father has the hardest time teaching me how to portray living people in gold. Somehow, the head of a knight always comes out looking more like a rock with a nose and a double neck!"

The couple's giggling induced Bella to nuzzle Robert in the back of his neck, which merely made the young couple laugh more.

Wiping the tears from her eyes, Aileen returned to her story. "Mother said that Mabel decided the most important figures shown at the climax of the work must be portrayed in as regal a way as possible. Thus it was that Mabel herself worked the figures of the king and the clerics in the final panel. She made sure the clothes were rich in texture and color and that the positions of the figures were as natural as could be."

"Your mother seems to know a lot about her revered ancestress," Robert said.

"It is a tale oft told within the family," said Aileen. "As soon as mother started talking about it after Bronnart left our house, I realized which way her mind was working."

"She believes that the cloth that the journeyman brought to St. Edmundsbury is the same as that on which Mabel worked?" Robert questioned.

"Mother believes it may be," responded Aileen. "She looked as closely at the design as she could given the condition of the cloth and the light. The linen is of the right age, and the design resembles that described in the family account."

"But what happened that a piece of such a grand design was torn from the whole?" asked Robert.

"You have put your finger on the question at the heart of the matter," said Aileen approvingly. "We cannot know the answer to that now, but, if this embroidery turns out to be the very same one on which Mabel plied her needle, would it not be a great adventure to find out?"

Speechless, Robert merely looked at his excited friend. Aileen never ceases to amaze me, he thought. No one else would think anything of a piece of dirty embroidery, let alone bubble over with enthusiasm at the idea of tracing its history.

If this is a piece of Aileen's family history, it would be thrilling for them all, of course, but only Aileen would think to search for the reason a torn piece of cloth had ended up in a buried box of cedar.

Aileen was looking at him, clearly waiting for him to say something.

Robert took a deep breath. "Aileen, whatever you need from me I will be there," he said. "We are a team, and I would not wish it any other way."

CHAPTER SIX

Here Duke William comes with Harold to his palace
where a cleric and Aelfgyva. . .

"WELL, I NEVER," EXCLAIMED Mistress Oliver, slapping down a trencher of bread and cheese in front of Durand. "I never thought to see anything like it in my living days. Did you ever see so many dirty beggars on the streets before?"

Giving the reeve no opportunity to comment, the tavern keeper's wife flicked an imaginary dust ball off the table with a towel and continued her thoughts on the current state of society.

"Pilgrims come and pilgrims go," she said, waving her hand around to include in her condemnation all her customers. "The townsfolk work hard to feed and maintain them, you know?"

Durand, aware that a response was not required, merely nodded his head.

Mistress Oliver scarcely noticed, her mind elsewhere. "Certain sure it is that we have seen more travelers in the last year than we have seen for many years past, do you not agree?"

Durand, his mouth full of the delicious cheese the tavern served, nodded again. I am not sure where this is going, he thought, but it may be that I will find out soon.

"Just the other day," continued the good woman, "I heard that John Turnbull found four strangers sleeping in his hay barn. They said they had come to pay their respects to the blessed Saint Edmund but that the inns were all full."

"Surely the travelers are good for the town and its coffers, are they not?" Durand offered tentatively, his expression serious but his dark brown eyes twinkling.

"Mayhap they are," the woman allowed. "But with the pilgrims come the thieves and the beggars. Why, yesterday, when the tavern was filled with people coming in from the Tuesday market outside the south gate, my husband had to chase two men out of here who looked only to beg coin or drink from our customers. Thieves and beggars, thieves and beggars. What are you going to do about it, that's what I want to know!"

Ah, here we come to it at last, thought Durand. I should have known.

"Mistress Oliver," he said. "I wish it were otherwise, but as long as we have the faithful visiting our great saint, there will always be those who come with bad intent. But I can assure you that the abbot and myself do take the matter seriously."

Tossing her head, Mistress Oliver opened her mouth to respond. Just then, the tavern door opened and in walked a tall man, strongly built with light brown hair and light grey eyes. He stood just inside the door looking around, his hand resting easily at his side, his expression proud and yet not arrogant.

Durand followed Mistress Oliver's eyes. This man has presence, thought the reeve.

As Durand thought that only such presence could still Mistress Oliver in full flow, the man's eyes met those of the reeve and ceased their roving. Striding over to the table, he turned first to Mistress Oliver.

"Mistress, a tankard of ale if you please," he said, giving her a lop-sided smile.

"Yes, my lord," she said, dropping a curtsey and bustling off to fetch his order.

Turning to Durand, who had risen as the man's order was given to Mistress Oliver, he looked him hard in the face. "I think you are the reeve, are you not?" he said.

Durand returned the look equably. "I am, sir," he said. "What may I do to help you?"

"I am Sir Roger FitzGilbert," said the man. "I am lord of the manor of Fitching, two day's ride east of St. Edmundsbury."

"Welcome to our Liberty," said Durand. "Please be seated and take your rest."

Sir Roger sat and accepted the tankard of ale that Mistress Oliver brought over.

"My lord, may I get you something to eat," she said. "You will find no better food in any tavern in this great town." The good woman beamed with pride.

"My thanks, mistress," said the knight. "I am not hungry."

Accepting the finality of the tone with reluctance, Mistress Oliver cast a frustrated look at Durand and left them.

"Methinks your mission must be urgent, my lord," said Durand. "Rarely does someone of the town seek me out at this time of the day. Rarer still does a traveler such as yourself do so."

"You speak truly," said Sir Roger. "My mission is urgent. I am come seeking a runaway serf who stole something of great value from me."

"This is indeed a serious offence, my lord," Durand said. "What was it that was stolen and when did this happen?"

"A cedar wood chest containing a valuable embroidered cloth," said the knight. "It was taken by one of my serfs, Bron, about two weeks ago."

Durand, scarcely even realizing that he had been frozen in place since the knight had mentioned the chest, let his breath out slowly. The town had been abuzz with gossip about the contents of the chest ever since its arrival, but Durand had been uneasy about the whole situation.

I have been doing this too long, he thought to himself. I can almost smell a lie. My nose has been twitching since Bronnart first told his tale. Why, even his name was a lie!

"I believe I may be able to help you, my lord," said the reeve. "I think that it will not be hard to find your serf."

Roger's eyebrows rose in surprise. "Truly?" he said. "You have heard tell of him being in this area?"

"More than that," said Durand, smiling the crooked smile that had sent many a female heart quivering. "I have seen the man and that which he carries."

Roger sprang to his feet. "Then indeed I guessed right when I rode to St. Edmundsbury," he said. "Where is he? Let us go and take him up now."

"Peace, my lord," said Durand. "Please be seated and allow this good woman to bring you some food."

Mistress Oliver was hovering nearby, disturbed by the sudden movement of her richly clad guest.

Sir Roger started to say something, but seeing the calm face of the reeve in front of him, he once again took his seat.

"I am hungry," he admitted, waving a hand at Mistress Oliver.

She bobbed a curtsy and hurried off to fetch the visitor some food.

"If we must wait," said Sir Roger, "I would be

interested to hear how you came to meet this man and what has transpired since his arrival in this town."

Durand nodded and began to tell the knight about the arrival of the "journeyman" a week ago and how the cloth was now residing in the abbey.

"Alack!" exclaimed the knight. "This is a tale indeed. I would not have thought Bron capable of such an artful scheme. Mayhap I have underestimated him."

An interesting reaction, thought Durand, and one I would not have expected from an angry lord chasing a fugitive serf.

"My lord," he said. "I have told you all I know, but I know little of this serf or of how he came to flee with this prize."

Sir Roger nodded and sat back on his stool, looking thoughtfully into the past. "My father was a fair man," he began. "I like to think that I learned well at his knee, yet it is hard sometimes to see ourselves as others do."

Definitely an unusual lord, thought Durand. Most think little of how others see them but only of their own interests.

Sir Roger was lost in his own thoughts and did not see the gleam of interest in Durand's eyes.

"Bron has an older brother, Cuin," said the knight. "Their father, Edric, was a good man and loyal to my father. He died the same year as my father, and thus it was that the brothers came to me to seek permission to work their father's holding."

"The two brothers wished to share the holding?"

asked Durand, aware that such an arrangement was unusual.

"Not exactly," the knight said ruefully. "Cuin takes very much after his father. He works hard, cheats no one, and offers his fealty as is due."

Sir Roger paused. "And Bron?" asked Durand, sensing there was something more to be said.

"Bron is lazy," Roger said. "His father did tell mine that he despaired of the boy ever facing life as it was. Even as a child, Bron would talk of sailing to foreign lands and finding a treasure that would make him rich."

"It is rare that a serf would talk thus to his lord," Durand said.

"It is," agreed Sir Roger softly. "My father was a rare man."

Taking a bite of the food that Mistress Oliver had laid in front of him, Sir Roger continued with his story.

"When the brothers were grown, both men came to my father and asked for permission to marry the same girl, Ardith. She was pretty and sweet and a good match for any man."

"They both asked for permission?" said Durand. "Were they so unaware of each other's feelings and those of Ardith, or was life always a competition between the two men?"

Sir Roger smiled and nodded. "Bron was ever resentful of his brother. He believed, possibly correctly, that their father favored Cuin."

"What did your father answer these brothers?" asked Durand.

"He brought the girl Ardith before him and asked her if she would select either man, given the choice," Roger said.

Once again, Durand was caught by surprise. "Not many lords would care so much about the feelings of their serfs."

"I agree," said the knight. "But my father did always seek to do good, and I believe he thought that where two men sought the hand of a woman, it would do no harm to ask that woman if she preferred one over the other."

"Let me hazard a guess," said Durand. "Ardith chose Cuin."

Sir Roger laughed. "Yes, she did," he said. "It was no great surprise to anyone that she would choose the hard-working, kindly man over the sour man who was never satisfied with anything."

"And I suppose that, after Edric's death, you granted the request of Cuin to be permitted to work the holding on which they lived?" Durand was beginning to understand where this tale was going.

"Yes," said Sir Roger. "Of course, that only increased the resentment felt by Bron, particularly as he had nowhere to live other than with his brother and Ardith."

"There was no other place for him?" said Durand.

"Bron had a well-earned reputation for laziness and carelessness," Roger said. "Only Cuin would tolerate him, and I do believe that was only for love of their father."

"An unhappy man with little to commend him to any," said the reeve.

"That is so," affirmed Sir Roger. "I believe that is why he took the opportunity to run when he found the chest."

"So he found it," said Durand. "I thought mayhap he had stolen it from another."

"He did steal it," said the knight sharply. "He found it buried in a field on my land, and thus it was my property. Cuin intended to bring it to me, but before he could do so, Bron took the chest and its contents and ran. I thought it likely that he would bring it to the nearest town where he could find someone to give him coin for it, and it would seem that my suspicion was correct."

"Indeed," said Durand. "We shall go together to the abbot presently and you can regain your property."

"And the thief," Roger said firmly.

"Yes, my lord," said Durand. "We shall also apprehend the thief."

Durand paused a moment. "My lord," he said. "From what you tell me, you have not seen the chest or its contents. You have come a long way to recover something that may be of little value."

The knight leaned back on his stool. "Master Reeve," he said. "I am come to recover something of a great value. A runaway serf cannot be permitted to so despise his master. Bron is a known troublemaker and sluggard, but if I were to leave him be, then others might believe I would do nothing should they run away. This I cannot allow to happen."

"So it is the serf rather than the chest that you seek most urgently," said Durand,

The knight smiled thinly. "You may have the right of it," he said. "However, even the lord of a manor may confess to a certain amount of curiosity when a buried 'treasure' is found on his land."

I like this man, thought Durand. He is an unusual lord. There are many who would count Bron lucky to be the serf of such a man.

Rising, he said to Sir Roger. "Then let us go to the abbey and satisfy your curiosity."

The knight smiled with real humor and, dropping coin on the table to pay for his food, rose to accompany the reeve.

"This is a disturbing tale, Sir Roger," said Abbot Samson.

Durand and the knight were seated in the abbot's chambers. The story of the runaway serf having been related, the two visitors kept a respectful silence as the monk, chin in hand and eyes looking deep into the fire, thought of how to proceed.

Rousing himself, the abbot turned to Sir Roger. "I

regret that our abbey has been an unwitting accomplice to such a crime."

The knight leaned forward and shook his head. "Father Abbot, in no way do I regard your venerable abbey to be complicit in this miscreant's deeds. Bron is more cunning than even I thought him to be. I do not hold you responsible for any part of this."

"Thank you, my son," responded the abbot.

"Father Abbot," said Sir Roger. "I have been told by the worthy reeve that the fabric is being restored by a woman of the town and that it is believed that it may be of some value."

"In part at least, that is so," said Abbot Samson. "We cannot tell whether there is value in the work until Mistress Arundel has completed at least a partial cleaning of the linen."

"If you permit, I would like to see this fabric that has caused so much trouble," said the knight.

"Of course, Sir Roger," said the abbot. "We shall go at once."

Before they could rise to their feet, Durand said, "Father Abbot, if it be your will, I would like to have the serf brought to us here so that there is no possibility of him absconding should word reach him that Sir Roger is here."

"A wise suggestion," said the abbot, smiling at his reeve. He picked up his bell and rang it. Brother Anselm, a young novice, softly knocked on the door and, upon being told to enter, came into the room, his hands in his sleeves and eyes on the ground.

"Please go to the guest hall, brother, and fetch the journeyman Bron . . . nart," said the abbot.

"Yes, Father Abbot," said the novice without lifting his eyes. Turning on his heel, he left the room at a greater pace than that with which he had entered.

While they waited, the Abbot told the knight what had transpired between him and the so-called journeyman. He also told Sir Roger that, should he wish to continue with the cleaning of the fabric, there was no better artisan for the work than Mistress Arundel.

"I shall certainly bear that in mind," said the knight. "Much will depend on what I see when we go and view the fabric."

"Quite so," said the abbot.

With that, silence fell. A few minutes passed, and then, just as the knight and Durand started shifting in their seats with some impatience, the sound of running feet came to those within the room.

Before they could say anything, there was a perfunctory knock on the door swiftly followed by the entry of two monks, Brother Jocelin and the novice who had been sent to fetch Bron. Both men were out of breath. Brother Jocelin looked puzzled. The novice looked scared.

"Brothers," said the abbot sharply. "Such an entry is not seemly. What has happened to cause such disorder?"

Brother Anselm looked as though he would rather have the floor swallow him up than stand in front of his abbot. Brother Jocelin flushed, but long years in the service of the Lord had made of him sterner stuff.

"Forgive us, Father Abbot," he said. "Brother Anselm came to the guest hall requesting the presence of the journeyman, Bronnart." He paused.

"Yes?" said the abbot.

"Only an hour ago I saw him sitting in the courtyard enjoying the late afternoon sun," Jocelin said. "I thought mayhap he was still there, so Brother Anselm and I went out to see if that was so."

The abbot merely looked an enquiry. Durand was beginning to have a suspicion as to what was to come. Sir Roger's face took on a stormy look.

The Guest Master was not oblivious to the growing tension in the room, but he had no choice but to continue.

"We did not find Bronnart in the courtyard, so Brother Anselm and I swiftly searched the guest hall and the cloisters. We then sought the journeyman in the church, thinking that he may have gone there to pray.

"Father abbot, we cannot find the man anywhere," Jocelin went on. "We could not keep you waiting any longer so have come to ask if you wish us to continue our search or if the matter is such that you would prefer to wait until the journeyman returns to the abbey."

"I doubt much that he will return to the abbey," said Durand gruffly. "Methinks he must have noted the arrival of Sir Roger and myself and fled."

The Guest Master and the young novice looked surprised but kept their peace.

"I thank you for coming so quickly to tell us of this," said the abbot. "There is, I believe, no need for you to continue your search. Return to your duties as before."

The two monks bowed their heads for the abbot's blessing and left the room. A moment's silence followed the quiet click of the door as the monks departed.

"I believe, Sir Roger," said Abbot Samson, "that there is little point in waiting any longer. Shall we go to the linen room so that you can see your treasure?"

"Yes, Father," responded the knight. "I am sure that the worthy reeve will institute a search for my runaway serf immediately. Until such time as Bron can be found, I would indeed be interested to see this embroidered cloth for myself."

The three men rose. Durand bowed and received the abbot's blessing, leaving with a determined stride to instruct his men in the search for Bron.

Abbot Samson and Sir Roger walked glumly toward the linen room. Twilight had wrapped itself around the courtyard of the great abbey. The hive of activity that was the norm during daytime had quietened to a low hum of voices from within the guest hall.

Arriving at the door to the linen room, the two men entered and walked toward the long table on which the cloth had been placed. The abbot held up the lantern he had brought with him so that the knight could better see the fabric and the work that had been done by Aileen's mother in the past few days.

"What is this?" said the knight.

"What dark deed has been wrought here?" said the abbot at the same time.

Lying on the table before them was a pale muslin cloth upon which the rescued embroidery had been laid. Mistress Arundel's tools lay neatly at the end of the table, but of the cloth there was nothing to be seen.

As Bron had disappeared, so had that for which he had risked all.

CHAPTER SEVEN

*Here Duke William and his army came to the Mount
of Michael and here they crossed the Couesnon River*

"WHAT WAS THAT SOUND?" RUTH stopped so suddenly that Avraham ran into her, dropping the trug he was carrying in his arms.

"Oh, I'm sorry Avraham," Ruth said, bending to help him pick up the basket and the mushrooms that had spilled out of it. "I was sure I heard something."

Avraham, ever ready to protect his gentle, petite friend, stopped what he was doing and searched the forest undergrowth with his dark eyes. "What did it sound like?" he asked.

"A rustling sound followed by something like a sob," she replied. "It did not seem like the movement of a fox as it moved through the brush. It was more like the careless steps of a man."

As she spoke, a heavy cracking sound reached them, swiftly followed by a cry.

"Let me go first," Avraham said urgently, holding his friend back from rushing toward the sound.

The young couple moved warily through the forest. As they came out into a clearing, they spied a man getting up off the ground. His clothes were torn as though he had caught them on bushes, and his face was scratched. Leaves and twigs were caught in his dark, greasy hair.

The man spotted the pair as they moved into the clearing. Crying out in fear, he turned and made as though to run away, but his ankle gave way and he fell to the ground.

Immediately, the stranger began to try and crawl toward the edge of the clearing, whimpering and looking over his shoulder. Avraham strode over to him with Ruth following close behind.

As the pair reached the man, he put up his hand to as though to shield himself from blows. "Do not hurt me, young master," he said. "I am but a poor traveler seeking shelter in the forest for the night."

"We would not harm you, sir," said Ruth. Her dark eyes were full of sympathy as she knelt beside the frightened man. "We heard your cry and came to see if we could help."

Not exactly what I came for, thought Avraham, his expression grim and his hand ready to strike should this man dare try to harm Ruth. But I will hold my peace for now.

The stranger looked uncertainly at both young people. Wisely choosing Ruth, he gave her a gap-toothed smile. "Thank 'ee, young mistress," he said.

"Your ankle is swollen, I think," said Ruth, looking at the man's foot. "Did you hurt it falling from that tree over there?"

A little shamefaced, the man admitted as much. "I did fear those who might come into the forest and thought to sleep in a tree. I chose the wrong tree."

It was all Avraham could do not to snort. There is something wrong here, he thought. No reasonable man climbs a tree for such a reason unless he wishes to hide from someone or has some other guilty deed on his conscience.

Ruth's thoughts had taken a completely different direction. "Sir," she said. "Let us bind your ankle so you may stand on it."

"I be all right," said the traveler. Turning to Avraham, he held up his hand. "Help me up, young sir."

Hesitating a moment, Avraham signed to Ruth to move away from the man. Then he put out his hand and pulled the stranger to his feet, stepping back quickly to ensure there was distance between them.

Wincing as he put weight on his injured foot, the man faced his two rescuers with a guarded expression on his face.

Avraham took stock of the stranger. He saw a bedraggled man with shifty eyes. His hands and nails looked as though he had been digging in the ground without the aid of any tool. Lying at his feet was a torn piece of sacking which contained nothing but a few mushrooms and roots he had clearly picked up in the forest. I do not trust this man, thought Avraham, gently pulling on Ruth's hand to get her further away from the traveler.

The man laughed, but the sound came out more like a raspy growl. "I be no threat," he said. "I told you, I was just looking for a place to sleep."

"Who is it that you fear?" said Avraham shortly.

When Ruth opened her mouth to protest, he gently shook his head.

Avraham knows what he is doing, Ruth thought. I will say nothing for now.

The stranger, seeing that he had fooled no one, crouched over as though in supplication. "No one person," he wheedled. "You know, young sir, that there are thieves and murderers who live in the woods. I was just being careful."

"I doubt that," said Avraham. His wide-legged stance, coupled with the scowl on his face and the abrasive tone of voice, was enough to make the traveler cower even more.

"Avi," said Ruth gently, laying her hand on his arm. "Pray do not be so harsh."

Turning to the man, she said, "I am sure, good sir, that you are only being cautious in front of two strangers. Is that not so?"

The man looked up at her and gave her a crooked smile. He slowly stood up straight and then, looking at Avraham's stormy face, backed off another step.

"You speak truly," he said.

"It is wise in these uncertain times to be careful," agreed Ruth. "Do you not think so, Avi?" she asked.

"Mayhap you are right," said Avraham, but his body language offered little comfort to the man in front of him.

Sighing a little, Ruth sat down on the grass and bade the two men do the same.

Eying each other suspiciously, both men complied with Ruth's request.

Pretending she had not noticed anything untoward, Ruth smiled upon both Avraham and the stranger equally.

"Sir," she said. "If you will not let us bind your ankle, may we not be of help in some other way? You are not of the Liberty, I think?" Cocking her head to the side, Ruth smiled sweetly upon the man.

Looking upon the young woman in front of him, the traveler found it impossible to withstand the kind look in her dark eyes. Few there were who had ever been so sympathetic toward him. Mayhap there was something to be gained by telling them something of his story.

"You are right," he said. "I am a traveler from afar who had thought to find some safety in the town of St. Edmundsbury."

Neither Avraham nor Ruth responded, but Ruth looked encouragingly at the man, hoping that he would go on.

"My name is Bronnart," the man said. His eyes

shifted to the right and then returned to fix upon Ruth's face.

"I am from Ireland, the Land of the Saints," he said.

"I know not of this land," said Ruth. "But I think you must have traveled far."

"I have," said Bron.

"Are you a trader?" asked Avraham, thinking that he would not believe the man if he said he was. No self-respecting merchant would be running around in the forest so dirty and torn.

Sensing that he had to be careful about what he said in front of this young man, Bron shook his head.

"No, good sir," he said. Sighing deeply, he threw his hands out as though in surrender. "I am a poor man falsely accused of murder in my homeland. I throw myself upon your mercy!"

Ruth's eyes opened wide, and her hands flew to her face in distress. Avraham, his face usually so still, showed his startlement as well.

I have these young people in the palm of my hand now, thought Bron. *Lucky it is that Sir Roger had a visitor only last year from Ireland. I learned many strange things from the servants who attended upon that visitor. I knew it would come in useful someday.*

I did not expect that, thought Avraham. *For sure the man is a liar, but why would anyone claim a murder charge if he is hoping to have help escaping capture and punishment.*

The poor man, thought Ruth. Our people know only too well what it is to be hounded by false accusations and threats of death. If this be true, we must help him.

"Will you tell us more?" asked Ruth softly.

Avraham merely scowled at the man and drew a little closer to his friend.

Bron eased his leg on the grass so as to lessen throbbing in his ankle. "Willingly, young mistress," he said. "If it will convince you that I am not guilty of any great crime, I will tell you all."

Bron did not look at Avraham and Ruth, but rather appeared to be fascinated by the mushrooms scattered around the torn sacking he had with him.

"I do not know if you have any knowledge of the law in Ireland," he said.

"We do not," said Avraham shortly.

Bron nodded. "It is as harsh, if not more so, than in your country," Bron said. "If a man be found to be a murderer, the law says that he is to be given to the family of his victim as a slave."

"Truly?" breathed Ruth. "That is indeed different from the law of this land."

"Yes," said Bron. "In Ireland, the victim's family may do as they wish with their new slave. It is written that the murderer may buy his freedom, but if he cannot do so, then the family has the right to execute him."

"Execution is more swiftly carried out in England," said Avraham.

"Aye, I know," said Bron. "But in either land an innocent man may be unjustly put to death."

"And you say that you are an innocent man?" asked Avraham. His tone implied he had his doubts.

"I am, good sir," said Bron. "I was accused of murdering a son of a powerful family. I know not who did the deed, but I was hastily charged, tried without any to speak for me, and given over to the family."

"That is terrible," said Ruth sympathetically. "You must have been greatly afeared."

Bron nodded his head. "That is why I took a chance to escape. I stowed away on a boat that came to England and have been making my way across the country since. I know not where the journey will end but I hope to find some safe place to stay."

Avraham was still skeptical. "That is a pretty tale," he said. "How did you come to be so running with desperation in our forest?"

Bron's brows drew together. I am not certain this young man is as easy to convince as I had believed, he thought. I needs must work harder to sway him to my side.

"I cannot deny that I was truly in fear when you came upon me," he said disarmingly. "Let me tell you how that came to be."

Avraham neither spoke nor moved a muscle. Ruth, sensing that her friend was not persuaded by the words of the stranger, held her peace as well.

"I arrived in St. Edmundsbury only a few days ago," said Bron. "I took shelter in the abbey. It has been a long journey, and I was able to rest and think about what I should do while I was within those walls.

"This morning," Bron continued, "I spied a man in the courtyard that I have seen before. He is a friend of the victim of the murder of which I was accused."

"He has followed you all the way from Ireland?" Surprise and horror were obvious in Ruth's voice.

"I cannot know for sure, but it does seem likely," said Bron. "In any event, I did not stay to find out his reason for coming to St. Edmundsbury. I ran for my life. That is how I came to be in the forest and why you found me in such a state of fear."

He is a skilled storyteller, thought Avraham to himself. It may be that he tells the truth, but somehow I still doubt him.

Ruth had no such inhibitions. "I can only imagine how you must have felt," she said. "I would have run away too."

You would never harm any living creature, thought Avraham. Goodness knows how many times we Jews have had to run from persecution, but I know you will never have cause to run from the consequences of any wrongdoing on your part.

Oblivious to Avraham's musings, Ruth impulsively reached over and touched Bron's hand. "We must help you," she said.

Bron smiled at her, but Avraham was horrified.

"How can we help him?" he asked. "You know how careful our people must be not to draw any attention to ourselves. What if the man from Ireland truly has come to find Bronnart and take him back with him? How do you think the Jews of Fornham will fare if we are found to have aided him?"

Ruth was undaunted. "I know we must be careful, Avraham," she said. "But it is our duty to help those in need, and Master Bronnart is in need."

Ruth is too kind for her own good, thought Avraham. It is one of the things I love about her but also one of the things that makes me fear for her.

"We must be very careful, Ruth," he said.

"I know, Avi," responded the young woman, smiling at her friend. "I promise I will not put us all at risk, but we cannot just leave this poor man in the forest."

I do not know why not, thought Avraham rebelliously.

"Master Bronnart," Ruth said, standing up. "Can you walk?"

"Aye, young mistress," he said. "I can." He gingerly rose to his feet and took a tentative step or two. His ankle was still sore, but he was sure it was not broken.

"Then come with us," said Ruth. "We will take you to my father. He is very wise, and I am sure he will know what to do."

Taking the lead, Ruth set off in the direction of Fornham with Bron behind her. Avraham, picking up the discarded trug, trailed along behind them keeping an eagle eye on Bron.

Come what may, he thought, I will protect Ruth from any harm this stranger may threaten.

CHAPTER EIGHT

Here Duke Harold dragged them from the sand and
they came to Dol and Conan turned in flight

"H E REALLY IS A GOOD LIAR, IS HE not?" asked Robert.

He and Aileen were sitting on the grass in the vineyard eating a late lunch. Aileen had just finished telling him all about how both the "journey-man" and the embroidery had disappeared the day before.

"I think he must be," said Aileen. "The abbot is not easily taken in, and neither is my mother. I think my mother sensed something that was not quite right about him, but there was nothing that would have led her to think he was lying about the whole thing."

Munching on their bread, the pair pondered a moment about the strange turn of events.

"I suppose everyone thinks the serf took the cloth before he ran," said Robert.

"It seems likely," said Aileen. "Surely it would be a great coincidence if both were to vanish at the same time and there be no connection."

"I agree," said Robert. "Mayhap he saw his lord entering the gates of the abbey and knew he had to run away before Sir Roger had a chance to catch him. Having risked so much to steal the cloth, he would be disinclined to leave without it."

"The punishment for a serf who steals and runs away must be quite severe," said Aileen.

"It is," Robert replied. "My father told me that, at the very least, any thief would be flogged. But for such a crime as Bron has committed, he is more likely to suffer the loss of an ear or a hand. He may even be put to death."

"That is dreadful!" exclaimed his companion. "The cloth may not have much value," she went on thoughtfully. "Why would a man such as he risk so grave a fate for something of such uncertain worth?"

"I do not understand it either," said Robert. "Mayhap this Bron was a man tired of his life and thought this discovery was the one chance he would have to escape to another."

Robert has depths to him I had little guessed at, thought Aileen as she looked at her friend. *He may well have the right of it.*

"My mother sensed something was not quite right about Bron when he first came to our house," Aileen said. "There was nothing definite she could put her finger on, but I do not believe she was as surprised to hear he had run away as were some."

"Was Mistress Arundel distressed about the disappearance of the cloth?" asked Robert.

"She was," replied Aileen. "Mother had been hurrying up to the abbey every morning as soon as her daily tasks were finished. She scarcely stopped to eat or drink, she was so focused on finishing her work."

"It sounds as though she had made a great deal of progress," said Robert.

"Every evening before I left the linen room, I would go over and see how far the cleaning had come," Aileen said. "Mother had, I believe, almost finished cleaning the cloth and the wools. The design was much easier to see. It was clear that the work was as fine as mother had believed."

"What about the part your mother thought had been completed by your great-great- . . . ." Robert paused, his face creasing in concentration.

Aileen laughed. "You mean my worthy ancestress?" she said in a tone not unlike that of the priest when he delivered his Sunday morning service.

The two burst out laughing and only stopped when they had to gasp for air.

"Yes," Robert said finally as he wiped tears out of his eyes. "That part."

Aileen sobered a little. "Mother was growing more sure that this piece of linen was taken from that work. She wanted to take a close look at it in good light as soon as that area of the embroidery was completely clean and dry."

"And did she do so?" Robert leaned closer in eager anticipation.

"Unfortunately, she was not able to do so before the fabric was stolen," said Aileen.

"Mistress Arundel must have been gravely disappointed at that," Robert said.

"Yes," said Aileen. "And frustrated. As you have said, mother is usually very calm. Right now, she is a little irritable, and I'm sure it's due to the embroidery's disappearance."

"It is frustrating for you as well, is it not?" said Robert, keenly aware of the play of emotions on Aileen's face.

"It is," she said. "If we cannot be sure that we are talking about a particular work, how can we even guess at how it came to be buried in a field?"

"Fear not," said Robert, sitting up straight and adopting a serious expression. "We are an unbeatable team. We will find the vanished embroidery, return it to the abbey, and solve the mystery of its journey to the field." Robert held up his hand as if he were swearing a solemn oath.

"Robert," said Aileen, unable to resist laughing again. "You do quite make me feel better. And you are right. We are an unbeatable team."

"Mabel, you are about as graceful as a cow trying to climb a tree!"

Anne's younger daughter looked up from the floor where she was gathering all the dried herbs that had just fallen out of the box she had dropped. It was the third time that morning that she had bumped into something and made a mess.

"I am sorry, mama," said the girl. Tears came to her eyes and she looked down, embarrassed at her clumsiness and the distress it was causing her mother.

"No, Mabel, I am sorry," said her mother, bending down to give the girl's cheek a brush and help her pick up the herbs. "I fear I am a little more irritable than usual these days. I should not have snapped at you so."

"I love you anyway, mama," said Mabel.

Her mother laughed and hugged her daughter. "I love you too," she said.

Mother and daughter continued with the lesson on mixing herbs and oils into healing balms. As the morning waned, Anne prepared the noonday meal for Mabel's father and her two young brothers. Mabel happily helped in the preparations, pleased at having learned so much and even more pleased that there had been no more accidents.

When Jude had gone back to his labors after lunch and the boys had been put down for their nap, Anne told Mabel to spend some time catching up on the chores that had not been done that morning due to the lesson on herbs. Then she picked up her basket and set off to make some purchases that should probably have been made during the past week while she was working on the embroidery.

Jude will be not be a happy husband if there are no candles to light this evening, she thought as she made her way up Abbeygate. Then there is flour to be purchased and quite a few other things that we will need in the next week. It seems as though I neglected much while working so hard on that embroidery. I am blessed to have a cheerful family that complains so little. Others are not so fortunate.

As Anne made her way through town, her thoughts were interrupted several times by people asking her questions. There was scarcely a person within the Liberty who did not know her connection with this mysterious cloth, and many wanted to know whether it was true that it had been stolen or if the stories that it was a treasure map were true. Some even wanted to know if she suspected some wizardry was responsible for the disappearance, given that it was rumored the cloth had magical powers.

To each of these questions, Anne merely responded that to her knowledge the cloth was merely an ordinary piece of linen with embroidery and that she had no idea who had taken it or why. Her answers were poor fodder for gossip and thus were a great disappointment to many of her inquisitors.

Gratefully, Anne turned into the chandler's shop. Arlo was not known to be a gossip, but he was rather a grumpy man. I doubt anyone will follow me inside to ask yet more questions, Anne thought.

She was right. The woman who had been dogging her heels for the past five minutes relentlessly seeking gossip about the cloth stopped short in the doorway, waited a minute with an exasperated expression on her face, and then, shrugging, turned on her heel and walked away.

"Mistress Arundel," said the chandler. "How may I help you today?"

Anne took in a deep breath of the warm scent of the shop. Were the chandler not so cold a man, she thought, I would be tempted to come in here more often. I love the soft fragrance of the candles hanging from the beams, the essence of honey and rose and lavender wafting through the whole establishment.

Forcing herself back to the matter at hand, she turned to face Arlo. "Master chandler, I have allowed my supply of candles to get too low," said Anne. "I must needs purchase more."

"Of course, Mistress Arundel," said the man. Pausing a moment, he continued: "I suspect that your labors in the abbey this past week have meant you have had less time to attend to such tasks as purchasing household supplies."

Arlo, a stocky man with a perpetually cross look, was well-regarded for his wares within the Liberty, but none would have described him as a talker. It was thus with some surprise that Anne realized he was initiating a conversation with her.

"It has been a busy week," said Anne. "But I hope that I have not been so engrossed in my work at the abbey as to neglect my duties to my family."

"Of course not, of course not," said Arlo, hearing the note of annoyance in the woman's tone. "I did not mean to imply such. Forgive me." Arlo's whole head seemed to flush with embarrassment, given that what little hair he had remaining was so wispy. His hands, soft from his constant use of beeswax, fluttered in conciliation.

"No, Master chandler, please pardon me," said Anne. "Methinks that I am tired and overly sensitive today. I take no offense at your enquiry."

Feeling as though she now owed the chandler some explanation, Anne decided she would tell Arlo something of the embroidery and what had become of the cloth and the man who had brought it to St. Edmundsbury.

"Cleaning such an ancient length of linen has been a challenge," Anne said. "I have worked on it each day since the abbot sent for me."

"You believe that your work has been successful?" asked Arlo, peering at the woman intently.

"Yes," said Anne, her eyes seeming to look into the distance rather than at the man before her. "I could see so much more of the design, and I do believe that I would have been able to bring the story back to life had the cloth not been stolen."

Forcing herself back to the present, Anne looked at Arlo. "Now I know not if all that work will have been in vain or even if the embroidery will be recovered intact," she said sadly.

The chandler seemed to be following a line of thought of his own. "Do you think the work is valuable?" he asked.

"I know some hope that it will be so," Anne said carefully. "You know that it was stolen by a serf of the lord FitzGilbert?"

Arlo looked down at the ground. Anne could not see his expression, but from his flushed color she suspected he was more than just curious. He is angry, she thought. Why would he be so?

"Master chandler?" she said softly.

Arlo raised his head, his emotions under control.

"Yes, Mistress Arundel," he said. "I had heard that the supposed journeyman was in fact a runaway serf from the land of Sir Roger FitzGilbert."

Fiddling with a piece of wax he had picked up from the top of the counter, Arlo looked into the serene face of his customer. "You know perhaps that my family came originally from east of here?" he asked.

"I have heard so," Anne said equably.

"My grandfather was from the area that is now a part of Sir Roger's land," he said.

"Truly?" said Anne. "I did not know that."

"Yes," said the chandler. "Before the coming of the Normans, my family farmed a large stretch of that land. The soil was fertile and the people wanted for nothing. Good, honest, hard-working folk were my ancestors." Arlo spoke with pride and seemed to stand up straighter as he remembered the stories of that time as they were told to him by his father and grandfather.

"I am sure they were," Anne said. "I am sure also that the Liberty is glad of the skills that you now bring to the townsfolk here." So many people were displaced after the Conqueror came to England, thought Anne. There are still many who carry bitterness in their hearts, but there are others who have learned new crafts and gained new homes.

"Mayhap you are right," said Arlo tightly. "My grandfather and father were glad to escape serfdom at the hands of the Normans, as am I, and yet it is hard to leave the land of your ancestors and seek a new life."

"Yes, I know," said Anne with conviction. Arlo looked at her, but she did not elaborate any further.

"So do you believe that the serf will be caught and the linen found?" he asked after a moment.

"I do not know," Anne replied. "I confess I am not sure how I feel about the serf. I spoke with him when he first brought the cloth to me, and it is hard to think of someone with whom you have conversed being taken back to his home in chains and potentially being executed by his lord."

"But he is a thief and a liar," said Arlo. "Do not thieves and liars deserve the punishment meted out to them by Norman knights?"

It is almost as though he is testing me, thought Anne. This is passing strange.

"That is the law of the land," she responded enigmatically. "And you, Master chandler, what do you say should be the end of Sir Roger, his runaway serf, and the chest found in the field?"

Arlo was a little taken aback at having the tables turned on him, but he found himself unable to resist giving his opinion to this highly-regarded woman of the Liberty.

"Bron may be both a thief and a skilled liar," he said. "But Sir Roger FitzGilbert has done nothing to deserve enrichment from whatever this fabric may be. The Normans are no less thieves than are serfs such as Bron. I say a pox on both their houses." Arlo's eyes flashed fire, and his fists clenched as he spoke.

Anne stepped back a little in the face of the man's fury.

The chandler, seeing her reaction, put out his hands in a placatory gesture. "Your pardon, Mistress Arundel," he said. "Methinks I do talk too much on occasion."

Once again finding herself astonished at how garrulous the chandler was being that day, Anne felt it was time to bring the conversation back to her reason for coming. "There is nothing to forgive, Master chandler," she said. "I have found our conversation most interesting. Mayhap I should give you my order now for the day is drawing on and I know we both have tasks to complete?"

Arlo cleared his throat, adopted his more usual grumpy expression, and nodded his head. "What size candles do you wish to purchase, Mistress Arundel, and in what quantity?" he said.

"I would like a dozen standard tallow candles," she said. "Do you also have some of your honey beeswax candles?"

"I regret that I sold the last of those this morning," Arlo said, not looking very much as though he regretted anything. "But I will have some more ready within the next three days."

"Then I will buy only the tallow candles today and return after the sabbath for the honey ones," said Anne.

The exchange of candles and coin being soon made, Anne left the chandler's shop to return home. What a strange encounter, she thought. I little thought to see such strong emotions in this man. He must have had a really bad day, she said out loud, and then laughed to herself at the thought of how anyone who had heard her would doubtless conclude she had taken leave of her senses.

Time to go home and take care of my family, said Anne, and suited her actions to her words.

CHAPTER NINE

Here the knights of Duke William fight against the men
of Dinan and Conan passed out the keys

"I PRAY YOU HAD A RESTFUL NIGHT," SAID
Ruth's father to Bron as he waved him to a
seat.

"I thank 'ee, sir," said Bron. "It was the first night's
rest for many days where I did not lie awake in fear."

Isaac could not fail to notice that the other man
was far from comfortable. Bron's eyes were shifting left
and right, and his muscles were tensed as if in readiness
for flight.

His eyes finally resting on his host, Bron saw before
him a grey-haired man with dark, warm eyes. His
daughter looks like him, thought Bron, but this man
has steel in him for all that he appears so mild. I must
take care.

"I regret that we were not able to talk with each

other last night when you arrived," said Isaac. "I believe that we should do so now."

Bron licked his lips, his mouth suddenly feeling dry as a bone. Has this Isaac of Cordoba discovered my secret? Is he going to give me over to Sir Roger Fitz-Gilbert?

Isaac saw the man's face turn pale, and the questions that had been raised by the story told him by Ruth and Avraham became more insistent in his mind.

"My daughter told me that you came to these shores from Ireland," Isaac said. "I have met only one man from your country before."

Bron swallowed. "I did not realize many men from my country traveled here," he said. His voice came out more as a breath than the strong tone he would have wished.

"Many men do not," said Isaac. "But the shrine of St. Edmund draws people from many lands to our Liberty. Thus it was that, one day many years ago, I treated the injury of a man from Ireland who had fallen down steps and gashed his face open."

"You are a physician?" Bron said in some surprise.

"I am," said Isaac. "But let us return to the matter of your arrival. You told my daughter and Avraham that you ran away from a false charge of murder."

"Yes, sir," said Bron. Again he swallowed hard and then adopted an expression that to Isaac seemed more like that of a conniving hustler than that of a grateful and innocent runaway.

"I thank 'ee much for your help, sir," said Bron. "I

do not want to trouble you more. If you could spare only a little coin to help me on my way, I will leave you in peace."

The more the man spoke, the greater Isaac's concern. This man speaks as does a man of Suffolk, he thought. I find it hard to believe he is from anywhere farther afield. He could bring great trouble to my house if he is a man running from the law of the Liberty. The Jews of Fornham cannot afford such trouble.

"Time enough to discuss what should be done, Master Bronnart," said Isaac. "The hour of the sabbath is drawing close, the women are preparing the evening meal, and soon it will be time to say *kiddush*. No further decisions can be made until after the sabbath."

Bron looked as confused as he felt. What is this "kiddush?" he thought to himself, and why is he saying we cannot talk more or decide on what I need to get away from here right now?

"Master Bronnart, I think you must have realized we are Jews, did you not?" asked Isaac.

"I did not think about it," replied the serf. "I suppose I realized you were not like the folk I am used to, and I know the priests always say that the Jews are not good people, but I do not know what it all means."

At least he did not spit on me as he insulted my people, thought Isaac. Many have done so.

"I hope at least that we have shown you proof that not all Jews are bad people," he said. "There are bad men of every faith and from every land. We are as other men are, tall and short, beautiful and ugly, good and bad."

Bron couldn't think of anything to say. He just stared at Isaac and wondered how he had come to be in such a place among such people. Most of all, he wondered how he was going to get out of the mess he was in.

"Let me tell you something of our sabbath, Master Bronnart," said Isaac. "You are welcome at our table, but you should know something of our traditions, else all will seem very strange to you."

I do not really want to know anything about their traditions, thought Bron, but short of getting up and running away, I do not see what else I can do. If I run, I think that big oaf Avraham will only chase me down and then I will be in even more trouble than I am now.

Isaac could see the calculation in the other man's eyes and had a shrewd suspicion what Bron was thinking. Receiving no response and seeing that the man was not moving, he began to talk.

"The sabbath is the seventh day of the week and our day of rest," said Isaac.

"But surely it is not Sunday already?" exclaimed Bron.

"The Christian day of rest is Sunday," Isaac said. "For the Jews, our sabbath begins at sundown on Friday and ends at nightfall on Saturday, after the appearance of three stars in the sky."

Bron thought this made no sense at all, but he said nothing.

"During the sabbath, it is forbidden to do any work. It is forbidden even to discuss business of any kind. That is why I said we would return to our discussion after sundown tomorrow.

"During the sabbath, we celebrate Yahweh's creation of the world and also the end of our slavery in Egypt," Isaac continued. "We shall begin the sabbath with a festive meal at sundown today. Before the meal we say a blessing, which is called *kiddush*, over a cup of wine. We will say another blessing, *hamotzi*, over two loaves of bread."

"You say two blessings before you eat?" said Bron, growing more bewildered by the minute.

"Yes," said Isaac. "The *kiddush* is to acknowledge the holiness of the sabbath, and the *hamotzi* celebrates the double portion of manna received by the Israelites in the desert each sabbath eve. That double portion meant that no labor was needed on the sabbath day to provide food."

I do not understand any of this, thought Bron, and I do not care what it is all about. All I know is that nothing is going to happen until tomorrow night. I have to get out of here else I will be caught.

"This be very interesting," said Bron unconvincingly. "But if it be all right with you, I think I would rather be on my way before you start this day of rest. If you can only spare a few coins, I can put more distance between the Irishman and myself before dark.

"I seek only safety," Bron whined, seeing from

Isaac's face that his argument was not being well received.

I would be happy to see this man gone, thought Isaac, but I must learn more before I can decide the right thing and how best to protect my people.

"It would be unwise for you to leave tonight," Isaac said. "If you are right that the man you saw is searching for you, I am sure someone told him you had been in St. Edmundsbury. Think you that he will have ceased searching for you in the area already?"

Bron paled. Sweat broke out on his brow.

This man is definitely running from something, thought Isaac. Whether it be from a false accusation of murder in Ireland or for some other reason I know not, but I dare not risk him telling those who are seeking him that the Jews of Fornham did hide him.

"There is also the matter of despising our hospitality," continued Isaac. "My family has extended to you a rare invitation to join us in our sabbath celebration. I am sure you do not wish to refuse to break bread with us."

Bron knew he could not counter such an argument. To refuse to eat with a man when you have accepted the shelter of his home was impossible. It is better to leave in daylight anyway, he thought.

"I thank 'ee, kind sir," he said to Isaac. "I will gladly join you and your family for your evening meal. I will leave in the morning when it is easier to see who and what is around you."

"I am afraid you will have to wait until Sunday, Master Bronnart," said Isaac.

Seeing the startled look in the traveler's eyes, Isaac continued: "As I said, the sabbath lasts from sunset to sunset. Tomorrow, we will have two more sacred meals. Then I think you and I will sit down after the sun sets and discuss further how we may resolve your problem."

These Jews are strange people, thought Bron. No wonder the priests tell us to avoid them. Yet it may be that if I do what this man wants, I will be able to escape with enough coin to be worth the delay.

"As you wish," said Bron, nodding his head more in agreement with his inner thoughts than with the words of the dignified man before him.

Isaac's eyebrows rose at the discourteous words of the other man, but he said nothing.

"Father," said Ruth as she came into the room. "The time draws near for the blessing."

The young woman looked at the two men. It was clear that there had been some serious conversation between them, but Ruth knew better than to ask questions at such a time.

"Thank you, Ruth," said her father.

Turning to Bron, the physician rose to his feet.

"Come," he said. "Let us praise Yahweh for His goodness and eat."

CHAPTER TEN

Here William gave arms to Harold

AILEEN SAVORED THE SILENCE OF THE linen room as she crossed its threshold. Motes of dust danced in the rays of the early morning sun, and the faint skittering of mice could be heard as the creatures made for their nests, disturbed by her unexpected arrival.

Fridays tend to be very busy days, thought Aileen, so I am glad that I came in this early. It does seem strange not to hear the sound of all the needlewomen chattering and Mistress Taylor shushing us all and telling us to get on with our work. But I really do want to have a little time to take a look around and see if there might be something left behind by the thief.

Unlikely, Aileen quietly chuckled, but you never know unless you try.

Aileen gathered up the muslin from the table, and

then, picking up a broom, she swept up bits of material and thread that had fallen to the ground.

"What was that?" Aileen said out loud as she saw something shiny skitter across the floor. Bending down, Aileen picked up a coin. Turning it over and over in her hand, she saw that its design, though similar to the silver pennies she had seen, was not quite the same.

The sound of women talking and laughing reached Aileen. Hastily, she put the coin in her scrip and finished sweeping the floor. I will give the coin to the robemaker later, she thought, after I have had a chance to take a better look at it.

"Aileen," called out Marion, one of her co-workers, as she came through the door. "You are here early. Have you done something for which you need to make amends, or are you just trying to make Mistress Taylor smile upon you today?"

Aileen joined in the laughter that followed the comment. She was saved from having to give an explanation by the arrival of Mistress Taylor. The robemaker, bustling in with her skirts flying and her round, motherly face flushed, was in no mood to tolerate any levity on the part of her workers.

"What is all the noise about,? she demanded. "A gaggle of geese would not make such a commotion. Get to your work, all of you."

Scattering to their tables, the needlewomen settled into their daily routine. Aileen became so engrossed in working the border of an altar cloth that she took little note of time. Before she knew it, Marion was nudging her to come outside and eat lunch.

"It is too nice a day to sit inside," said Marion. "Besides, we are all bursting to talk about the stolen cloth and that lying serf who brought it to the abbey."

Aileen was only too glad to discuss the cloth with her friends. *Mayhap I will learn something new,* she thought. *Even gossip sometimes provides information.*

The women sat outside in the courtyard, soaking in the warm rays of the sun, chewing on their bread, and taking a well-earned rest.

"Aileen," said Marion, "We all saw what fine work your mother did on the embroidery. The design was becoming easier to see and the colors were coming to life."

"Yes," said Alice, one of the ladies who rarely said anything. "Your mother is very talented."

Aileen beamed with pride at the praise for her mother. "I am glad you were able to see the work she did," said Aileen. "She would be happy to know that it brought you pleasure."

A moment's pause ensued while the women ate a few more bites.

"When we looked at the design," Marion said, "it did seem as though there were many fighting men, but there was no battle scene."

"My mother believes that this is a part of a larger story," Aileen responded. "As you saw, one end is torn and frayed, so it would seem likely."

"Does your mother know what the story is that is being told?" asked Marion.

Aileen hesitated. Even were my mother certain of the origin of the embroidery, it is not my part to make it known. But there is no harm in talking about some of the ideas that everyone has been prattling about.

"She is not sure," Aileen said. "But I think she also believes that a great battle is a part of the story. The first panel of the cloth, the part that is frayed, shows men lying on the ground with arrows all around, and the second seems to show a surrender to the commander of the fighting men. But who is the victor and who it is who is surrendering is not clear."

"What about the words stitched on the fabric?" asked one of the women. "They might indicate who it was that won and who lost."

"It was hard to read them though," said Marion. "Mistress Arundel's work was bringing them out, but the last time I looked they were still hard to make out."

"It did seem to me that the name 'William' was one of the words," Alice said, once again surprising the other women with her entry into the conversation.

"I think you may be right, Alice," said Aileen. "Before the cloth was stolen, the writing did seem to include the name 'William'. But of course, we cannot be sure which William was meant. It is not an uncommon name."

"No, it is not," said Marion. "At least, it has not been uncommon since the time of the Conqueror. There are lords of manors in this area with that name, and of course the lord William de Warenne became known within the Liberty due to the murder last year.

"Aileen," Marion continued. "Did your mother say how old she believes this embroidery to be? That might help us think of a more likely Williem to be recorded in such a work."

"Of course, mother could not be certain," replied Aileen, thinking that Marion was asking all the right questions and might be a good ally. "It is old though, and has been buried for many years."

"That tale of the chest being buried and dug up by the serf was so interesting, I thought it could not be true when I first heard it," said Marion. "Bron was a fool to think he could get away with running away with the chest."

"Do you think he stole the cloth before he ran away?" asked one of the other women. "I heard they think he saw Sir Roger in the courtyard and ran away in a panic."

"That does seem likely," said Aileen. "If I were in a panic though, I am not sure I would think to run across the courtyard to the linen room to gather up the embroidery before I ran away."

"That is a good point, Aileen," said Marion. "But I heard Mistress Taylor talking to one of the brothers this morning, and they were saying that the serf also had stolen a candlestick before he ran away."

Aileen was surprised. "It's a wonder he had the time to run all over the place stealing things without being seen," she said.

"I agree," Marion said. "You must admit, though, that this is all rather exciting!"

The women laughed and, seeing that their time was almost up, gathered up their scrips, dusted off their skirts, and made their way back to the linen room in good humor.

It was as Aileen left work that afternoon that she realized she had forgotten to give Mistress Taylor the coin she had found on the floor.

"Bother," she said under her breath.

Aileen paused, wondering if she should go back and find the robemaker now. I think I will wait until tomorrow, she thought to herself. If I make my way home by way of Robert's house, I can show it to him. He may have a better idea of what it is than I do. After all, his father is the goldsmith and so they see a lot of different coins.

Glad to have a good reason to visit the Palgrave house, Aileen set off happily, making her way past the carts rolling home from the market and the children running and laughing as they played.

As Aileen arrived at the Palgrave house, she saw Robert coming down the street. As soon as he saw her, the young man sped up and waved.

"Aileen," he said as he drew level with her. "I did

not expect to see you here this evening. Is all well?" His face, initially alight with pleasure at seeing her became creased with concern.

"All is well, Robert," she said. "Do not be worried. I am here to show you something I found. Mayhap we can talk for a little while?"

"Come in," he said, opening the door and waving her inside.

"Mother, father," Robert called. "See who has come to visit."

"Aileen," Jane Palgrave said cheerfully as she came from the back of the house, the smell of baking wafting in with her. "Glad I am to see you. It is a while since you have visited us."

"Welcome, Aileen," added her husband as he ambled behind Jane, licking his fingers.

Aileen tried hard not to smile. Jane Palgrave's gingerbread was known throughout the Liberty as the best in town. Many people had tried their best to learn her recipe, but Jane always smiled and said it was a secret passed on from mother to daughter and it was not her part to share it with others.

"Thank you," Aileen said. "My mother was saying only the other day that it has been too long since our families shared a meal."

"It has indeed," said Jane, brushing a blonde hair out of her grey eyes and smiling. "Mayhap you would like to take some gingerbread home with you as an invitation to sup with us soon?"

"I am sure such an invitation would be well received," said Aileen demurely.

The laughter that resulted from this response was brought to an end by Jane returning to the kitchen to cut gingerbread for Aileen to take home with her. John Palgrave's piercing blue eyes looked gravely at the pair before him.

Robert's father ran his hand through his thick brown hair, a sure sign to his son that he was busy thinking.

"Aileen," John said eventually. "Of course I am glad to see you. But I doubt not that it is neither my wife nor I that you came to see this late in the day." The goldsmith was a stern man, but a small smile lit his face as he spoke.

Aileen blushed and Robert shuffled his feet.

"Sir," Aileen said, "I am always happy to see everyone in the Palgrave family. But true it is that I came to talk to Robert, if that be possible."

"It is near the hour for us to eat, Aileen," said John. "As I am sure it is for your family."

Aileen hung her head and nodded. She could think of nothing to answer.

Taking pity on the pair, John laughed. "Why, I think the two of you look miserable enough to make a dove cry."

Aileen couldn't help but giggle, and Robert smiled at his father, glad to know that he was not really irritated with them.

"Go on, the pair of you," said John. "Take a little

time to talk. But mark you, Robert, your mother will have supper on the table a short time from now, and I expect that you will be there on time."

"Yes, father," said Robert. Turning to Aileen, he grinned and gestured for them to go out into the garden at the back of the house.

"What is it you have to show me?" said Robert eagerly, getting straight to the point.

"It is something I found in the linen room this morning," responded Aileen, just as earnestly. "I meant to give it to Mistress Taylor today, but I forgot. I will give it to her tomorrow, but I thought to show it to you first and see if you have any idea what it might be."

Aileen pulled the coin out of her scrip and gave it to Robert. The young man turned it over in his hand several times, seeing initially only a dirty coin with two different crosses in the center of either side and text around the edges.

"Where did you find it exactly?" he asked.

"It came from under the table upon which the embroidery had been laid," said Aileen. "I can see it is silver, but it looks a little different from the coins I have seen before."

"I agree," Robert said. "It is very old as well, so I am not sure if it actually is a coin of the realm or if its value is personal to whoever dropped it."

"Robert, how clever of you," she said. "I had not thought of it being something personal. If it is so, then it may well lead us to whoever took the cloth."

Robert's face flushed with pleasure at the praise from the young woman he counted as his best friend.

"Of course, it may just be a coin from across the South Sea," he said offhandedly. "Pilgrims bring many different coins with them when they come to the shrine of our blessed saint."

"Even so, we may be able to learn much about whoever dropped it if we can understand more about the coin itself," said Aileen.

Heads close together, the pair bent over the coin. I like the scent of Aileen's hair, thought Robert. It smells like lavender.

"I see the Latin word for king, but I am not certain what king it is talking about." Aileen's words brought Robert back to the present sharply.

Clearing his throat, Robert looked more closely at the text on the coin.

"It looks like a cross with GRATIA D-I REX after it," said Robert. "I have seen that on other coins. It just means 'King by the grace of God.' That does not help much since we are not sure whose name the cross represents."

"What does it say on the other side?" said Aileen. "Mayhap that will help a little more."

Robert turned the coin over.

"I do not think this is any better." Robert sounded dejected. "All I can tell is the word for town: CIVITAS. But I do not recognize the rest of the text. It must be the name of the town where it was minted."

"If you do not recognize it, then that must mean it

was brought here from Normandy or some other land over the South Sea," Aileen said. "You would recognize the name of a town in England."

"Probably," said Robert. "I do not think there are so many mints in England that I would not recognize the name."

"Then we must find someone who can tell us where this coin was made," said Aileen.

"Mayhap I could ask my father," Robert said. "He has seen many coins in his time as a goldsmith."

Aileen's brow furrowed.

"What is it?" asked Robert.

"This coin is worth more than a penny," she said. "Anyone we ask will want to know how we have come to have it in our possession."

Robert was nothing if not practical. "Tell him the truth," he said. "There is nothing strange about finding a coin and picking it up. You can let my father know that you plan to give it to the robemaker on the morrow but that you thought to satisfy your curiosity first."

"I think I have become too used to mysteries," laughed Aileen. "I made of the puzzle something too complicated. As usual, your solution is the simplest and, in this case, the best."

Joining in Aileen's laughter, Robert stood up, and the pair went into the house where they found John Palgrave sitting at the table.

"I was just about to call you," said Robert's mother, coming into the room holding a platter.

"Aileen, I would ask you to join us, but I am sure your mother will want you to sup with them."

"I am leaving for home now," said Aileen. "But first, would you mind if we asked you a question, Master Palgrave?"

His eyebrows rising, the goldsmith rose from his stool.

"I am happy to help you, of course," he said. "What is it that you wish to ask?"

"Father," Robert said. "Aileen showed me a coin she found on the floor this morning. It is not like the coins we have seen, so, before she gives it to Mistress Taylor on the morrow, we thought to ask if you know anything of its history."

Interested, John took the coin from Robert. He walked over to a candle and turned it over and over in his hand.

"I have not seen one quite like this before," he said.

Seeing the disappointment in the faces of Aileen and his son, John smiled and put up his hand to stop them from saying anything.

"I have seen one similar to it however," he said. "Many years ago, I was commissioned to make a goblet by a man who came to the shrine from over the South Sea. He paid me with silver coins very like this, but they were obviously made more recently."

"Do you know where the coins were made?" asked Robert.

"Yes, and I recognize the name of the city on this

coin," replied his father. "This coin comes from the mint at Bayeux in Normandy."

"Bayeux?" Aileen was surprised. "I am not certain I know anything of this place."

"There is a great cathedral there," said John. "The half-brother of the Conqueror was once bishop there, I do believe."

"The Conqueror," Aileen breathed, lost in thought at this news.

"Yes," said the goldsmith. "But Aileen, you must take this to Mistress Taylor in the morning. This is a denier and worth more than 200 pennies. Whoever dropped it may well be seeking it, and thus it is important it be placed in the right hands."

"Tomorrow is Saturday, Master Palgrave," said Aileen. "And the abbot has said that all may take the day off in remembrance of the blessed St. Edmund's sacrifice."

"Then I would suggest you keep the denier safe until you can give it to her when you return to work," said John.

"I will do so," Aileen said. "Thank you very much for all your help."

"As long as you and my son are not putting yourselves at risk on one of your expeditions, I am always happy to help," replied Master Palgrave.

It is just as well that we are not involved in the search for the runaway serf, thought Robert. I would not like to have to suffer my father's disapproval again.

Aileen turned to leave.

"Aileen," Jane Palgrave called. "Do not forget to take the gingerbread to your family." She picked up the wrapped treat and handed it to Aileen.

"Thank you, Mistress Palgrave," said Aileen. "I know we will all enjoy it very much. "Fare thee well and thank you all for everything," she said.

"Fare thee well," called three voices as she went out the door and headed home, thoughts racing in her mind and the scent of a mystery to solve wafting in the air around her.

CHAPTER ELEVEN

*Here William came to Bayeux where Harold made an
oath to Duke William*

"I T MUST BE DISTRESSING TO YOU,
FATHER Abbot, that such shame should be
brought upon your abbey."

Abbot Samson paused as he was about to take a sip
of wine and looked at the proud man sitting before
him. He saw a man used to commanding obedience
but with little empathy for others. Ambition is one
thing, thought the abbot. The Good Lord forgive me
if my ambition has ever led me astray in the long years
of my calling. But I pray I have not been so contemp-
tuous of other men that I have failed to honor God's
commandment to be compassionate toward those who
are not so blessed as have I been.

"Why would you say so, Brother Lanfranc?" the
abbot said mildly. "I see no shame to our abbey in the

sheltering of pilgrims who travel from far and wide to visit the shrine of our blessed St. Edmund."

Lanfranc's piercing cold blue eyes bored into those of the abbot.

"But you gave shelter to a thief and a liar," he said. "This man did steal from his lord and tried to make of you an accomplice."

"I dare say even the great cathedral of Bayeux has, in the course of its long history, given sanctuary to some who have been less than honorable." Nothing in the abbot's manner could have been said to have been critical, but Lanfranc's pale face flushed and his lips pursed.

"The rules of sanctuary are not a matter of choice," Lanfranc said icily. "The Holy Father has ordained that we must permit those fleeing punishment to claim sanctuary within our cathedral walls. That is different from permitting felons to lodge within your guest hall, eating and sleeping next to honest men who come to trade or worship."

Ah, thought the abbot, his pride is offended at the mere thought of his having potentially encountered the serf.

"Many come to our abbey and ask for shelter," Samson said. "I doubt not that among these there have oft been some whose motives were suspect. It is our part, as far as it is possible, to ensure that nothing untoward happens while our guests are within our walls. We cannot do more, other than to pray for all those souls who enter here."

Lanfranc's lips twisted in derision, but before he could say anything, the abbot smoothly continued: "I am sure that you did not come to discuss with me the relative merits of hospitality and sanctuary, Brother Lanfranc."

Lanfranc took a deep breath and smiled thinly, accepting defeat. There is little to be gained by antagonizing the abbot, he thought to himself. Provincial though this burgh may be in comparison to the great city of Bayeux, Abbot Samson holds much power in this region.

"My lord abbot," Lanfranc said. "Of course, you are right. Interesting though such philosophical discussions may be, I craved audience with you to bring greetings from the bishop of Bayeux and to ask if there might be some reply you would wish me to carry back to him upon my departure."

By no sign did Samson show any surprise or disbelief at the cleric's words. Not even a raised eyebrow or a twitching of the lips was revealed in the abbot's face, although he did think it somewhat strange that Lanfranc had not presented these greetings when first they spoke. I doubt not there is some other reason for this meeting, thought Samson.

"That is most kind," said the monk. "Please do convey my compliments to Bishop Henri and let him know that we have been honored to have you as a pilgrim to the blessed Edmund's shrine."

Samson smiled benignly upon Lanfranc. The

Norman cleric took a sip of his wine, all too obviously thinking about what to say next.

"Father Abbot," he said at last. "I am most interested in your views upon this stolen embroidery. I did visit the room in which the embroidery was laid a few days ago and was most intrigued by what I saw. I would be glad if I could provide the solution to the puzzle when I report to my bishop upon my return from this pilgrimage."

Now we have arrived at Lanfranc's real reason for joining me in my chambers, thought the abbot. But from the look in his eyes I think his interest is more than mere curiosity. I wonder what it is that concerns him about this cloth.

"I too am intrigued by this embroidery," the abbot said. "I visited Mistress Arundel as she was working on the linen only the day before it was stolen. Her opinion that these panels were torn from a larger work remains unchanged and I agree with her. The removal of the dirt is revealing fine work and, I would say, the end of an epic tale."

"You interest me greatly," said the cleric. "Have you concluded what epic tale the embroidery may represent?"

"That is impossible to say," responded the abbot. "Unfortunately, unless the fabric is recovered and the work of Mistress Arundel completed, we may never know for certain."

"What about the theft?" said the cleric. "Is the serf assumed to be the thief, or is there suspicion of another?" Lanfranc's staccato delivery made his words sound more like an interrogation than an enquiry.

"If I knew who had done this deed, I would have sent the reeve after the thief and we would have had him in custody and the cloth recovered already." Abbot Samson was beginning to grow irritated.

"Your pardon, Father Abbot," said Lanfranc. "I did not mean to annoy you with my questions."

The abbot studied the man before him. "You seem rather more interested in this matter than I would have expected a traveler such as yourself to be," he said, drawing a sharp look from the cleric.

"I confess I am much affected by the discovery of this cloth and by the tale it may tell," said Lanfranc. He paused, clearly unsure of how to proceed.

I do not think this man often displays anything other than pride and authority, thought the abbot. I must probe this a little further.

"Brother Lanfranc," said Samson gently. "I think perhaps you need to tell me why this is so."

Lanfranc reared up in his seat, his back straight and his head chiseled like a statue, chin jutting and eyes burning. "I am not weak," he almost shouted. "I have no need for confession beyond that which is my duty to God."

"I did not say anything about weakness, brother," said the abbot. "It is you who came to me and began to ask so many questions about a matter that surely little concerns you."

Lanfranc said nothing, breathing fast, fists

clenched.

"Very well," said the abbot coldly. "I will answer your questions and then mayhap you will answer some of mine."

Receiving no reaction from the other man, Samson went on. "It is true that many believe Bron saw Sir Roger FitzGilbert arrive in the abbey courtyard and that he took the chance of taking the embroidery from the linen room and ran away with it."

"Is that what you believe, Father Abbot?"

"I do not know. Certain it is that Bron took great risk if he did go to the linen room. He could not be sure he would not be seen or that there would be no one in the room to prevent him taking the cloth.

"There is also the matter of the missing candlestick," the abbot continued.

Lanfranc's brow furrowed. "Candlestick?"

"A fine silver candlestick went missing from the Lady Chapel three days ago, the same day on which Sir Roger arrived and Bron fled," said the abbot. "The obvious culprit is, of course, Bron."

"Yet you do not seem to be convinced that the serf is responsible for both disappearances, Father Abbot?" Lanfranc's interest was caught.

"If Bron saw Sir Roger arriving at the abbey and decided to flee, it does seem strange to me that he would take time to steal two items from totally different places in the abbey. Did he not thereby greatly increase his risk of being caught?" The abbot's bushy eyebrows raised in inquiry as he spoke.

"So you believe another is responsible for at least one of these thefts?" Lanfranc spoke slowly, as though he was thinking through the ramifications of what the abbot had said.

"I do not know," responded the abbot.

Interesting, Samson thought, watching the other man closely. It is as though he has drawn back inside himself after that one explosion of passion. Now his face is impossible to read. What is it that he is thinking?

"Brother," the abbot said. "What is it that concerns you so about this embroidery? "Come," he said as Lanfranc shook his head. "I have been honest with you and answered all your questions. Will you not allow me the same courtesy and tell me why you are so interested in this needlework?"

For a moment, Lanfranc was still. Then, shaking his shoulders as though to lift a weight from them, he turned to the abbot. "Father Abbot," he said. "I am, as you know, an official of the great cathedral of Bayeux."

Samson nodded his head.

"I am not the first of my family to be so honored as to be treasurer of Bayeux," the cleric continued.

"Truly," said the abbot. "Your family has a long tradition of service in Bayeux then?"

"Yes," Lanfranc replied. "My ancestor, Conan, was the treasurer of Bayeux during the bishopric of Duke Odo."

"Duke Odo?" Now the abbot was truly surprised. "The half-brother to the Conqueror?"

"Yes," replied the cleric simply. "He was bishop of Bayeux for many years."

"I have heard so," said Samson. He started to say something further about the long-dead bishop but changed his mind.

"Those were very unsettled times," the abbot said, aware that Lanfranc was waiting for him to say something. "Your family must have passed down many interesting stories concerning the events that unfolded before the eyes of your ancestor."

"Indeed," agreed Lanfranc, his bearing once again one of pride and authority.

The Norman cleric paused a moment, apparently gathering his thoughts.

"Father Abbot, do you know about the work commissioned by Bishop Odo to celebrate his brother's victories against the unlawful king, Harold?"

Unfazed by the hard stare directed at him, Samson smiled. "I have heard many tales of the spoils of war and great monuments to the victory at Hastings," he said. "It was long ago and there are few accounts that grow less impressive with the passage of time."

Lanfranc shrugged his shoulders and gave a wry smile.

"That is true," he said. "Yet there is one account of a commemoration of that great victory which I know to be truth."

"You interest me greatly," said Samson encouragingly. "Pray continue."

"The great cathedral my family have had the honor

to serve was built not long after Duke William had been crowned king. It was dedicated some eleven years after the Battle of Hastings.

"Bishop Odo became a man of great power in the early years of King William's reign," the cleric went on. "He was given much land as a reward for his loyalty to his brother, including some in this part of the country."

"Yet perhaps his heart remained in his native land," suggested Samson.

"I do believe one of his proudest achievements was to be granted the title of Bishop of Bayeux," agreed Lanfranc.

"Forgive my interruption," said the abbot. "It was not my intention to speak my thoughts out loud."

"It is of no matter," said the man from Bayeux with a casual wave of his hand. "Your words in fact lead me to the central part of my account."

Samson raised his eyebrows but said nothing.

"Bishop Odo wanted to commemorate his brother's victory in grand fashion," Lanfranc continued. "He commissioned a great tapestry to be displayed in the cathedral upon its dedication."

"A tapestry?" enquired the abbot.

"Yes," replied Lanfranc. "It depicts the entire story of Harold's betrayal of his oath not to take the throne upon the death of King Edward and his eventual death at the hands of the soldiers of the Conqueror. The tapestry is still hung on the walls of the cathedral on special occasions."

Lanfranc paused.

"The tapestry is worked in wool embroidery on plain linen."

Samson was startled. So this is why the man is so eager to know the origins of Bron's discovery, he thought. But surely he cannot think this is a part of the Bayeux tapestry if he has seen the original in the cathedral there.

"I understand your interest in the embroidery now, brother," said the abbot. "But assuredly you do not believe that this dirty cloth found in the field by Bron somehow belongs to the tapestry that hangs in your cathedral?"

Warming to his theme, Samson continued: "There must be many tapestries worked in this way. I have myself seen hangings in cathedrals that would qualify as similar works."

"I agree that there are 'similar' works elsewhere, Father Abbot," said Lanfranc. "But I have yet to reveal to you one very salient point. The tapestry as we know it in Bayeux is incomplete."

"Incomplete?" the abbot repeated. "In what way is it so?"

"The end of the story is missing," Lanfranc said. "One end of the work is torn and frayed."

Samson's eyes opened wide, and for a moment he was unable to frame a response. "So you believe that Bron's find is the missing piece of the Bayeux tapestry," he breathed finally.

"It is possible," Lanfranc replied. "As we both

know, Bishop Odo held lands in this part of the country."

"Yes," said the abbot. "But why would he have damaged such an important work when he took so much trouble to have it made in the first place, and why would he bury it so far from Bayeux? These are questions that must have occurred to you in the past days."

"They have," said Lanfranc. "I do not have all the answers, but I do wonder if the bishop could no longer stomach the final glorious panels of the tapestry once he fell from grace and thus decided to remove them. Mayhap he could not bring himself to destroy them completely, so he hid them where they would not be found by anyone then living."

"'Final glorious panels'," quoted the abbot. "You know then what was depicted in the final panels?"

"It is said that the missing portion of the tapestry portrays the coronation of King William in Westminster Abbey on Christmas Day of 1066," said Lanfranc.

The abbot let out a breath he had not realized he was holding in. "I see," he said. "But we do not know for sure what is contained in the final scene of the embroidery brought to the abbey by the serf. Mistress Arundel had not finished her work at the time it was stolen from the linen room."

"I realize that," Lanfranc said. "However, I have visited the room where it lay on several occasions since the woman began her work. The improvement in the condition of the embroidery had encouraged me to think that possibly the final scene could be the coronation of King William I. If so, then this tapestry belongs in Bayeux, not St. Edmundsbury."

So we come to it at last, thought Samson. "Since we cannot know for certain what is portrayed in this work until we have recovered it and Mistress Arundel has had the opportunity to finish her repairs, it is premature to discuss where it should reside," said the abbot.

Lanfranc's face darkened. Were he a child, thought Samson, I would describe his expression as rebellious. A man who has not outgrown childish habits can be dangerous.

"I believe that any further discussion regarding this work at this time is fruitless," said the abbot. "We must hope that it is found soon and returned to the abbey."

"And when it is returned to the abbey," Lanfranc said insistently, "will you seek to keep it for your house?"

"That is a discussion that must be had with Sir Roger FitzGilbert," said Samson. "From what you have told me, the tapestry was damaged many long years ago, and Bayeux would have no absolute right to claim it. The law of the land gives that right to Sir Roger FitzGilbert. It is to him that all requests will have to be made."

Lanfranc grunted. "Then it is to him that I will make my case in the event that the tapestry is found," he said.

"I thank you for your time, Father Abbot," he

went on, rising and placing his goblet on the table. "I will take my leave of you for now. I know you must have many tasks to complete and prayers to say before the mass tomorrow."

Waiting only to receive a blessing from the abbot, Lanfranc strode out of the room, closing the door behind him with a definite click.

A strange, possibly dangerous man, the abbot mused, staring at the door. He is arrogant and certain of his right to claim whatever he believes to belong to his cathedral. Is it conceivable that he would go so far as to steal the tapestry himself if he had doubts that either Sir Roger or myself would agree to his taking the tapestry back to Bayeux?

The abbot mentally shook his head. That is a grave allegation to make against an official of a great cathedral. In any case, the timing of the theft and the disappearance of the runaway serf makes it hard to believe that anyone but Bron took the embroidery. How would Lanfranc have known to take such a small and unexpected opportunity to remove the work from the linen room? And yet, this is a clever man who would not shy away from risk to get what he wants.

Samson sighed. I am ignoring my own advice, he thought. Further deliberation is pointless unless and until the serf is caught and the cloth is returned safely to the abbey.

Turning his focus onto more pressing matters, the abbot returned to his duties until such time as he had to prepare for the evening mass.

CHAPTER TWELVE

*Here Duke Harold returned to English land and he
came to King Edward*

"Mmmm," said Robert. "This pie is delicious."

Aileen smiled. It had been Robert's suggestion that they take advantage of time away from work this Saturday afternoon by exploring the different booths that had been set up on the site of the festival fair that had arrived in town that week. They had enjoyed looking at items for sale at the pottery and jewelry stalls, stared wide-eyed at the fortune teller sitting outside her tent inviting passers-by to come in and have their palms read, and watched jugglers moving through the crowd, encouraging all the good citizens of the Liberty to part with a little of their hard-earned money.

Aileen was the first to see the pie stall. Touching Robert's elbow, she watched his face light up as she pointed it out to him. Robert's appetite for pies and pasties was so prodigious that sometimes Aileen wondered where he stowed it all in his lanky frame.

"Come on, Aileen," he said eagerly. "Let us see what kind of bake metes they have."

Grabbing Aileen's hand, Robert almost ran to the booth.

"You look like a young man who appreciates good food," said the stall owner. "I take my oath you will not find a better pie in all of England."

A little dramatic, though Aileen, but Robert was so happy to see such a choice of baked goods that he scarcely heard the vendor's greeting.

"What are those?" he asked the man, pointing at a stack of pies smaller than usual. "The coffins are so small I cannot see how there could be anything inside them."

"A very noticing young man," said the stall owner cordially. "Let me tell you that these pies are a sensation in London right now."

"Really?" Aileen said doubtfully. "What is so different about them other than the size, sir?"

I really do not want Robert to get carried away, Aileen thought. The man is a fast talker and Robert is so easily tempted by baked goods.

"I am glad you asked, young mistress," said the man. "You would never guess, but I have a recipe for a container that can be eaten together with the contents."

Robert's head came up and his eyes opened so

wide he looked rather like a deer startled by a careless hunter. "Truly," he breathed. "But how does it taste? I mean, you can break a tooth on most coffins and they taste so bad no one would want to try and eat them anyway."

"I have a secret ingredient," said the man. "Come, let me give you just a very small piece of the coffin and you can see for yourself before you decide to buy one of my pies."

Reaching down to the counter, the man handed Robert a small piece of golden brown crust. Robert sniffed at it and fingered it between his hands, delighted to find that it broke in two. Tentatively, he licked the morsel and then, a big smile coming over his face, he popped it into his mouth and chewed on it.

"Aileen, you simply must try this," said Robert. "It is delicious."

Thus it was that the pair found themselves sitting on a wall near the East Gate to St. Edmundsbury, tucking into meat pies that Aileen had to admit tasted better than anything she had bought from a vendor before.

"It is delicious, Robert," she said. "I am glad you persuaded me to try one."

The pair sat back, basking in the afternoon sunshine and happy just to be in each other's company. Since the time when they were small children, they and their friends had always spent time together when they were allowed time off for any reason. Sometimes they would fish, sometimes they would collect herbs or mushrooms for their mothers, and sometimes they would just play.

As time went by, their friends had gone their own ways, but Robert and Aileen had discovered that they enjoyed their time together too much to change what they were doing. Sometimes they did the same things they had done as children, but at other times they just sat and talked. On occasion, they would even meet up with Ruth and Avraham in the forest after the Jewish sabbath was over.

Now that the pair were older, their parents would sometimes ask them to run errands on their time off. On those occasions, Robert would often borrow his father's cart, blushing at the teasing of his brother that Aileen was his "sweetheart" and at his father jokingly asking if they needed a chaperone. Deny it as he might, Robert had to admit he enjoyed spending time with Aileen more than with just about anyone else.

On this day, their conversation turned naturally to the missing embroidery and the man who had run away.

"A candlestick was stolen at the same time as the embroidery," Aileen informed her friend.

"Truly?" said Robert. "That serf was really busy on the day he ran away. How did he manage to do all that without being seen?"

"That is just what I said." Aileen beamed at her friend.

"Somehow, none of this seems to make any sense."

The two sat in thought for a moment, trying to put the puzzle pieces together in their minds.

"I feel as though the coin I found must be the key to the mystery," said Aileen at last, pulling the coin out of her scrip.

"I thought you were going to take that to Mistress Taylor," Robert said.

"I was," said Aileen. "But when I showed it to her, she went all fluttery and said the coin was far too valuable for her to risk losing it. She told me to take it straightway to Master Durand."

"You did not do so?"

Aileen almost laughed at Robert's puzzled face. The way his eyebrows rise and his nose crinkles is really very becoming, she thought to herself.

"I did try to do so," she said, coming to herself. "He was not at home last night when I went there after work. I thought we might go together this afternoon and give it to him."

"I would like that," said Robert. "Mayhap he can tell us something we do not already know, something that will help us solve the riddle and put everything right again."

Aileen laughed. "You are ever the eternal optimist," she said. "But of course that does not mean that you are not right."

As Robert joined in the laughter, the pair heard a slight cough behind them. Turning around they were astonished to see an old friend from over the South Sea.

"Mistress Aileen, Master Robert," said William de Vere, his thin face alight with laughter and his fair hair flopping over his forehead as he leant forward in a mock bow.

"Sir," Aileen exclaimed in pleasure, running to greet him.

Robert was not so pleased to see the return of the young lord who had so captivated his friend at the time of the theft of the holy relic. I thought I was over being jealous, he thought, but now I am not so sure.

His innate good humor returning to him as suddenly as it had departed, Robert stood and went over to greet the man. William was clearly delighted at the welcome he had received and asked if he could join them.

"Of course, sir," said Robert generously. "We were just enjoying the sunshine and talking."

Settling himself on the ground, William sighed with pleasure.

"It is so good to see you again," he said. "I feel as though my cares roll away when I am in your company."

"That is kind of you to say, sir," said Aileen, blushing a little in embarrassment.

Robert felt it was time to change the subject. "What brings you to St. Edmundsbury, sir?" he asked.

"Please," said the young man. "I feel as though we are old friends. Certain it is that without you I would not be where I am today. I would prefer that you call me William since we are much of an age."

William looked at Aileen as he spoke, sparking another blush from her and what sounded like a faint growl from Robert.

"If you insist, we will try, sir. . .William," responded Aileen.

Robert tried again. "It must be something important if you have returned to the Liberty."

"I came at the behest of my father," William said, tearing his eyes away from Aileen and looking at Robert. "You will be glad to know that we have reconciled after so many years of estrangement, and now he trusts me to carry out his business."

"I am very glad to hear that," said Aileen, smiling broadly. She remembered well the sorrowful young man who so bitterly regretted the actions that had driven him and his father apart. That they had been able to help William regain his dignity and the confidence of his father was something of which she could be proud.

William smiled. "Then, when mother asked that I come visit our relatives in this part of the country while I was here I was only too happy to do so. I have to say, my willing acquiescence to the suggestion seemed to puzzle my mother somewhat."

Even Robert joined in the laughter at that. He well remembered the tangled relationships between William's family and that of Sir Henri du Lac. Had they not learned those details, they might not have been able to solve the crime that almost cost their dear friend Ruth and her family their lives.

"Had mother only known that I was eager to return to this area in order to see again the friends I made here, she would have been horrified. This is so in particular because I believe that mother was hoping that I would form an attachment with my cousin, Elanora," said William.

"Your cousin, sir. . .William?" said Aileen wondering at how close the kinship was. I know that some noble families have a history of marrying members of their family that are too close a relation, she thought, but I have always heard that doing so is not good for their line.

"I think she is a cousin once-removed, or mayhap it is twice-removed," he continued, screwing up his face in concentration. Aileen was relieved to hear this. I like William, she thought. I would have him marry well and be happy in his offspring.

"How did your mother's plan fare?" asked Robert hopefully, completely oblivious to Aileen's musings.

William laughed. "Not well, I fear," he said. "Elanora is fair of face but fierce of temper. I do not believe we would be compatible."

"For shame, sir," said Aileen, but she could not keep the laughter out of her voice, and soon all three of them were in the best of tempers, laughing so hard they had to hold their sides.

"Aileen," Robert said at last. "We have dallied long enough. If we are to see Master Durand, we needs must go before the afternoon wears away."

"Master Durand," said William. "The reeve? I was

going to ask if you had had any more adventures since I was last within your town walls."

"I am not sure you would call them adventures," laughed Aileen. "But come, let us walk toward the abbey together and we will tell you all about it."

"How exciting," William said happily, leaping to his feet.

"Now," said the young lord after they had set out along the road from the East Gate. "Tell me all."

"'All' might take a little too long," said Robert, entering into the spirit of the moment. "But I have to say that the last year has been anything but dull."

"That is certainly true," Aileen said. "First of all, we got involved in finding who murdered a pilgrim and then. . ."

"A murderer," exclaimed William. "That is even more than I could have imagined."

"We really only had a small part in the solving of that mystery," said Robert, embarrassed at the admiration for them that was clear in William's eyes.

"Yes," affirmed Aileen. "We were just in the right place at the right time to put a few of the clues together."

"So you say," said William. "I know you better than that. If Master Durand is not careful, he will have to look out for his job."

Aileen and Robert were aghast at such a suggestion. The looks on their faces only made the young lord laugh more.

"Oh very well," he said when he realized that the

other two had stopped in their tracks and were simply looking at him. "We will leave that aside for now. Come, let us walk on."

Once again, the trio set out for the abbey but this time in silence. William, however, could not contain himself for more than a minute or two.

"I believe I may be able to guess what adventure you are involved in now," he said teasingly.

He held his hand to his forehead as if trying to read the thoughts of Aileen and Robert.

"Could it be that you are searching for a lost embroidery and possibly even an escaped serf?"

"How did you know?" Aileen said, truly surprised at the apparent knowledge of a visitor so recently arrived in the Liberty.

"The guest hall of the abbey is abuzz with news of the panel and speculation as to what it is and who stole it," he said. "I arrived in St. Edmundsbury last night and scarce had time to stable my horse before I heard all about it."

"That does not surprise me," said Robert. "Everywhere I go in town, that is all people are talking about."

"And what is it that they say happened?" asked William. "According to the tale being passed around in the guest hall, the runaway serf saw his lord arrive and ran for his life, taking the linen cloth with him."

"Many in town believe that to be the truth," Robert said. "Others say a terrified man would scarce take the time to snatch the cloth up before running."

"That is one of the things that Robert and I have discussed," Aileen said. "But really we are only talking about it, just like all the other people in town. We are not involved in the search at all."

William raised an eyebrow. "I find that hard to believe, knowing all that I know about you," he said. "Surely you have discovered more information than that."

"A candlestick was taken at the same time," confessed Aileen. "We really do have to wonder if Bron could possibly have taken both things before running away."

William laughed. "I knew it," he declared. "Tell me more."

"There really is not much more to tell," Aileen said. "Is there, Robert?"

"No," her stalwart friend said. "I am sure you heard that Aileen's mother was the one who was restoring the embroidery, did you not?"

"Yes, I did," replied William. "That is one reason I thought you would know more about what is going on than do any of the people staying in the guest hall."

Aileen smiled. "My mother had not completed her work before the linen was stolen," she said. "She does believe, as do many people in the town, that this is a part of a greater work that celebrates a victory in battle of a great lord."

"Does she know what battle?" asked William, his interest quickened.

Aileen hesitated a moment before saying: "She

cannot be sure. I will tell you, however, that my mother thinks this work is old, and that mayhap it comes from a time when an ancestor of hers was a part of a great needlework tradition in Canterbury."

Robert looked at his friend, surprised. Aileen had been so careful not to say too much about her mother's thoughts, and yet here she was, sharing close-held information with a relative stranger.

Neither Aileen nor William noticed Robert's reaction. William seemed to absorb the information as a matter of course. Aileen was thinking that it would be no bad thing if they could get the opinion of someone from the outside. I believe William de Vere to be trustworthy, she thought. Mayhap he would put his finger on something they had missed.

"This is all very intriguing," William said. "So you believe that this serf found a buried treasure, realized it had some worth, and brought it to St. Edmundsbury in order to try and sell it?"

"I doubt he had any idea about its value," said Aileen. "If my mother and the abbot are unsure of its worth, I do not think Bron could have any greater surety. He probably just saw it as a way of escaping his master."

William nodded. "Then, according to the gossip, he saw his master enter the abbey courtyard and ran away to avoid the harsh punishment he would receive, taking the embroidery with him?"

"That is the common belief," said Robert. "Aileen

and I are not certain about the exact sequence of events however."

"Yes, I can tell that you have doubts," said William. "Is it that you have doubts about the serf seeing his master enter the courtyard or that you do not believe he stole the cloth twice?"

"I do not think we are certain where our doubts lie," said Aileen, turning to Robert to see if he agreed.

"I think we just find the whole account as gossip would have it occur rather. . .convenient," Robert said.

"Exactly," Aileen said approvingly.

"I see," William said. "We could take a look at the individual parts of the story, could we not?"

"Or at least at some of the parts that are in the background, if that makes sense," said Aileen.

"The background," Robert said thoughtfully. "The background to the whole story is the serf's actions."

"I think perhaps it goes further than that," said Aileen encouragingly. "What about Bron's master. Mayhap we could consider Bron's behavior in light of the actions of Sir Roger FitzGilbert."

A little doubtfully, Robert nodded his head. Aileen's instincts are always good, he thought to himself. Besides, I would not like William de Vere to get the idea that there could be any split between Aileen and myself.

"Have you met Sir Roger?" Aileen asked William. "He lodges within the walls of the guest hall, I believe."

"I have not met him yet," said William. "I do hear

tell though that he is a generous man not given to arrogance or anger."

"He is not angry at what has happened?" Aileen asked in some surprise.

"Oh yes, I am sure he is," responded William. "After all, he rode all the way to St. Edmundsbury to reclaim his serf and the chest. What I meant to say," he went on, "was that he has not been roaring around the abbey like a lion threatening all sorts of terrible consequences to the serf and his family. Apparently his comments have been more about ensuring that his villeins and serfs know they cannot thwart the law than bringing upon Bron's head fatal consequences."

"That is interesting," said Aileen. "It sounds more as though he is a lord who is capable of showing mercy than anything else."

"That may be true," said Robert, "but Bron may have thought otherwise."

William grimaced. "Even though this Bron is a foolish serf who has transgressed against the laws upon which society stands, I would have Sir Roger show mercy to him as I myself was shown it not so long ago."

Aileen smiled at him. "Sir. . .William, you have repaid the mercy shown you ten times over. Of that I am certain sure."

William gave an embarrassed cough and flushed to the roots of his fair hair.

Surprised to find himself feeling sorry for the young man, Robert turned to Aileen. "Why do you not show him the coin before we take it to Master Durand," he suggested.

Pulling it out of her scrip, Aileen handed the coin to William, explaining what it was that John Palgrave had told them about it.

William turned the coin over in his hand a couple of times.

"I agree with your father," he said to Robert. "This is a coin minted in Bayeux. I have family in the area of Lower Normandy, which is where Bayeux is located, and I have seen coins like this when I have attended upon them in that area."

"Is there anything remarkable about it, William?" asked Aileen.

"No, not really," he replied. "I would say that this one is very old, not only because of its condition, but because the design is not the same as those I have seen before. This coin may be several hundred years old."

"As old as that," exclaimed Aileen. "Surely a coin as old as that would not be in use now."

"I would not think so," said William. "It could, of course, be a remembrance to someone of a person or an event."

"Or it could just be something a pilgrim found along the way and decided to give to the shrine of St. Edmund," suggested Robert.

The other two nodded.

"Either way, I do not think we can take this discussion much further now," said Aileen.

"I agree," said William. "We are almost at the

courtyard gate of the abbey anyway. I will bid you both farewell for now. Mayhap we could meet again before I leave in a few days," he continued in a hopeful tone. "It would give me great pleasure if I could be of some service to you in this matter."

"Of course, sir," said Robert politely. He kept his doubts as to the usefulness of the young lord in their endeavors to himself.

"I would be glad if we could work together," said Aileen happily, choosing to ignore Robert's clouded brow.

William turned toward the abbey gate. Aileen put her hand in Robert's, smiled at him in such a way that his heart seemed to skip a beat, and said, "Shall we make our way to Master Durand's now?"

Robert gladly turned in the direction of the reeve's house, content to know that his friend was still the same Aileen he had known and loved like a sister his whole life.

CHAPTER THIRTEEN

*Here the body of King Edward is carried to the Church
of Saint Peter the Apostle*

I would that Ruth had not said this man could come with us, thought Avraham. I do not trust him.

The sabbath had ended. It was Sunday, and some of the young members of the Fornham community were going into the forest to find mushrooms and to cut grasses and vines to make baskets.

Bron, whose sullen appearance all the previous day had hardly been lifted by a further talk with Isaac of Cordoba in the evening, had come up to Ruth and asked to go with the group to help.

"Of course, Master Bronnart," said Ruth happily. "We are always glad of extra help."

Somehow, I doubt his motives, thought Avraham. When he has not lifted a finger to help ever since he arrived and has only sat in a corner moping, why would he suddenly offer to help. I will have to keep an eye on him, Avraham sighed.

Avraham was only slightly mollified by Bron's apparent eagerness to help get the harness on the donkey and the traces set. Eventually, the group set out for the forest, Avraham driving the cart with Bron walking with the others beside it.

As the morning wore on, Bron showed himself to be an efficient gatherer, even if he remained mostly silent. By the noon hour, the cart was filling with grasses and vines, and the group had gathered very nearly enough mushrooms and berries to provide for each of the Fornham households.

"Shall we sit awhile and eat our lunch?" suggested Ruth, and the others gladly agreed.

Avraham, feeling a little ashamed of his attitude, sat next to Bron and opened up a conversation: "It must be strange for you to be so far from home," he said. "Where is your home?"

"I come from a small place not far from Clare," replied Bron, forgetting himself as he bit into his bread and swallowed a couple of berries.

"Clare?" Avraham looked up sharply. "But that is but two days journey from here. I thought you said you were from Ireland?"

"Nay, young sir," Bron said hurriedly. "I do not mean any Clare that is nearby here. This Clare is in Ireland."

I suppose there must be more than one Clare in

the world, thought Avraham. Yet he did look startled when I talked of the village close by here. Was that startlement because he had not known of it, or was it because he had been caught out in a lie?

And while I am thinking about it, I still cannot shake the suspicion that there was something more to his volunteering to come with us into the forest than just helpfulness. I wonder what else I can find out if I press him a little more.

Trying to relax and show his more friendly side, Avraham said sympathetically: "It is an awful thing to be falsely accused of such a crime as murder," he said. "How did it come about that this charge was laid against you?"

Bron's expression was surly. I need to be more careful, he thought to himself. Almost I was trapped by this addlepate. Best I say nought else.

"I do not want to talk about it," he said. "It is painful to think of it, let alone talk about it." He wiped an imaginary tear from his eye, leaving a berry stain smeared across his face.

"I understand," said Avraham in a voice which sounded as though he was talking through clenched teeth. "Yet you must realize that it is impossible not to be curious about a land where such a punishment as you have described can be carried out."

Bron nodded grudgingly but said nothing.

Avraham tried again. "Isaac of Cordoba did tell me that he has heard of such a thing being done in other countries, but none of us have ever seen a case such as yours."

Silence.

Growing desperate, Avraham tried another tack. "I know that Ruth's father told you something of our traditions," he said. "Did he tell you of the times we have been enslaved and of the many times we have been exiled from countries we had thought to call home?"

"You were slaves?" Bron was startled. "I have never heard of it."

Bron paused for a moment.

"Was it because you deny Jesus Christ is the Messiah?"

"No," Avraham said. "We have been made slaves more than once. Yahweh sent Moses to bring us out of enslavement by the Egyptians. I am sure you have heard your priest tell you of Moses?"

Bron nodded.

"Long after that time, the Assyrians and then the Babylonians invaded our homeland and took us away to make of us slaves. We suffered thus for hundreds of years. All of this was long before Jesus of Nazareth's time."

Bron's eyes were wide. "This sounds like one of those tales told by jongleurs on their travels," he said.

"Yet it is the truth," said Avraham. "You will see now why we are interested in your tale of unjust accusation. Will you not tell me more?"

"There is little more to tell than I have told you

already," Bron said. "I would like to hear more about these nations that made of your people slaves though."

If I can make him talk about his people, thought Bron, mayhap he will stop asking me questions. Sometimes it is hard to remember what I have told one man when faced by another. Easier it is to just say nought.

Avraham was not so easily put off however.

"If you want to know more, then Isaac is the one you should ask," he said. "I know a little, but he is an elder and knows the whole history of our people. You could perhaps talk to him this evening."

Bron's eyes shifted.

"I told him I would leave today. Your sabbath is over and few of my people travel on Sunday. This is a good day for me to leave the Liberty."

I wonder why he chose to come with us into the forest if he intends to leave, thought Avraham. Then it occurred to the young man that mayhap the Irishman had thought to use the group as cover and see what route would be best for him to take.

Bron was fidgeting, his fingers drumming on the ground beside him and his legs constantly crossing and uncrossing. Avraham saw that the man's eyes, which had been shifting left and right, fixed on the cart.

An alarming thought came to the young man. Surely the stranger could not be thinking of stealing the cart while we were all away collecting food and grasses!

Avraham leapt to his feet and ran to the cart. Bron, alarmed, jumped up and went after him.

Reaching into the front corner of the cart, Avraham dug under the pile of sacking that was kept there in case of need. His hand felt something hard, and his face became dark and angry.

Ruth and the others, seeing the two men racing to the cart, got up and wandered over to see what was going on.

"What is this?" demanded Avraham of Bron, holding out his hand in which a leather bag lay opened. Within the folds lay some dried meat, cheese and, bread along with a stoppered jug of wine. The Fornham companions gathered around, murmuring to each other.

"Did you think to steal away from us? Did you think to take the cart?" Avraham's anger was so clear that Ruth went over and put a hand on his arm.

"Avi," she said. "Be calm. I am sure Master Bronnart has an explanation."

All eyes upon him, Bron swallowed, and he found it hard to look any of them in the eyes. "I told your good father that I would be leaving today," he whined. "I thought to thank 'ee for all you did by helping you today. That be all."

"There, Avi," said Ruth. "I said he would be able to explain."

Even now Ruth believes what men say too easily, thought Avraham. I thought by now she would be a little more wary of men's motives, but, of course, her trust in others is one of the things that makes her special.

"What about the bag and supplies?" Avraham said, avoiding Ruth's eyes. "Did you ask permission to take these?"

"I did not think you would begrudge a poor man a few bites to eat and sips to drink," said Bron, still sniveling.

"Of course we will not," Ruth said robustly. "I am sure father would agree with me."

She looked daggers at Avraham, who flushed to the roots of his hair but held his ground.

"I think you should return to Fornham with us, Master Bronnart," he said. "I do not know what conversation passed between you and Ruth's father, but I am certain we can make sure all is well."

Before Bron could say anything else, Avraham continued: "Besides, the afternoon drags on now, and it would be foolish for you to try and find your way through the forest at night."

There was really no argument Bron could muster to that, particularly as Ruth and the others loudly agreed with Avraham on the folly of traveling through unknown woods after dark.

Thus it was that, however reluctantly, Bron rode back to Fornham on the cart with Avraham.

If looks could kill, thought Bron, this big dolt would be lying on the ground writhing in pain and I would be riding off in the cart while all those other fools attended to him.

If looks could kill, thought Avraham, this lying

rascal would surely have struck me to the ground by now. Just as well he is all bluster and I unnerve him.

A small smile lighted Avraham's lips, and he happily flicked the donkey's reins, eager to get home and talk to Isaac of Cordoba.

CHAPTER FOURTEEN

*Here King Edward in bed speaks to his faithful followers
and here he died*

"Master Durand, it is five days since my serf and the chest disappeared. Have you any news for me?"

Durand ruefully shook his head. The day after the sabbath was always a busy one, but now he had been summoned to come to the abbot's chambers. It never rains but it pours, he thought to himself.

When he arrived at the abbey, he found the abbot and the knight waiting expectantly for a report from the reeve.

"My lord, I regret not," he said. "It is strange, but there have been no sightings of him since the day he ran away. Usually when you are searching for a missing person, several people will claim to have seen them. The problem is that most often the information provided means the person for whom you are searching must have traveled faster than a horse gallops."

A thin smile lighted Sir Roger's face. Abbot Samson, knowing his reeve would not be sitting idly by waiting for something to happen, simply asked, "What steps are you taking to discover the serf's whereabouts?"

"My lords, I have men scouring the surrounding countryside and asking after the man in the neighboring hamlets," he said. "It is tedious work, but it must be done, and I believe it is the method most likely to produce success."

Sir Roger, chin in hand, looked gravely at the reeve. "Would a reward help?" he asked.

"A reward..." Durand said. "That could be a double-edged sword. It well may open some mouths, but it would be hard to know if what was said was truth or just someone hoping to win the reward."

"I understand that," said Sir Roger. "But I cannot wait here forever hoping for news, and I will not return home without a serf. As I said before, I cannot afford to have other discontented serfs try my authority as has Bron." Sir Roger's face, usually so calm, darkened with anger.

"We will not cease the search, Sir Roger," said the abbot. "Of that you may be assured."

"I thank you, Father Abbot," the knight said, his color fading as his anger cooled. "I made the offer of a reward in an effort to perhaps encourage the willingness of some to give up any knowledge they may have concerning this matter."

Turning to Durand, he continued, "Let it be known that I will pay three silver pennies to the first person who provides information that leads to the capture of Bron. If the chest is recovered, that is well, but it is Bron that is of the most importance to me."

"That is a generous reward, my lord," said Durand.

Sir Roger nodded. "For the past couple of days, I have been thinking about an appropriate sum," he said. "From what I could see of the exchange of goods and coin at last week's market outside the south gate, I believe three pennies would be valuable to most people in this area."

"It would indeed, my son," said the abbot. "As the reeve has said, there will no doubt be those who will come forward with false leads as a result of the offering of this reward, but I believe it will garner good information as well."

"What say you, Master Reeve?" asked the abbot, turning to Durand.

"I am certain sure you are right, Father Abbot," he said. "I will make sure that it is made known to all that the reward is being offered. ...Speaking of coins," he continued, taking a coin out of his scrip. "Mistress Arundel's daughter has recently brought this to me."

"Aileen gave this to you?" the abbot asked, taking the coin from Durand and holding it up so that the knight could see it as well.

"Yes, Father Abbot," said the reeve. "She and

Robert Palgrave came to see me. Mistress Aileen told me she had found this on the floor in the linen room."

The monk's eyebrows rose. "Truly, these young people have a talent for involving themselves in mysteries," he said indulgently.

Sir Roger and the abbot looked closely at the coin. They could see that it was silver and that one side depicted a cross while the other looked as though it described a wreath and a saltire cross. It was obviously a very old coin, given that the pattern was not totally clear.

"What else did the enterprising young Aileen tell you?" asked the abbot.

Durand smiled. "She told me that the young lord de Vere has returned," he said. "Apparently he had business in the area and thought to see the friends who had helped him."

"You are full of surprises today, Master Durand," said the abbot.

Sir Roger was looking from one to the other of them, puzzlement writ all over his face.

"Who is this Aileen?" he asked. "Who is this master de Vere?"

"Aileen is the daughter of Mistress Arundel," the abbot explained. "She is an embroiderer here in the abbey. Master Palgrave is her friend, and the two of them have been helpful in solving a few mysteries in recent times."

Durand picked up the tale: "William de Vere was present at the time of one of these mysteries," he said.

"He was known for sowing wild oats. According to Mistress Aileen, he is much changed and now well-regarded by others."

"I see," said the knight, although he did not look as though he was much enlightened by the explanation.

"According to William de Vere, this coin was most likely minted in Bayeux many years since," the reeve said.

The abbot looked a little startled. "That is very interesting," he said. His tone conveyed that conviction, and both Sir Roger and Durand looked at the monk closely.

"Why so, Father Abbot?" said the knight.

The abbot shook his head. "I did not mean to imply anything by my words," he said. "It is merely that we have a visitor from Bayeux within the precincts of the abbey at this time."

"That is interesting," said Durand. "Has he been here long, Father Abbot?"

"He arrived almost exactly a week before you," said Samson.

"Then he was here when the cloth was stolen," Sir Roger said.

"He was here when Bron brought it to the abbey as well," Durand said.

"Yes," said the abbot. "But he is the treasurer of the chapter of the great cathedral in Bayeux. He is come on pilgrimage."

"Not a man one would think likely to steal such an artifact then," said Sir Roger.

"Not likely to commit such a crime, I agree," the abbot said carefully. The reeve, who knew the abbot better than the knight, looked hard at the monk. Samson returned the look blandly.

"Father Abbot," Durand said. "What can you tell us about this cleric?"

"As I said, he is an official of the cathedral in that city," the abbot said. "He is proud of his family's history of service to the bishop's seat."

Samson paused a moment to collect his thoughts. "Lanfranc, for that is his name, has been showing great interest in the embroidery and in the progress of Mistress Arundel's work," he said.

"Most of the people in town have been showing a great deal of interest in this tapestry," said Durand. "Has this Lanfranc paid more attention to the mystery than would seem normal, Father Abbot?"

"It is hard to say," replied Samson. "We have talked several times since his arrival. The last time we spoke, he told me a tale that would explain his interest in the embroidery but could perhaps also lead suspicious minds to question his potential involvement in the work's disappearance." Samson looked at Durand as he spoke.

"One of the reasons I summoned you, Master Reeve," the abbot went on to say, "was to inform you of this conversation."

"I understand, Father Abbot," said Durand. "Pray continue."

Sir Roger and Durand listened attentively as

Samson gave an account of his conversation with Lanfranc two days earlier.

"So this Lanfranc believes that the work my serf found may be the final part of this tapestry commissioned by Odo," said the knight when the abbot finished. "I confess, I would find this to be an extraordinary coincidence if it were so."

The abbot inclined his head. "I agree with you, but Brother Lanfranc did make the point that Bishop Odo was granted more than one demesne by King William, some of which were in this part of the country. It is not impossible that the embroidery could have found its way here."

Sir Roger looked doubtful. Durand, who had been looking thoughtful ever since the abbot told his tale, looked from one man to the other and nodded.

"I too agree that it is unlikely," he said. "Yet young Aileen found a coin from Bayeux in the room from which the fabric was stolen, and now we find that we have a pilgrim from that city within the abbey walls whose family history links him to a tapestry that may be the original from which the embroidery was torn. I think we must consider that this cleric may be a suspect in the theft," he concluded.

"Master Reeve, you put the situation very clearly," said the abbot. "But we must also consider that Brother Lanfranc may have dropped the coin innocently at any time in the past week. He did say that he had visited the linen room to inspect the work in progress. There is no necessary connection between the coin and the theft."

"That is true, Father Abbot," said Durand. "I would still be grateful if you would ask Brother Lanfranc to attend upon you in your chambers and permit me to ask him some questions."

"Of course, Master Reeve," said the abbot. "I would have been surprised had you not made such a request."

Sir Roger rose. "I will leave you to this task," he said. "I thank you both for this information and look forward to receiving good news regarding the capture of my serf and the recovery of my stolen property."

Nicely put, thought the abbot. He makes it clear where he stands on both issues without being disagreeable.

Well said, thought the reeve. I continue to find this knight an unusual lord. Yet something about this whole conversation troubles me. I wish I could put my finger on whatever was said that does not strike me as quite right.

Shrugging his shoulders and putting the matter aside for the moment, he turned to the abbot and asked if he could speak to the treasurer from Bayeux now.

"I will send for him," said the abbot. Smiling, he picked up his bell and rang for a brother to fetch Lanfranc.

"I think this will be a very interesting conversation," said Samson. "Mayhap I should not look forward to it as much as I do, but pride meeting persistence can sometimes produce an intriguing result."

With that, the two men sat back in their seats and waited patiently for the arrival of the cleric from Bayeux.

CHAPTER FIFTEEN

*Here they gave the king's crown to Harold and here sits
Harold King of the English*

"You would have thought I had stepped on his toe," said Mistress Taylor indignantly.

Aileen looked up from her work to see the robemaker in conversation with the wife of the chandler, Margaret. The two were old friends, and they often took advantage of Margaret's delivery visits to have a little chat.

Aileen smiled. Mistress Taylor would have been horrified if anyone had so much as suggested that she liked to gossip. "It is important that we keep up with the goings on in the town," she would have said. "That is not gossip!"

Bending once again over her needle, Aileen paid little attention to the conversation going on at the door. Why is it that we always seem to spend the day on Mondays repairing vestments that have been stepped on or smeared with wax? She sighed.

Focused as she was on her work, Aileen only half-heard Margaret's sympathetic murmurs supporting her friend in her distress and the snorts of Mistress Taylor's scorn for whoever it was who had so annoyed her.

"Thinks he is better than all others just because he is a Norman from faraway Bayeux," the robemaker exclaimed. "Men!"

Aileen's head snapped up. Bayeux? Mistress Taylor had come across a man from Bayeux? I had better listen a little more closely, she thought to herself. One never knows from where new information will come.

Unfortunately, Mistress Taylor and Margaret had decided they had better get back to their duties and were hugging each other and saying their farewells.

How frustrating, thought Aileen. I will have to find an opportunity to talk with the robemaker this morning. Knowing that that would not be a task too difficult to accomplish, Aileen went back to her work, keeping an eye out for Mistress Taylor to approach.

It was only fifteen minutes later that the robemaker's rounds brought her to Aileen's table.

"That is good work, Aileen," she said, reaching out to turn the cloth over, making sure the embroidered stitches were neat on the back as well as the front of the rich fabric.

"Thank you, Mistress Taylor," Aileen said. She opened her mouth to ask the robemaker a question about her conversation with Margaret but found at the last moment that she did not know how to introduce the subject without appearing nosy.

"What is it, Aileen?" asked Mistress Taylor. "Speak up. I cannot abide people who just dither and quiver."

How fortunate am I that the robemaker should give me the very opening I need, thought Aileen.

"I did not mean to listen to your conversation this morning, Mistress Taylor," she said. "But I could not avoid hearing you mention Bayeux when you were talking to the chandler's wife."

For a moment it seemed as though the robemaker was going to take offence at Aileen's curiosity but then her expression cleared.

"I think that mayhap I did speak a little too boldly," she said. "But I was affronted by the behavior of this. . .Norman." Mistress Taylor positively spit out the word, as though the mere fact of being Norman was something beyond the pale.

Trying hard not to smile, Aileen adopted a sympathetic expression and asked the obvious question. "What was it that this man did to so distress you, Mistress Taylor?"

"Let me tell you," said the robemaker, drawing up her shoulders and puffing out her cheeks. "I was crossing the courtyard this morning on my way to work, minding my own business and wishing evil to no man."

Mistress Taylor's face is becoming alarmingly red,

thought Aileen. I hope she does not do herself an injury in this remembrance.

"All of a sudden, this great lout appeared right in front of me, looming over me and throwing out his hands as though he would strike me."

"That is terrible," Aileen said feelingly.

Thus encouraged by the younger woman's appreciation, Mistress Taylor perched on the edge of the table and continued.

"I came to a sudden halt, as you may imagine," she said. "Though none could say the encounter was my fault, I am, as you know, nothing if not amenable. I offered a quiet apology to the man, expecting him to return it with one of his own."

"He did not apologize?" Aileen guessed.

"Not only that," the robemaker huffed. "He scorned my apology and made loud comment about country-bred women who did not know their place and stood in the way of their betters."

"No!" Aileen knew that if there was one thing Mistress Taylor could not abide it was people who gave themselves what she called "airs." Usually she applied the term to those who were "no better born than was I or my mother, God bless her soul." Somehow Aileen suspected that this offender did not fall into that category.

"Country-bred?" she offered. "Was he of the town then?"

"Not of this town," said the other woman. "I had seen him throwing his weight around before, looking down his long nose at the lay servants and demanding their immediate attention. When I asked one of the poor women who this man was, they told me he was from Bayeux."

"I have heard the name before," said Aileen. "But I know little about it. It is a city in Normandy, is it not?"

"I believe so," said Mistress Taylor. "I did hear tell that it was an important place in the time of the Conqueror. Of course, I suppose it must have been if his brother wanted to have a great tapestry made for the cathedral there."

The robemaker missed the startled expression on Aileen's face, focused as she was on the behavior of the man who had so offended her.

"Tapestry," Aileen said, trying not to appear too obviously eager to hear more. "What tapestry do you mean?"

"I do not know that much about it," said the robemaker. "I do not even remember where I heard tell of it. All I know is that King William had a brother who was made bishop of Bayeux."

"Please go on," said Aileen when Mistress Taylor stopped.

"There is not much more to tell," said the robemaker. "I did hear tell that the bishop ordered a large piece of embroidery to hang on the wall of the cathedral. He commissioned the work here in England and then took it to Bayeux. That is all I know."

Suddenly realizing that she had paid scant attention to the progress of the work in the room for perhaps too long, Mistress Taylor turned around, clapped her hands and said, "Come, come. The afternoon is fast waning. Let us get on with it!"

Most of the women in the room bent over their work, smiling to themselves. Aileen too returned to her work, trying hard to focus on the embroidery in front of her and not the information she had just gleaned.

"Mother," said Aileen that evening as they sat at their evening meal, "I was talking to Mistress Taylor today and she told me about a great tapestry that was commissioned by the brother of the Conqueror for the cathedral at Bayeux."

Anne put down her spoon and smiled. "Mistress Taylor spoke truly," she said. "Bishop Odo, for that was the name of King William's brother, did order such a work."

"And it was made in this country?" asked Aileen.

"Yes," said Anne. "The embroiderers in this country were well known to be the best at the time. As history has told the tale, Bishop Odo wanted to celebrate his brother's victory with only the very best work, so he commissioned the tapestry to be made in England. When it was complete, he took it back to Bayeux."

Aileen looked at her mother. Anne's eyes were

twinkling, and her face bore the expression of one who was waiting for her clever daughter to ask the right question.

"You believe the piece of embroidery upon which you have been working is a part of that tapestry, do you not?" said Aileen.

Her mother smiled. "Yes," she said simply.

Everyone at the table was now looking at her, clearly waiting for more.

"I told you of our family tradition regarding Mabel, did I not?" she said.

Jude, Aileen and Mabel all nodded. Aileen's younger brothers, Richard and Henry, had no interest beyond filling their stomachs and paid no attention to the conversation at all.

"I am named for your ancestor, am I not, mama?" asked Mabel, giving Aileen a smug look.

"Yes, Mabel, you are," affirmed her mother. "It is my hope that you, like Aileen, will become a skilled plier of the needle."

Aileen tried not to smile at her mother's gentle way of reminding Mabel that humility was to be preferred to pridefulness.

"Mabel was a most skilled needlewoman," Anne said. "She was also very devout."

Aileen was puzzled. She was not quite sure what the one had to do with the other when it came to this discussion.

"You may wonder why I would comment on her faith when we are talking about embroidery," Anne went on, unconsciously echoing her daughter's thoughts. "It is necessary, however, to help explain what I am going to tell you."

"Please go on, mama," said Aileen as her mother picked up her spoon.

"Let us finish our meal first," said Anne. "What I have to say may take some time, and we must first clear the table and put Henry and Richard to bed."

Patience is a virtue, Aileen thought to herself, but I am not sure it is one I have in large measure. Stabbing her spoon into her food, she said: "Yes, mama."

Anne, who knew her daughter well, hid a smile and calmly continued with her meal.

In less than an hour, all the chores had been completed, and the two young boys were in bed fast asleep. Aileen, Mabel, and their parents gathered in front of the fire, Jude contentedly puffing on his pipe, Aileen plucking leaves off the woad plant to ready it for dyeing in the morning, and Mabel practicing stitches on a little scrap of linen.

"Now where was I?" said Anne, sitting down with some mending on her lap.

"You were saying that your revered ancestress was a devout woman," said Jude helpfully.

"And you told us that her strong faith was important to this story," added Aileen.

"It is so," said Anne.

Turning on her stool a little so that the light from the fire would make it easier to see what she was doing, she began to darn the hole in the cloth before her as she spoke.

"My great-grandmother wanted to make sure that this commission was as splendid as it could be, not only because the great lord who ordered it was a man of influence and power but also because of her considerable pride in the work of the English artisans."

"I can see how that would be," said Aileen. "That must have been a hard time for all people of this land, and I am sure those who could wanted to show the Normans that we had great skills."

"Well put, Aileen," said her father. "There was much upheaval in the land for many years after the defeat of King Harold. Much was asked of your mother's ancestress, but pride in her country and its people would have required of her an even greater effort."

"Is this right, mama?" Mabel was a little lost in all this talk of pride and hard times. She was more interested in her mother's approval of her efforts.

"Yes, Mabel," said Anne, taking a look at the stitching. "That is much better than it was. Just make sure you concentrate on not pulling the needle tighter on any of the stitches."

"Yes, mama," Mabel said. She returned to her work, her forehead creasing in concentration and the tip of her tongue working its way around her lips as though it could help her fingers as they plied the needle.

Anne smiled at her younger daughter and then continued with her mending and her story.

"As I said, Mabel wanted the work to be exquisite, but she also felt strongly that only our Lord God could produce perfection. That was why she did what she did."

"What did she do?" Aileen was leaning forward in her eagerness to learn more.

"From the amount of cleaning and repair work that I had already completed, you could see that there was a border in the design top and bottom, could you not?" Anne said.

"Yes," replied Aileen. "All your hard work was really bringing out the whole picture."

"In the top border of the last panel, I believed I saw ships portrayed," her mother continued. "I had not quite finished cleaning them, but on the last day before the cloth was stolen, I had been able to bring out the outlines of ships to the point where I could see most of the prow of each one."

By now, Jude and Aileen were hanging on every word uttered by Anne. Even Mabel had stopped her stitching and was watching her mother.

"I was waiting until the fabric was dry before I tried to pick out the final details," Anne continued. "Unfortunately, I did not get the opportunity to complete my work. I can only hope that the tapestry is found in good condition and that I will be able to return to my task."

"If you are so able, mother, what is it you hope to find?" asked Aileen.

"According to my grandmother, Mabel found a

way that she could include an error in the stitching without it being noticed," said Anne. "That way God was glorified in the work and no man could say that any artisan was guilty of blasphemy in trying to attain perfection."

"And that error is in the border of the last panel," guessed Aileen.

"Yes," said Anne. "It is family tradition that my great-grandmother filled out the prow of each ship with stitches. All except for one prow. That was left empty. Only someone looking for a mistake could possibly see it, but Mabel was satisfied that it would not detract from the quality of the final product."

"I understand why you were so perturbed by the disappearance of the piece," said Aileen.

"We can only pray that it will be returned to the abbey safe and sound," responded Anne calmly. "If so, then we may have the joy of seeing a piece of our family history. If not, well then I still have the joy of my own family."

Anne smiled upon her husband and children.

Jude leaned over and took his wife's hand. "I believe there is no joy greater on this earth," he said sincerely.

Mabel rolled her eyes.

Aileen smiled to herself. Father is a man of few words, she thought, but he and mother are so obviously still in love after all these years. I used to think it silly when I was Mabel's age. Now I wonder if I could ever find someone who will love me like that.

Jude, looking quickly at his children, cleared his throat and sat back. "If this is indeed the tapestry Bishop Odo took to Bayeux, the next question must be how this fragment make its way to Suffolk soil," he said.

"As I walked up Abbeygate today, many people asked me about the cloth," said Anne. "They were interested in many things: Whether the serf stole it, what it was, and, as you just said, how it came to be buried in a field in Suffolk."

"And how did you answer?" Jude asked, smiling.

"You know very well how I answered," Anne responded, smiling in her turn. "I could tell them little about the embroidery itself and nothing about its travels to our county."

"Do you have any ideas, father?" asked Aileen. "You know so much more about what has happened in the past than do the rest of us. I am sure you have some thoughts as to the cloth and its history."

"You flatter me, Aileen," Jude said. "I believe your mother has far greater knowledge about this fabric and its history than do I. However," he went on. "I have been thinking about the fact that the same man who may have commissioned this tapestry also happened to be lord of lands not too distant from here."

No one said a word. Jude looked around the room. Three pairs of eyes looked at him expectantly.

"I have heard that Bishop Odo did fall out of favor with his great brother toward the end of the

Conqueror's reign," Jude continued. "I wonder if that might have some bearing on the matter."

Aileen thought about it for a moment. "You mean that it may have been the bishop himself who returned the fragment of the tapestry to Suffolk?" she asked slowly.

Jude gave his elder daughter a nod of approval.

"Yes," he said. "I believe that Bishop Odo was exiled from England by King William after he had tried to usurp his power. Mayhap he decided a celebration of his brother's victory over good King Harold stuck in his craw once he was caught and punished."

"So he tore off the end of the great work he had himself commissioned?" Anne sounded as though she was scandalized at such vandalism.

"But father," said Aileen. "If he was banished, how did he come to bring the fragment of the tapestry back to England?"

"I do not say that this is the truth," said Jude. "I just pose it as a possibility. And remember, Aileen, even though this man may have fallen from grace with the king, he still held power and had many knights and servants sworn to serve him. He might have sent the panels that were found to this country to avoid his brother finding them."

"You mean that he would count on the king not thinking to seek the tapestry right under his own nose?" Aileen asked, fascinated by the suggestion.

"As you see," her father said, laughing. "You are

not the only one in the family who can think of complicated solutions to puzzles."

"I have always wondered where Aileen got her talent for solving mysteries," said Anne, joining in the general laughter. "Now I know!"

CHAPTER SIXTEEN

These people marvel at the star

"Had the abbot not been present, it is certain I would have given that jobbernowl a piece of my mind."

Sir Roger nodded gravely at the explosion of words from his red-faced companion. He had tarried in the guest hall that Tuesday morning in hopes of seeing the Norman cleric. Seeing the expression on Lanfranc's face when he entered the room, he was uncertain as to whether this was a good time to approach him but decided to do so anyway.

"Good morrow, sir," he said as their paths crossed. "I hope that your time in this great abbey is proving fruitful."

Lanfranc looked the other man up and down. The bearing and the garb of this tall, strongly-built man denoted at the least a Norman lord. He bowed his head and attempted a smile.

"Good morrow, my lord," he responded. "Rather would I have been making my prayers in my home abbey which is, I firmly believe, of far greater standing than this gray lodging."

Abbot Samson said this man was prickly, thought Roger. It will be hard to have a worthwhile conversation with anyone whose very smile seemed barbed with thorns, and yet I will persevere.

"You interest me greatly, sir," said Sir Roger. "Mayhap we could sit and talk a while and you can tell me all about this place of which you speak?"

Seeing hesitation on the face of the cleric, Roger went on smoothly: "Allow me to introduce myself. I am Sir Roger FitzGilbert, lord of the manor of Fitching."

Lanfranc's interest quickened. The serf's lord, he thought. It may be worth my time to sit and talk with this man.

Fixing his face into as genial an expression as was possible Lanfranc waved to some seats close by and said he would be glad of the opportunity to converse with Sir Roger.

If that is an example of his friendly side, thought the knight, then I would not like to be there when his mood turns dark. Hiding a rueful smile behind his hand, Roger took the seat offered by Lanfranc and asked a passing servant for two tankards of ale.

"I am tardy in introducing myself, Sir Roger,"

began Lanfranc. "I am treasurer of the chapter of the great abbey at Bayeux." His voice filled with pride as he announced his title.

"A noble title indeed," said Roger in as reverent a tone as he could bring himself to adopt. "It is, then, of this abbey you speak?"

"It is," affirmed Lanfranc.

"Did you then come to St. Edmundsbury on pilgrimage to the blessed shrine of St. Edmund?"

Lanfranc's face darkened. "I did," he said shortly.

"Your experience has not been as you had expected?" said Sir Roger tentatively.

At that question Lanfranc's fists clenched and his cheeks puffed out. "It has not," he said. "In seeking to give of my wisdom and knowledge to help this abbey and the town's reeve, I have been offered nothing but offence and suspicion. Indeed, I can scarce believe what that officious oaf had the nerve to say to me last night."

"The reeve interviewed you last night?" said Sir Roger, only to be regaled with Lanfranc's declaration of what he would have said to the reeve had Abbot Samson not been present.

"It is certainly not the place of such a lowly official to disoblige a lord such as yourself," Roger said. "How did it come about that the reeve was in a position to so aggrieve you?"

Lanfranc paused, regaining his composure. If I wish to learn anything from this knight, he thought, I needs must be cautious in what I say.

"My lord," he said. "I think that you are the lord of

the serf who stole a chest that was dug up in a field, are you not?"

"I am," said Sir Roger. "I have come to St. Edmundsbury to retrieve both serf and that which he stole."

"There has been some gossip in the town concerning the cloth found within the chest," said the cleric. I am not sure how much he knows, Lanfranc thought, but I mean to find out.

He is testing me to see what I have heard, thought Roger. I wonder why.

"Yes, I have heard talk that it is part of a rich tapestry that may have come from your hometown," he said, cutting to the chase.

The Norman cleric looked somewhat surprised to be so easily rewarded with the information he had sought.

"Quite so," he said.

"It was about this that the reeve wished to speak to you last night?" asked Sir Roger.

Lanfranc's color began to rise again. With much effort and several deep breaths, he was able to regain his composure.

"It was," he said a little more snappily than he intended. "I had previously told the abbot about my family's history and that I thought the cloth might be a fragment of a tapestry well known in Bayeux," he continued in a more temperate tone.

"That is most interesting," said Sir Roger. "Then

the abbot thought that you might be of help to the reeve in solving the mystery of its whereabouts?"

The knight's manner was so deferential and sympathetic that Lanfranc found himself talking about last night's encounter in far greater detail than he had intended.

"Mayhap that was the abbot's intent," he said. "The reeve's tone, however, was suggestive of suspicion rather than collaboration."

"That is shameful if such be the case," Sir Roger said, his eyebrows rising in professed surprise.

Thus encouraged, Lanfranc continued.

"Abbot Samson asked that I attend upon him in his chambers," he said. "When I arrived, it was to find that the reeve was with him. I was somewhat surprised to find that the abbot was not alone, but I supposed that the abbot had sent to ask for my presence before the man had arrived."

"Such was not the case?" asked the knight.

"No," said Lanfranc. "It soon became clear that I had been asked to attend upon the abbot solely for the purpose of discussing this matter with the reeve.

"I had no objection, of course," Lanfranc assured the knight. "It would have been more courteous to inform me of the presence of the abbot's man within the monk's chambers when extending the invitation to me, but of course not all men are raised with such gentle manners."

I can understand now why the abbot seemed restrained in his description of this cleric, thought

Roger. His self-esteem rises to the height of the steeple of the abbey church.

"You speak truly," he commented, mentally apologizing to the abbot as he spoke.

Mollified by the supportive attention of this knight, Lanfranc continued with his account. "The abbot explained that he had communicated some of what I had discussed with him some days before concerning the possible origins of the tapestry. I confess I was surprised at this breach of confidence, but, since I had nothing to hide in this regard, I merely raised an eyebrow and waited for what was to come."

The cleric paused to take a sip from his tankard. His pursed lips indicated that he thought little of the drink in front of him, but he was resigned to the fact that a dry throat will suffer whatever beverage may come.

Collecting his thoughts, Lanfranc picked up his tale. "Abbot Samson explained that he had thought it best to include me in the discussion he and his servant the reeve were having since I seemed to have superior knowledge regarding the history of the embroidery."

I somehow doubt that those were the abbot's words, Roger thought as he tried to hide the smile that came to his lips. But it is best if I keep my peace since Lanfranc is obviously unaware of the fact that I too have been made aware of his views on the identity of the tapestry.

"Pray continue," he said to the cleric. "As you can imagine, I am most interested in hearing anything you may know regarding the origin of this embroidery. From what you say, it would appear that you have a greater insight into its identity than do any others within these walls."

Lanfranc frowned. He had not meant to be the one handing out information, but after all, there was no harm in engendering trust in this minor lord. He would have to know sooner or later if the tapestry was to be returned to its rightful owner.

"I do not know how much you have been told about this cloth, my lord," he said finally. "But the reason the abbot's servant wished to speak with me was because I had told the abbot that my family history has led me to believe that the contents of the chest found by the runaway serf are part of a great tapestry that was commissioned to hang in the cathedral of Bayeux."

Interesting, thought the knight. He cannot bring himself to name the reeve, but he has a very ready explanation for his interest in the stolen embroidery. How far does that interest extend, I wonder? Pride cometh before a fall, but it is hard to believe that this man's pride would be so weening that he would stoop to theft of a tapestry of as yet unknown origin.

"I see," said Sir Roger noncommittally. "So the reeve wanted to hear from you about this history?"

"That is what he said." Lanfranc's voice was ragged, and Roger could almost hear his teeth grinding. "But the first thing he did was ask me if I had visited the linen room during the time the woman of the Liberty was working on the cloth."

"And had you?"

"Of course I had," snapped Lanfranc. "Half the town and most of those within the abbey walls wanted to see this dirty cloth brought to Abbot Samson by a thieving serf. As soon as I heard the rumors about what it could be, I knew I had to see it for myself."

"That is only natural," agreed the knight.

Mollified, Lanfranc went on. "After the tapestry was taken from the abbey, I felt it was my duty to inform the abbot of my suspicions regarding the nature of this work."

"Of course," said Roger. "You are obviously a man of integrity. You could not do otherwise."

The cleric glanced at the knight, but Sir Roger's blameless expression encouraged him to continue.

"I demanded to know why the reeve should be asking me to explain my movements," Lanfranc continued. "I am a man of position, of honor and piety. He had no right to speak to me so."

"What was it he said that so enraged you?" Roger asked.

"As if he were a jongleur, he pulled a coin out of his scrip and held it beneath my nose," said Lanfranc. "He told me it had been found on the floor close by the table upon which the tapestry had been laid and asked me if it was mine."

"A coin?" said Sir Roger.

"You can be sure that I put that clodpate in his

place," Lanfranc said. "I took the coin from his hand and examined it, finding it to be a very old coin from the mint at Bayeux. Ignoring the yokel, I spoke to Abbot Samson alone and told him as much."

"What did the abbot say?" asked the knight.

"He said he had been informed it might be from the Bayeux mint and said that, since it appeared to be very old, he wondered if perhaps it was a memento of mine."

"Mayhap the abbot simply wished to ensure that the coin was returned to its rightful owner," said Sir Roger.

"I know not for sure the abbot's purpose in asking me to attend upon him in his chambers," said Lanfranc. "I only know that his man was offensive and needs to learn the limits of his authority."

"It is sad indeed that there are those whose conduct toward others is so lacking in proper respect," said the knight carefully.

The two men sat in companionable silence for a moment.

"But, Brother Lanfranc," said Sir Roger. "You have not said whether you did in fact recognize the coin. Was it a memento you had accidentally dropped when viewing the tapestry?"

"It may have been," said Lanfranc. "I could not say with certainty that the coin was mine, for there are many pilgrims to this benighted town who may have such coins within their possession. However, I do have such a coin that I often take with me as a sort of talisman when I travel."

"Did you bring it with you to St. Edmundsbury?" Roger asked.

"In truth, I cannot say for sure," said Lanfranc. "I did check my scrip when asked about the coin and found nothing. I cannot remember having seen it during this journey, so it may be that the coin that jobbernowl showed me is, in fact, mine."

"What happened to the coin once your discussion was finished?" Sir Roger was genuinely interested in hearing Lanfranc's answer.

"The reeve held on to it," the cleric said carelessly. "The man said it was evidence and he must retain it until the serf has been captured and the cloth returned to the abbey. Only when that is complete will the abbot make a decision as to the final disposition of the denier."

Sir Roger nodded absently. "The coin aside," he said, "your scrutiny of the cloth gave you indication that it may be a part of this great work that was commissioned for your cathedral?"

Now we come to the part of the conversation that interests me, thought Lanfranc. It is tiresome having to explain myself to this provincial knight, but if it gains me my objective it will have been worth it.

"My examination of the cloth showed that the style of the decoration was identical to the great tapestry that belongs to the cathedral in Bayeux," he said.

"How did a part of this work come to be separated from the whole?" asked Sir Roger.

"There are rumors," responded Lanfranc, "but none can be certain of the truth of any one account. It has been missing for many years and I am sure most have thought it long since destroyed."

"Certain it is that few could have imagined this outcome," said the knight.

I may as well be direct in my inquiry, thought Lanfranc. This Sir Roger FitzGilbert seems to be a man who appreciates such an approach.

"May I ask how the embroidery came to be found?" he said to the other man. "I have heard rumors, but, as with all gossip, the story only grows with repeated telling. I would rather have the correct account from someone such as yourself."

"I cannot fault you in that," Sir Roger said agreeably.

Taking a drink from his tankard, the knight continued: "Bron, for that is the name of my wayward serf, dug the chest up out of a field he was ploughing. The field had been covered with brush and brambles for many years and was only now being prepared for crops. I suspect that is why the chest was not found until now."

"I see," said Lanfranc. "And the serf decided to steal the box and run from his duty?"

"He did," Roger said. "This man's father was well-regarded, as is his brother, but Bron has ever been headstrong. I fear he has gone too far this time however."

Lanfranc paused.

"What is it that you intend to do with the tapestry, should it be recovered?" he said.

"I have made no decision as yet," returned Sir Roger. "I wish to see it for myself first, and, thus far, that has not been possible."

"But you have not decided whether you will retain it in your own manor or allow it to be taken elsewhere?" pressed the cleric.

"Excuse me, good sirs," said a voice beside the two men.

Looking up, slightly startled at the interruption, Sir Roger and Lanfranc saw a tall, somewhat lanky young man standing before them. His dress proclaimed him to be of good rank, but neither man knew him.

"Good morrow, sir," said the knight, a slight smile of welcome on his face. Lanfranc raised his eyebrows and said nothing.

"Pardon my interruption," said the young man, flushing slightly. "I would not have disturbed your conversation, but I am newly arrived in St. Edmundsbury and have been informed that an official of the great cathedral at Bayeux is currently staying in the guest hall. I believe that may be you, brother," the man continued, inclining his head in a slight bow.

Lanfranc, happy to see someone according him due respect, returned the bow and spoke graciously to the stranger. "I am indeed Lanfranc, treasurer of the chapter of the cathedral of Bayeux."

Waving his hand in the direction of his companion, he introduced him as Sir Roger FitzGilbert, lord of the manor of Fitching.

"My lords," said the young man. "I am honored to make your acquaintance. My name is William de Vere. My father is lord of lands in France."

It was clear from the expression on Sir Roger's face that he was unfamiliar with the name but perfectly willing to have conversation with this young lord. Lanfranc's face, however, showed first surprise, then confusion, calculation, and finally the resignation of a man aware that whatever may have been his present plan would have to wait.

He knows my family is close to the crown, thought William. That will ensure that I am not unceremoniously dismissed from their presence.

"Of course I know of your family, my lord," said Lanfranc, confirming William's impression. "We would be honored to have a member of a family so close to the French king join our company."

Restraining the crow of triumph that almost escaped his lips, William asked if he could sit a while with the two men.

"Of course," said Sir Roger, rising to offer his seat to William. "Do you wish to speak with this worthy cleric alone?"

"My lord, not at all," said William. "Pray do not disturb yourself thus. I merely thought to pass some time in the hall speaking with someone who is from a place of which I have such fond memories."

The good Lord forgive me for such rank exaggeration, thought William. Bayeux is pretty enough, but rarely have I met such a group of haughty clerics filled with the assurance of their own superiority.

Preening himself in the warmth of such discernment, Lanfranc forgot his annoyance at the interruption of his conversation with Sir Roger and smiled at the young Lord de Vere.

"Bayeux is indeed a place renowned for its beauty and its holiness," he stated in a reverent tone.

William cleared his throat. "When I arrived, there was little else being discussed but the disappearance of a certain cloth and a runaway serf," he said. Lanfranc frowned slightly.

Adopting an expression of interested innocence, William continued. "Mention was made of a rumor that the cloth may have come from Bayeux, and that was when I heard that there was a great official here from that beautiful city."

Roger took pity on the cleric whose face clearly displayed a struggle between his desire to snap at the nosy young lord and his awareness of the exalted family of which that same young lord was a member.

"You are well informed, Sir William," said the knight. "The cloth which you mention was brought to St. Edmundsbury by a runaway serf of mine. Both serf and cloth have now vanished, and Brother Lanfranc, who had seen the cloth while it was within these walls, was good enough to give the abbot his thoughts on its origin."

"I would be most curious to hear your thoughts on the matter, brother," said William, turning to the cleric. "Bayeux is justly famous for its cathedral and for the tapestry that was commissioned at the time of the first King William. Your insight would be valuable to anyone interested in solving the mystery of this fabric."

This is not the way I envisioned this conversation, thought Lanfranc frustratedly. I can scarce refuse to answer this young lord, however. Preferment by his family is something of great value and, while I know not how it may benefit me at this time, to deny him the information he seeks would be foolish.

Sighing, Lanfranc forced himself to smile and told William about the conversation with the abbot concerning the possibility that the fragment of embroidery was a part of the tapestry that had hung in Bayeux for so many years.

Lanfranc completely missed the twinkle in William's eye. He hates having to do this, thought the young man. Were he not so well aware of my family's position, he would doubtless have told me to mind my own business.

"From your account, brother, it would seem to me that there is a good possibility that this twice-lost cloth is a part of the great tapestry commissioned by Bishop Odo," said William.

Roger nodded. "I agree," he said.

William turned to the knight. "May I ask if you

know whether your land was one of the manors held by Bishop Odo under his brother?"

"I believe so," responded Sir Roger. "The borders of manors that have oft changed hands over the course of time cannot always be calculated exactly, but the records of the great survey carried out by the Conqueror do suggest that at least a part of my land was held by Bishop Odo at one time."

"Could he have brought the fragment of tapestry back to England with him at some point?" mused William.

"I have never heard that Bishop Odo returned to this country after he fell out of favor with his brother," said Lanfranc. "Surely it would have been dangerous for him to do so after he had been exiled?"

"That is a good point," William said approvingly. "But do we know when the missing piece of the great tapestry of Bayeux was torn from the whole?"

In spite of himself, Lanfranc was becoming interested in the discussion. The two knights were hanging on his every word. Recognition of his importance at last!

"I fear not," he said regretfully. "The chapter accounts and the history told me by my family do show that the tapestry was in its place in the cathedral before Odo's ill-conceived revolt against his brother. After Bishop Odo's fall from grace, there was a period of confusion and the cathedral accounts are not complete."

"That is unfortunate," said Sir Roger.

"The main part of the tapestry was still within the cathedral walls," Lanfranc said hurriedly, not wishing the others to think that he had exhausted all his knowledge. "It was brought out on special occasions for many years and hung with pride."

"Mayhap we can solve at least a part of the mystery then," said William eagerly. "When the tapestry was hung on those occasions, was there a part of it missing?"

"I do not know for certain," said Lanfranc. "It is many years since it has been seen in public. There has been a tradition in my family, however, that there was a part of the great work missing from the time of my distant ancestors."

The three men were silent for a minute, each focused on his own thoughts.

"Think you it is possible that Bishop Odo, so angered by his brother's banishment, tore the tapestry in two?" asked William.

"From what I have been told, the last few panels of the work were a splendid representation of King William's triumph and his coronation in Westminster Abbey," said Lanfranc. "I suppose it is possible that he might wish to remove such a reminder of victory and yet not destroy the entire work."

"Would such an act be characteristic of the bishop?" asked Sir Roger.

"I know only that my family tradition is that Bishop Odo was a proud man," responded Lanfranc.

"Whether that pride would lead to such destruction, I know not."

"Yet we still have the problem of how the fragment came to be in a field on my land," said Roger.

"I think that is not such a hard thing to figure out," said William. "After all, even in exile, Bishop Odo would have had faithful servants. How better to hide a part of the great tapestry from his brother, should William wish to search for it, than under the Conqueror's very nose?"

"You mean that the bishop may have sent one of his men to England to bury the treasure in a field on what is now my land?" Roger said in surprise.

"Why not?" asked William, laughing. "It is the kind of thing a proud yet clever man might do."

"Mayhap you have the right of it," said Lanfranc, surprised by the young man's astuteness.

Sir Roger's thoughts had turned to a more recent history of the embroidery.

"Bron is a proud man, too," he said. "He is not a clever man however."

"A serf who runs away from his lord is a fool," Lanfranc said forcefully. "How far does he think he can go before he is captured and receives his due punishment? Why forfeit your life for a find of unknown value."

Roger looked at the cleric thoughtfully?

"His punishment is not yet decided," he said. "I do agree, however, that he is foolish. Even were he to escape the Liberty with the tapestry, how will he ever find someone to give him good value for it? Word of the theft will go from manor to manor and town to town. No one will give him succor for fear of being punished themselves. Indeed, there will be many who will give him up for the reward I have offered."

There seemed little more to be said. The three men rose and took their leave of each other.

What should I do with this feebleminded serf when he is captured? thought Roger as he walked across the courtyard. I am loathe to send any man to his death, but there must be a fitting punishment if I am to retain control of my peasants.

I am more and more convinced that this buried cloth is a part of our great tapestry, thought Lanfranc. It must be returned to Bayeux.

This has been most interesting, thought William. I must seek out Aileen and Robert tomorrow and talk to them more before I leave. Wouldn't it be exciting if we could solve the mystery of the tapestry together.

CHAPTER SEVENTEEN

Here an English ship came to the land of Duke William

"Avraham," exclaimed Robert. "I little thought to see you today. Is all well?"

"All is well," said Avraham. "I am sorry to have startled you."

Robert carefully put down the crucible of molten silver he was holding. His father, John Palgrave, looked up from the exacting scroll work he was applying to a bracelet and smiled.

"Avraham," he said. "Good morrow. How is your family?"

"Very well, sir," Avraham responded. "Forgive my interruption."

"It is no matter," said John. "I am sure you have a purpose for your visit though. Is there something we can do to help?"

"Isaac of Cordoba did send me to St. Edmundsbury today to seek information regarding a visitor to our community," said the young man. "I thought to start with my friends, for I know there is little that happens in the Liberty that has not come to the attention of Aileen and Robert."

John barked a laugh. "Nicely put," he said. "True it is that both of them have more curiosity than is always good for them." The smile he bestowed upon his son took the sting out of his words.

"Robert, you have worked well the past two days," John said. "Take you a little time out to talk with Avraham."

Turning back to their visitor, he continued: "If there is anything I can do to help, please let me know." So saying, he turned back to his bench and bent over his work once again.

Gesturing to his friend, Robert led the way out of the workshop and round to the back of their house. Sitting down on a bench, he asked Avraham what it was that had brought him to St. Edmundsbury.

"Master Isaac wanted me to find out what word there is within the Liberty of the Irishman," said Avraham. "We need to be certain that in giving him shelter we are not putting our own community at risk once again."

"What Irishman?" asked Robert. "I do not believe I have heard tell of someone from that country."

Avraham's brow creased. "Mayhap he did not come to St. Edmundsbury before finding his way to the forest and thence to us," he said. "But I would have expected the men chasing him to have asked questions of the townsfolk."

Robert shook his head, his puzzlement unabated. "Your pardon," he said. "I really do not know anything of this man or indeed of any outsiders asking questions about an Irishman."

Avraham was alarmed. Isaac had confided in him that he was becoming concerned about the truthfulness of Bronnart's tale. Avraham's account of the expedition to the forest two days before only served to heighten Isaac's anxiety. Thus it was that he had asked Avraham to make the journey to St. Edmundsbury in search of information regarding Bronnart.

"Be discreet," had been Isaac's parting words to the young man. Do not worry about that, thought Avraham. I know how to be careful both in my choice of people with whom I speak and my choice of words. Why else would I start with Robert Palgrave.

"This is worrying," Avraham said now to his friend. "This man Bronnart did tell us he was falsely accused of a murder in his country and that he was fleeing men who would take him back to certain death."

"Bronnart," said Robert. "That is his name?"

"It is," Avraham replied. "Or at least, that is what he has told us."

Robert was becoming eager. His face was flushed and his hands waved in the air as he asked Avraham to describe the man.

"He is not very handsome of face," said Avraham.

"He is shorter than I and has the dirt of long acquaintance with soil ground into his skin and nails. He has lank, black hair and an expression that would make milk curdle."

"Bron," exclaimed Robert. "You are describing Bron."

"Who is this Bron?" asked Avraham.

As Robert told his friend about the runaway serf and the embroidery that had presumably been stolen twice by the man, Avraham's face grew dark and his eyes sparked with anger.

"By all that I swear by, I am glad this. . . this wretch is not within my reach," he said at last. "If he were, I would myself be had for murder."

I do not think I have ever seen Avi so angry, thought Robert. I cannot blame him, of course. The Jews of Fornham have ever been the target of those who seek scapegoats. Finding out that Bron is a cuckoo in the Fornham nest must wrench his gut.

Robert laid his hand on top of Avraham's clenched fist. "Avraham," he said. "Be still. Let us sit together and see what we can do to make sure your people's generosity does not cause you suffering. There must be some way to handle this without letting anyone know where Bron has been all this time."

Avraham's tension started to drain away. He and Robert sat for a moment, both thinking furiously.

"I know what we should do first," said Robert at length.

"What is that?" said Avi.

"We should find Aileen," Robert said. "Three heads are better than two. In any event, I always find it easier to come up with good ideas when Aileen is around."

Even in the midst of his worry and anger, Avi almost smiled. Robert's fondness for Aileen was apparent to nearly everyone who knew them. The only ones who did not seem aware of the subtle changes in their relationship were the two young people themselves.

"Very good idea, Robert," said Avi. "Do you know where we shall find her at this time of day?"

"It is close to the noon hour," replied Robert. "I think that she may be in the courtyard taking the sun and eating her lunch."

The two young men repaired to the abbey courtyard and, sure enough, found their friend sitting in the courtyard talking to some of the other women of the linen room. Aileen exclaimed with pleasure at the sight of the young man from Fornham and rose immediately to greet them both.

"Avi," she said. "This is a pleasant surprise."

"Good morrow, Aileen," said the young man. "It is pleasing to me to see you both as well. Would that the reason for my visit was more agreeable than it is."

"What is wrong?" Aileen's voice was as concerned as the expression on her face.

"Come, let us find somewhere more private," said Robert, leading the way to a quiet corner of the courtyard.

"What has happened?" Aileen said as soon as they reached the spot Robert had selected.

It took but a minute or two for the two young men to tell her of the reason for Avraham's visit to St. Edmundsbury.

"So that is where Bron has been for the past six days," said Aileen. "I doubt that Durand thought to search for him in Fornham."

"I am sure that the Jews of Fornham are the last people your worthy reeve would expect to be sheltering this man," Avi said ruefully. "Yet it is a part of our tradition to welcome strangers and offer succor to those in need. This man had a pretty tale to tell that awoke memories of the past in us."

"Yet Master Isaac has grown suspicious of him," said Aileen. "Ruth's father is a man of great wisdom. It must be hard to deceive him for long."

Avi smiled. "Few there are who would try."

"But now we must discuss how to bring this man back to justice without risking blame being placed on your people," said Robert.

"You said that Bron was intending to leave Fornham soon," said Aileen. "Do you know when and where he intends to go?"

"No," said Avi. "Master Isaac wanted to find out more about him before encouraging him to leave. He is mistrustful of this man's story and thus he is concerned that, should he be captured, he may still pose a threat to our community."

Robert looked up quickly at Avi's comment, but it was Aileen who responded first.

"I would say that his concern is well-founded," she said.

Robert spoke slowly. "I do not know why I did not think of this before, but I think I may have met this man."

The others were shocked.

"When?" said Avi.

"How?" asked Aileen.

"Your pardon," said Robert. "It was but a brief encounter with a stranger, and it was not until just now that I thought of it."

Robert went on to tell the others about a man he had met walking down Churchgate Street a couple of days before the embroidery was taken from the abbey.

"The man stumbled over something in the street, and I put out my arm to stop him from falling," said Robert. "The man thanked me and said something like 'there be few in this town who are as kind as you, young sir.'"

"And you think this man was Bron," Aileen said with little doubt in her voice.

"I do think so now," said Robert. "I told him that it was nothing and that I was sure most of the good people of St. Edmundsbury would have done the same."

"What did he say to that?" asked Avi.

"He grunted a little and told me that only that day he had asked begged charity of several people to help a poor journeyman who was in need until payment be made to him for his services. He said that none of them had been gentle in their answer."

"I know you, Robert," said Aileen. "You gave him a farthing, did you not?"

Robert flushed a little. "Well, yes, I did," he said. "It may have been a mistake because the man insisted on wringing my hand and telling me all about the shopkeepers who had refused him aid. He said one of them had even gone to far as to squint at him suspiciously and say that he did not look like a traveling craftsman but more like a peasant working on the land."

"If that was the serf," said Avi. "I doubt not he must have been fearful of such an accurate description."

"I think you are right," said Robert. "Apparently the shopkeeper told Bron that, had he actually been a peasant working for a feudal lord, he would have been more like to help him but that he was not going to give aid to a lazy journeyman."

"How tempting it must have been to admit his identity," laughed Aileen.

"Truly," said Robert. "I am certain sure now that the man was Bron. Everything Avi has said about his appearance and his behavior would indicate so."

"I agree," said Aileen.

She stood for a moment, chin in hand and eyes looking through the barrels stacked in front of her.

"From everything we have learned about this

man," she said. "I think that we should not be in too much haste to form a plan. In this situation, too much haste may pose as great a risk to you and your friends as does Bron."

"But how long can we wait to take action, Aileen?" said Robert. "Every minute that passes may result in Bron's capture."

"If Durand and his men have not sought out Bron in Fornham thus far, there is little likelihood they will do so today," she replied.

Turning to Avraham, Aileen continued: "I suggest that you return to Fornham and tell Master Isaac about the runaway serf and the stolen tapestry. Mayhap he will hatch a plan better than anything we can devise, and, in the meantime, your people can ensure that Bron is kept out of sight in case someone from the Liberty should visit Fornham."

"I will do so," said Avi.

"What are we going to do, Aileen?" asked Robert. "Mayhap we should see if we can find out where the searchers are going to look next and dissuade them from going anywhere near Fornham."

"I think it is a good idea to find out more about the progress of the search, Robert," said Aileen. "We need to be careful not to make anyone suspicious about our motives in asking questions of them, however."

"Yes," Robert said. "I fear I am not as expert as you in asking seemingly innocent questions."

Aileen laughed and lightly touched Robert's hand.

"One of your best qualities is your transparent honesty," she said.

Robert wasn't sure that was much of a compliment in the circumstances, but he was always happy to hear that Aileen thought well of him. Avi, in the meantime, was trying hard not to laugh.

"When shall we meet again?" he said, filling in the small gap of silence.

"Let us meet at the edge of the forest tomorrow at noon," said Aileen. "It is best if Robert and I go about our usual business in the morning, but no one will think it strange if we leave our work at the noon hour."

"Let us pray that between us we will have found a solution to this dilemma by then," said Robert.

With a solemn nod, the three turned to go back to their various duties.

"Your pardon, sir," said Aileen, stopping suddenly as she realized that she was about to collide with Sir Roger FitzGilbert.

Starting as though he had been so deep in his own thoughts he was unaware of his surroundings, the knight looked hard at the three young people standing there. For a moment, he looked as though he was about to say something, but then he merely grunted and marched toward the stables.

"Who was that?" asked Avi.

"That is Sir Roger FitzGilbert," said Robert. "He is Bron's master."

"I think I have never seen such a scowl on his face

before," said Aileen. "It is an expression which ill suits him."

"What do you think he is so upset about?" asked Robert.

"I know not," Aileen said. "Always before, in spite of all that has been going on, he has been mild in manner. I wonder what it is that has led to that calm abandoning him."

Shrugging, and with more on their minds than the temper of a visiting knight, the three young people went their separate ways.

CHAPTER EIGHTEEN

*Here Duke William ordered ships to be built and here
they drag the ships to the sea*

"MISTRESS ARUNDEL," SAID ARLO. "I expected you on Monday, and here it is Wednesday already."

Why do I feel guilty? thought Anne to herself. After all, my schedule is mine to keep and alter as I choose.

"Master chandler," she said. "Life sometimes makes it hard to carry out one's plans on any given day."

Arlo scowled but had no audible reply. Anne ignored the complaint that was uttered under the man's breath.

"I hope that you have not sold out of your latest batch of honey candles," Anne said, changing the subject as quickly as possible.

"Nay," said the chandler grudgingly. "I still have a

goodly supply. Not everyone is willing to pay the extra price for a quality candle."

"Then I will take a dozen," Anne said. She smiled at Arlo as she spoke, and even the irritable chandler could not resist a slight warming of his expression.

"I will fetch them for you," he said, moving into the back room.

Returning with the candles in his hands, Arlo put them in the basket Anne had placed on the counter.

"Have you heard anything more of the search for that serf and the cloth he stole?" Arlo asked.

Once again, Anne was surprised at the man's unusual willingness to enter into a conversation with her. But this time she was prepared with her answer.

"No," she said. "I know nothing beyond the common knowledge."

Arlo pursed his lips.

"I think I am not the best person to ask," Anne continued in an attempt to soften her unsatisfactory response. "I am sure that there are many people within the Liberty who can discuss nothing else, but most of what they have to say is gossip. I pay little attention to such chatter."

"Aye, that be true," acknowledged Arlo. "You were given special access to the embroidery by the abbot though, so I thought that you might have better information than the common run."

"I am afraid not," said Anne firmly. Digging in her scrip, Anne drew out the money to pay for the candles and offered it to Arlo.

The chandler seemed reluctant to accept the money.

"I hear tell the fabric is valuable," he said. "There are those who declare it be part of a great tapestry that has been missing for many a long year."

"That may be the case," Anne said carefully. I just do not understand why he is pressing so hard for more information from me, she thought. I am beginning to feel uncomfortable.

"If it be what they say, then it must be very valuable, think you not?" said the chandler.

"It may be," said Anne. "But you must remember that condition will affect the value of any item. I had not completed my work before the embroidery was stolen. At that time, the condition was improving but not where it should be. Who knows what state the cloth will be in now?"

"Aye," said Arlo. "I can agree with that. But think you not that a tapestry of such fine quality as is rumored, one that includes the first Norman king, must be valuable in any condition?"

"You have heard that the tapestry depicts the first King William?" asked Anne.

"I have, as I am sure have you." Arlo was getting a little red-faced, and his words grew more angry. "He that defeated our good King Harold and caused great suffering for all the people of the land."

So many generations since this battle was fought, thought Anne, and yet the bitterness remains.

"The Good Lord knows how much suffering has

been inflicted by man against man," said Anne rather more severely than was her usual wont. "Yet we must live the lives we have been given and count the blessings bestowed upon us."

Arlo looked a little taken aback by this statement but rallied quickly.

"That's as may be," he said heatedly. "But to my way of thinking, the descendants of the Saxons that were so foully displaced from the land that Norman now holds have as much right to that old tapestry as does Sir Roger FitzGilbert." He almost spat out the name of the Norman knight.

"Even were that so, who now knows the names or the whereabouts of those displaced farmers?" Anne said reasonably in an attempt to cool the atmosphere.

"Certain sure that Norman has no idea what suffering his kind has inflicted on those descendants, whoever they may be," the chandler said as though that was the end of all argument on the matter.

Anne took a deep breath. "Master chandler, I know that many families were displaced at the time of the invasion, and my heart bleeds for the suffering they went through. But all we can do now is be charitable to those who fare worse than ourselves and always remember to be kind and affectionate to those we love."

Arlo looked horrified at the idea of giving to the poor. He mumbled something that sounded like "Harrumph." His face, which had been suffused with the blood of his anger and resentment, gradually faded to his usual rather pasty white.

"Mistress Arundel," he said. "Pray take no note of a testy old man whose dinner last night was poorly digested." His face screwed into a poor attempt at a smile which came across more as a leer.

"You are right, of course," the chandler continued in an ingratiating tone. "That Lord of Fitching cannot know who it was that was deprived of their land all those years ago. Why, the land of my forebears was given to a Gundulf of Caen. I am sure that those who now rule that estate do not know where my family and I now live. I am certain sure that, if they ever give it a thought, they do not care where we live either."

Arlo swallowed, aware that he was having a hard time holding back his anger and resentment in front of this customer.

Anne chose to ignore the temper of the comments.

"Master chandler," she said. "I am honored that you should choose to discuss your opinions on this matter with me. But now we must each attend to our duties, and so let us conclude our business."

"Be it as you say," said Arlo, his customary frown back in place.

The price of the candles having been paid, Anne left the chandler's shop, thinking that it was obvious Arlo was more on the side of the runaway serf than that of his lord. Surely the chandler cannot be hiding Bron, she thought, stopping in her tracks. But no. I do not see him risking so much for so little gain, even if his anger against the Normans is so sharp.

"Your pardon, Mistress Arundel," she heard a voice say behind her. "I was so close I near stepped on your heels when you stopped."

Turning around, Anne saw the butcher, cap in hand, staring at her.

"No, Master Aelred," she said. "The apology is mine to make. I was thinking so hard I scarce realized I had stopped so suddenly."

Aelred was a tall, thin man with rheumy grey eyes and the muscles of a man used to wielding a big cleaver. The wisps of grey hair in a ring around his head had given him the nickname of the "monk," a name which gave rise to a great deal of mirth among all those who knew him well.

"Mayhap you stopped because you remembered that you needed to purchase some meat from my shop," Aelred said hopefully.

Anne realized they were standing only a few yards beyond his shop so, while it seemed unlikely that any merchant would chase her down the street to offer her their wares, the comment was not so unlikely as it might seem.

"I am sorry, Master Aelred," she said. "I do not require any meat today."

"No sausages?" the butcher said regretfully. "You know my sausages are the best. Guaranteed not to contain any dog or cat meat. I will take my oath on that."

"No, no sausages," said Anne kindly. "I am sure I will visit your shop soon though."

As Anne turned to go, Aelred put out a hand to stop her. "Your pardon," he said, withdrawing his hand quickly. "I merely wished to ask if you have heard anything more today about the search for the missing tapestry or the serf who ran from his master."

Anne sighed. If many more people ask me about this, I will have to send Mabel out to do my errands. It is taking me twice as long to do everything these days.

"No, Master Aelred," she said. "I know nothing more than does anyone else within the Liberty."

"It is a pity," the butcher said cryptically.

In spite of her haste to return home, Anne could not resist responding to his words. "A pity that the cloth has been stolen, or a pity that nothing has been heard of it or the serf in almost a week?"

"A pity that we have come to a time when a man is so afeared that he believes he has no choice but to steal from a cruel master and run," said Aelred.

Anne was a little surprised. This interpretation of events was not one she had heard much discussed.

"I think that the Commandments tell us we should not steal," she said, straightening her shoulders and speaking as the good Christian she was. "Whatever reason this man Bron may have believed he had to take what was his lord's property cannot justify the theft."

Aelred realized he had perhaps spoken too boldly. "Nay, of course not," he said hurriedly. "I did not mean that stealing is right. I meant only that a man may be driven right out of himself by a situation beyond his control."

Anne's look was dubious, and Aelred began to feel that he was talking himself into a hole even though he felt compelled to continue explaining his meaning.

"I mean," he said, "good men and women were reduced to poverty by their Norman overlords when the Conqueror came to power. This serf may be descended from free men who had no choice but to accept the pittance of a living from a powerful Norman."

"You speak as one who has experience of being brought low," said Anne more sympathetically. I think I may have sounded too harsh, she thought. After all, Aelred is not a man used to expressing deep opinions. Mayhap he misspoke when he talked of Bron stealing the tapestry.

"Not I," said Aelred. "My great-grandfather, though, was brought low by the invaders."

Anne's compassion was written on her face, and Aelred felt impelled to continue. "My family came from the area of Barfreston in Kent," he said. "We were free men, farmers of good land."

Aelred's eyes were looking into the distant past, and Anne would have believed that there were tears in those eyes had they not always been a little damp.

"When the Conqueror took over the land, he granted much of Kent to his half-brother, Odo," said Aelred.

Anne was startled by his words and Aelred smiled wearily.

"Aye, the same Odo that rumor has it ordered that tapestry to which this missing piece may belong," he said.

"I can understand why you might be interested in what happens to it," said Anne.

"Yes," said the butcher. "I knew nothing of this tapestry until this past week, but I cannot deny that I hold resentment in my heart toward the family of the first King William."

"What happened to your ancestors?" Anne asked.

"The new lord threw them off our land," said Aelred. "Of course, they hoped that one day they would be able to return, should the Normans be defeated in battle, but it was not to be."

Anne's face showed her compassion for the ancestors of this tradesman.

Aelred's eyes took on a sad look as he thought back to the past. "There is a tale handed down in my family, as in many others, that what wealth they could collect before the arrival of the Normans was buried for the time of their return." His words were said softly, almost as though he was talking only to himself. Then he came back the present and turned back to Anne.

"My ancestors were reduced to traveling the roads until they settled here and became butchers. My grandfather said his father and mother never recovered from the horror of the invasion. They died only a couple of years after they were banished from their land."

"I am so sorry, Master Aelred," said Anne. "I will pray for their souls and will, of course, let you know if I hear anything of the recovery of the serf or the tapestry."

She turned to go.

"I saw it, you know," Aelred said.

Anne turned back around.

"Aye," he said. "When I first heard about the chest dug up in a field, I thought mayhap it might be something buried by the Saxon farmer before he fled. Then I heard tell that it might be connected with that brother of the Conqueror, so I had to see it for myself. I went to the abbey and took a look at it when the women left the linen room for their noonday meal."

Anne looked an enquiry at the butcher.

"I could see it was a fine piece of work," he said. "Your skill in the cleaning of it was clear."

"Thank you, Master Aelred," said Anne. "I hope to be able to complete that work."

"It will be very valuable if you do," said the butcher. "Any man in possession of it might anticipate good fortune and a much more comfortable existence than he likely has today."

So saying, Aelred doffed his cap to Anne, turned on his heel, and went back to his shop, leaving Anne to return home with a great deal on her mind.

CHAPTER NINETEEN

These men carry arms to the ships and here they drag a cart with wine and arms

"YOU HAVE TOLD US NOTHING BUT LIES."

Bron recoiled from the anger that was evident on Isaac of Cordoba's face. Few had ever seen the old physician this angry. Avraham, standing behind the serf, was glad that he had never been on the receiving end of the fierce flash from his eyes. Ruth, who had ushered the peasant into Isaac's study and was now standing beside her father, laid a gentle hand on his shoulder.

Before the peasant could think of anything to say in reply, Isaac continued: "Your deceit has put at risk all of my people. You have proven yourself to be a man without a vestige of honor."

By now Bron was all but blubbering, his lips trembling and tears in his eyes. "I knew nought of your people afore I met you," he said piteously. "How could I know anything about your troubles. I had enough of my own."

"You dare to speak to me of your troubles?" roared Isaac. "Had you spoken truth to us, we could have considered how best to respond without putting our wives and children in danger. But your lies have made that impossible."

Isaac took a deep breath. I will accomplish nothing with this fury, he thought. My efforts are better spent seeking a solution to this conundrum.

Bron, in the meantime, was desperate to find a way out of his situation.

"I be in danger, good sir," he whimpered. "Your pardon if I did not feel I could trust strangers when first I came upon you. But I am still at risk, even if it not be for quite the same reason as I first said."

"Your danger is as nothing compared with ours," Isaac said more quietly than before.

"My lord will like to kill me for this," wailed Bron.

"You are a thief and a runaway," said Isaac. "As Jews we are sympathetic to the poor men who labor for their feudal lords. But you had no right to risk the lives of my people for your own dishonest interests.

"Even more, how can we now believe anything you tell us?" Isaac continued without allowing Bron any response. "How can we even believe that your lord will execute you?"

Bron was becoming frantic.

"I told 'ee," he said, wringing his hands. "I only lied

because I knew you not. Now I know you, I would tell you truth."

Avraham could see his own doubts reflected in Isaac's eyes.

"What truth would you tell us now that could be believed?" Isaac said.

"Ask me anything," said Bron wildly. "Ask me anything and I will answer truly."

Isaac thought for a moment, hand stroking his grey beard. "This tapestry that you stole from your lord has been stolen again, this time from the abbey," said Isaac at last. "When you ran from St. Edmundsbury, did you take the cloth also?"

"I did not," said Bron, his eyes growing large and his tone one of indignation.

Turning to Ruth, Bron spoke as though in challenge: "Did you see such a thing in my hands when you found me in the forest?" he said. "You know I am telling truth."

Almost I am tempted to believe him, thought Isaac. Yet this is a man skilled in cunning and deception. I will not be taken in again.

Ruth, ever one to believe in the essential goodness of men, surprised both her father and her friend by speaking up.

"When Avraham and I found you in the forest, sir, you had mud all over your hands," she said. "Mayhap you buried the treasure before we saw you trying to climb a tree."

"Nay, young mistress," said Bron. "I had had

nought to eat all day. I was digging in the earth for food, not hiding treasure."

Isaac sighed. The man is a miserable wretch, he thought. I would like to believe him, but I cannot.

"Once a man has proven himself to be a liar, I find it nigh on impossible to regain any trust in his word," he said. "I fear that our only option is to take you to St. Edmundsbury ourselves and hand you over to the reeve."

"Nay," howled Bron. "If you take me back in chains, it will mean certain death. After all you have told me about your story, you cannot do such."

"It is not we who are condemning you to whatever punishment Sir Roger chooses, but rather your own conduct that condemns you," said Isaac gravely.

He paused for a moment. "I am loathe to involve us in the affairs of gentiles, but the reeve is a good man, a fair man," he said. "In delivering you to him ourselves, it is my hope that he will understand we did nothing other than offer respite to a cold and hungry traveler. If I have read the character of the man correctly, he will believe us and take the matter no further."

Bron thought furiously. "Good sir," he said, the wheedling tone back in his voice. "I would repay you for your kindness toward me. I see now that my actions have indeed put you and your people at risk. Let me try to set things right."

Isaac's skepticism was written all over his face.

Avraham almost smiled when he saw Ruth's expression mimicking that of her father.

"How do you propose to do such a thing?" Isaac asked.

"If I go myself to St. Edmundsbury and turn myself in," Bron said, "it might go easier for me when my master decides on my punishment. When I tell him I had nought to do with taking the cloth from the abbey, he might even be grateful that he can now seek the real thief."

Isaac's expression was not encouraging, but the serf could do nothing but go on with his plea.

"There would be no need for me to mention you or your people if I go to the reeve thus," he said.

"You have a smooth tongue," said Isaac. "I can see how you have managed to cajole others into doing your will before now."

Bron's eager face indicated his hope that Isaac was going to approve of his plan, but Avraham and Ruth knew better.

"You will not coax me to bend my will to yours however," Isaac said. "We cannot trust you to keep your word, and thus I will not permit you to leave Fornham unaccompanied."

Bron's misery was complete. How am I going to get out of this? he thought. I must find a way. I must.

"Avraham," Isaac ordered the young man. "I would that you will go and prepare the cart. You will make sure that this serf reaches St. Edmundsbury and the reeve safely."

"Yes, Master Isaac," said Avraham. Smiling encouragingly at the sad-faced girl standing beside her father, he turned and left the room.

"My daughter," said Isaac, turning to Ruth. "Pray do not be so sorrowful. It is as I said a moment ago. This man has chosen his own path. It is not our part to take responsibility for that path. We can only do what is right."

"Yes, father," said Ruth. "I understand."

Isaac stroked the girl's cheek and smiled at her.

"Shall I prepare some food for Avi to take with him, father?" Ruth asked. "He will have a long day, and I would make sure he has food and drink for the journey."

"That is a good idea," said her father. "Go now and prepare it, for I doubt Avraham will take very long in readying the horse and cart."

Ruth rose and left the room. Isaac and Bron were left alone, silence stretching out between them.

Bron was hunched over, staring at the floor. Isaac gazed gravely at the serf for a moment and then, frustrated that he could think of no other solution to the problem at hand, reached out to pick up a scroll that lay by his right hand. I see no other course of action but the one I have laid out, he thought as he unrolled the scroll and began to read, and yet I am loathe to become involved in the affairs of those who have oft persecuted my people, knowing that the punishment meted out for Bron's rebellion may well be death.

Mayhap the wisdom of the Torah will provide some other way to resolve my dilemma.

As Isaac picked up the scroll, Bron rose to his feet quickly and lunged toward the older man. Caught by surprise, Isaac had no time to react. Bron shoved him hard, and Isaac fell over, the table and stool crashing to the ground as the physician uttered a shout of shock and pain.

Bron had no intention of waiting for anyone to respond to the commotion. He turned, wrenched open the door, and took to his heels, running as fast as he could into the forest and beyond the reach of the people of Fornham.

CHAPTER TWENTY

Here Duke William in a great fleet crossed the sea and came to Pevensey

THAT WEDNESDAY NOONTIME, WHILE Bron was running for his life, Aileen was sitting on the riverbank with Robert and William.

Robert had hidden his chagrin at the appearance of the young lord well enough for Aileen's uncritical eye, but not quite well enough for William's gaze.

"Your generosity in allowing a mere acquaintance to spend this time with you both is greatly appreciated," said William, looking at Robert.

"It is our pleasure," said Robert, flushing to the roots of his hair.

Why is he embarrassed? Aileen asked herself. He is not usually so stiff around strangers, let alone those we know. He is cute when he blushes though.

"William found me as I was leaving the abbey this evening," Aileen told Robert. "He wanted to tell me about the conversation he had with Bron's master and the man from Bayeux. I told him the best thing to do would be to come with me to meet you here."

"It is very exciting to be included in your mystery-solving partnership," said William. Looking around he asked: "Is this where you usually get together to plot your strategy?"

Aileen laughed. "Since childhood, we and our friends have met on this bank. Robert and I have never given up the tradition, that is all."

"And we are not really involved with this search," added Robert, hoping that William would become bored and leave them alone.

"That is true," said Aileen.

"I am certain sure that both serf and tapestry would have been found by now if you were so involved," said William.

"I must confess that the mystery concerning the embroidery itself intrigues me," said Aileen, a little flustered by the young lord's words. "I would very much like to be able to know for certain what it is and how it came to be buried in that field."

"That is why I thought I should find a convenient time to talk with Sir Roger and Lanfranc," said William. "What you told me yesterday piqued my interest. I wanted to join in the fun of searching for clues."

Robert clamped his lips together and strove to

keep his face expressionless. Why does he have to involve himself in our lives? he thought. Come to that, why did he have to come back to St. Edmundsbury at all?

Neither Aileen nor William took note of Robert's expression. Aileen listened to William's account of his discussion with the two men in the guest hall with rapt attention, and even Robert was interested to hear about the conversation between Durand and the cleric.

"It would appear that everyone is convinced that Bron took the tapestry when he ran from the abbey," said Aileen. "I am still not sure about the timing, but my father often accuses me of unnecessarily complicating things. It may be that he is in the right when it comes to this matter."

"It would be so much easier to solve the puzzle if we knew where the serf and the tapestry were to be found," said William.

Robert grinned. "As to that, I think we may be able to provide you with some information ourselves," he said with some satisfaction.

He could not complain of William's reaction. His head swiveled toward Robert and his eyes grew wide.

"Pray tell," he said. "You know where the villain and the embroidery are to be found?"

"Not the fabric," said Robert. "We have good reason to think we know where Bron is to be found."

"We just cannot tell the reeve yet," explained Aileen, a little anxious in case William should take it into his head to run straight to that honorable official.

"Why not?" William asked reasonably.

When Aileen and Robert filled him in on Avraham's story, William nodded his head. "I see," he said. "I remember the last time I was here, the Jews of Fornham were at great risk because of false accusations laid against them. I can understand their reluctance to become involved in any more controversies, and, since your affection for them runs deep, I also understand why you wanted to wait."

"Thank you, sir," said Aileen.

"That is one reason we have gathered here today," Robert said. "Avraham should be here soon. We are going to make a decision as to how to tell Durand where he can find Bron."

Before William could respond, the trio heard the sound of running footsteps. Turning, they were surprised to see Avraham and Ruth running toward them in clear distress.

"What has happened?" Aileen asked sharply, rising to her feet.

"Bron has run away," Avraham said succinctly.

"Oh no," said Aileen.

"What happened?" asked Robert.

"By my troth," exclaimed William.

Not knowing to which of the simultaneous reactions he should respond, Avraham said nothing more. Aileen looked at Ruth, who then explained what had happened that morning.

"Is your father injured?" asked Aileen.

"He was a little bruised, but I think his pride was hurt more than his body," said Ruth.

Avraham picked up the tale.

"By the time we had run back to Isaac's house and helped him regain his feet, Bron was long gone," he said. "Of course, we searched for him in the forest, but we did not find him."

"We will have to think of a new plan now that he is missing," said Robert.

"Yes," said Aileen. "It may be that the reeve's men will capture him now, but, if they do, he may say something about where he has been all this time."

"That would not be good," said Avraham.

Aileen was thinking back to the young man's account of what had occurred between Isaac and Bron. "Did you believe Bron when he said that he had not taken the tapestry from the abbey linen room?" she asked.

"None of us did," said Ruth quietly.

Aileen and Robert, knowing their friend so well, looked as surprised as had Isaac and Avraham that morning.

William, who did not know her well at all, merely nodded his head. "Once a liar, always a liar," he said solemnly.

"Mayhap, if he says that he has been hiding in Fornham for the past week, no one will believe him either," Robert said.

"We cannot take that risk," said Avraham. "We

need to think of something we can do to ward off any danger to our people."

"I think we need to find Durand as quickly as possible," said Aileen. "As your father said, Ruth, he is a good and fair man. I suggest we need to tell him something of what has happened."

"You are right, Aileen," said William. "It is more likely now that the serf will be caught. Better to prepare Durand for what he may say than be quiet and hope he says nothing."

"But how do we explain where Bron has been, and how do we protect Ruth's people?" Robert's brow was creased with anxiety.

Aileen thought about it for a moment. "I do not think it wise to lie to him," she said. "Durand may not like the way we become involved in some of his cases, but I am certain sure he trusts that we are honest in our dealings. We do not want to lose that trust."

"Father would never support us lying to the reeve either," said Ruth.

"Well then, why do we not go to Durand together and tell him truly that the two of you came across the serf in the forest," Aileen said. "You can give him all the details of that meeting, leaving out only the date."

"And if he asks when we found Bron in the forest?" Avraham said.

"I will think of something to say to interrupt the flow of the conversation," Aileen said, waving her hand in the air.

"From what I have seen of the man, I think it likely

he would take the hint and not return to the question," William said, laughing.

Aileen smiled at the young lord's understanding, prompting a stab of jealousy in Robert that, try as he might, he could not suppress.

"If we do this, we must hope that Durand is as perceptive as you think he is," Robert said.

"I too am uncomfortable with going to the reeve in this way," said Ruth. "I cannot think of a better plan though, and I think we are out of time to devise some other plan that would pose any less risk to our people."

Avraham had been thinking quietly during their discussion. "I believe that it need not be so complicated," he said. "Remember, the Jews of Fornham knew nothing of this runaway serf and the cloth he stole from his master's land until yesterday."

Three pairs of eyes looked at him quizzically.

Avraham blushed slightly at all the attention. "If the reeve wants to know why we did not report the discovery of the serf until today, I will be telling the truth if I say that it was only when I talked to Robert yesterday that I found out about Bron's crimes."

Aileen nodded approvingly. "You are right," she said. "And if Durand asks why you did not go to him at once, you can tell him that you believed it was important that you report back to Master Isaac and that he be the one to bring the villain to St. Edmundsbury."

"Yes," Robert said eagerly. "Durand would understand your reluctance to act on your own after the false accusations made against your people at the time of the theft of the holy relic."

"It is decided then," said Avraham. "Shall we go now?"

"Better to delay no longer," agreed Aileen.

"Is there anything I can do?" asked William a little plaintively. He could not help feeling left out in this group of longstanding friends.

"Mayhap this good knight could accompany us to see the reeve," said Ruth shyly. "His support would lend great weight to what we have to say."

William smiled at her.

Aileen started to agree, and then another thought came to her. "Sir. . . William," she said. "Ruth speaks truly, but you may be able to help us in another way."

"Your wish is my command," said William, lifting her hand and kissing it.

Aileen blushed, and Robert managed not to snort too loudly.

"It does seem likely that this serf is a thief two times over," she said. "Yet there remains a small amount of doubt about that."

"Indeed," said William. "You want me to try and find out whether or not he hid the tapestry in the forest?" The tone of his voice demonstrated the misgivings he felt concerning such a task.

"No, not that," said Aileen, laughing at the expression on William's face. "I was thinking that keeping an eye on Sir Roger and the man from Bayeux would be no bad thing."

"That is a task much more suited to my capabilities," William said, relieved.

"It is not likely that either man is involved in stealing the tapestry from the abbey," said Aileen. "Yet they both have an interest in the value of the cloth. Mayhap we should not discount them entirely."

"I am happy to be of assistance," said William sincerely.

With good wishes for success exchanged between them all, the party broke up, William to return to the abbey and the others to find the reeve.

CHAPTER TWENTY-ONE

Here the horses leave the ships and here the knights have
hurried to Hastings to seize food

UPON HIS RETURN TO THE GUEST HALL after the meeting with Aileen and her friends, William had sought out the man from Bayeux. He had wanted to talk to Sir Roger Fitz-Gilbert first, but the knight was nowhere to be seen, so William decided to go with what he had.

There has to be a way of starting a conversation with this proud cleric without giving the game away, William thought. A moment's rumination and he had it.

"Good morrow, brother," he said to the man sitting eating his evening meal. "I hear there is a rumor going around that the serf has been found. Have you heard anything of it?"

Lanfranc's head snapped up at William's words,

and a light came into his eyes. "Where?" he said eagerly without bothering to offer any greeting.

"I am not sure," William said airily. "It is just something I heard."

Frustration showed clearly on Lanfranc's face. "Where did you hear the rumor then?"

William screwed up his face in a pretense of concentration. "I don't know," he said finally. "On the street somewhere, I suppose."

Lanfranc looked as though he wanted to throttle William, much to the latter's amusement.

Taking a deep breath and smiling brittlely, the man from Bayeux asked, "Did you hear if the tapestry was found as well?"

"No," responds William. "I did not hear."

This really is too much fun, William thought. The man is so easy to provoke.

Opening his eyes wide in an innocent stare, William said "Mayhap I should have paid more attention."

Lanfranc's fists clenched. With an obvious effort, he took a deep breath and unclasped his hands. "It is of no moment," he said unconvincingly. "Small town gossips will make up any tale." Waving his hand as though to dismiss such tattle, he continued, "I am sure that the reeve would have informed the abbot had the serf been captured, and then we too would have heard."

"I am sure you are right," said William reassuringly. He paused, as though considering the statement further. "And yet," he went on, "sometimes the people in small towns are the first to know any news. They seem to have an uncanny ability in that regard."

Lanfranc was about to respond to William's goading comment when Sir Roger FitzGilbert came through the door, spotted the two men in conversation, and came over to them.

"God save you," he greeted the two men.

William smiled and greeted the knight in return. Lanfranc grunted.

"I see that something has happened to disturb your good humor," Roger said blandly.

William had a hard time not bursting into laughter at the statement but managed to restrain himself.

"The lord de Vere has heard a rumor about your serf being found, but unfortunately he seems to have little more than one sentence to give of the account," said Lanfranc.

Roger looked at William. "Truly?" he asked.

Smiling, William repeated his tale of hearing a rumor in town.

"Where did you hear this?" asked the knight, sitting down and looking hard at William.

"I do not know for sure," said the young lord, thinking happily that he was beginning to know how Mistress Aileen and her friends must feel when they investigated mysteries. "I simply heard that he had been captured. I think it must have been somewhere on the streets as I was walking."

"And the tapestry Bron stole?" Roger pressed on.

"I do not know," William said.

The knight was beginning to understand why the cleric from Bayeux was looking the way he did. This young lord's manner was enough to make even a grown man throw a tantrum like a child.

"Well," he said, taking a deep breath. "If it be true, then I will be glad to have the man back so I can take him home and return order to my lands."

"Curious," thought William. His concern seems all about the serf and the running of his estates. I would have expected him to be as interested in the tapestry that was the beginning of this whole drama.

As if he were reading William's thoughts, Roger added in a rush, "And I will be glad of the return of the property Bron stole from me, of course."

"Do you believe that, if this is indeed a remnant of the great tapestry commissioned by Bishop Odo, that it is yours to keep?" Lanfranc put in.

Roger looked surprised. "Of course it is," he said. "It was found on my land."

"But do you not think that the cathedral of Bayeux has a greater claim on it?" said Lanfranc.

"I do not," said the knight sharply. "As I understand it, the tapestry has been lost for many years. Who can tell now if this embroidery is indeed a part of this aged masterpiece? No one alive has seen the complete work."

Lanfranc's mouth opened as if to interrupt, but Roger did not allow him the opportunity to do so.

"We may speculate about the origin of this find,

but there is none with a better claim to it than myself," the knight continued.

There was a pause, the cleric's expression inscrutable as he studied Sir Roger's face.

Almost to himself Lanfranc said: "That is what I thought you would say."

Rising, the man from Bayeux bid the other two men farewell and walked slowly out of the hall.

Roger and William looked at each other with raised brows. Then, rising in his turn, the knight smiled thinly at William.

"I will bid you good night, sir," he said. "I have business to take care of before I can rest this night."

Watching Sir Roger stride out of the room William decided he was probably going to see if the abbot had any news regarding this so-called rumor. Mayhap he will find that Lanfranc has reached the abbot's chambers ahead of him.

Laughing to himself, William rose and went to bed in high good humor. Tomorrow, I will have much to tell Aileen and her friends, he thought to himself. What a grand adventure I am having!

Bron shivered as he carefully poked his head out of the pile of twigs and leaves under which he had slept Wednesday night.

Why did it have to rain all last night? he thought disgustedly. And it was that nasty cold rain that makes one long for a cheerful fire and a mug of Ardith's mulled ale.

Bron stood up stiffly and brushed the dirt and leaves out of his hair and off his clothes. It was just too bad I had to run, he thought. Curse that young man and his chattering friends!

There is no way I am going to get caught though. Now that I have got away from Roger FitzGilbert, I am not ever going to return, not even if I never see any money for the cloth I worked so hard to save.

With such virtuous thoughts, Bron set off with a determined look on his face, checking the shadows on the trees so he could be sure he was going in the right direction. It took him a while to find the place he sought, but at last he came upon a clearing that was familiar to him.

Softly congratulating himself on his cleverness, he walked across to a big oak tree, swept aside a pile of brush, and started digging with his hands in the dirt. It did not take him long to find what he was looking for. It was not buried deep.

Pulling a piece of sackcloth out of the hole, he stuffed it under his arm and set off in the opposite direction to that of St. Edmundsbury, whistling under his breath. Now I am on my way, he thought. There's none so clever as to find me once I'm out of this pesky wood. I will be free as the birds and safe forever.

Had he not been so pleased with himself, he might

have paid more attention to his surroundings. His mistake in being so careless became evident as he came out of the trees beside a small river, snapping the twigs as he strode down to the water to drink.

A short, grey-haired man sitting on the riverbank fishing heard the sounds and turned to look, thinking that he would see a deer coming down to drink.

It would be hard to say which man was more startled. Unfortunately for Sergeant Ralph, the abbey's gatekeeper, Bron was not only younger but more fit. He ran back into the trees before Ralph could even get halfway across the distance between them.

Ralph was not to be deterred however. He knew this country well and Bron did not. Seeing the direction in which the other man was running, Ralph started off at a trot in a slightly different direction.

I know that man, Ralph thought as he moved silently along the path between the trees. That is the missing serf, the thief everyone is looking for. What glory will be mine when I bring him through the gates of St. Edmundsbury. Too many people in the Liberty think of me as just a fat old fool, doing nothing but open and close the gates of the abbey morning and night. They will know better soon.

Ralph sped up a little, knowing exactly where he was heading. That fool peasant has no idea I am closing in on him, he thought. Soon I'll have him in my clutches, and the reward his master offered will be mine. He trotted softly on, breathing a little more heavily than he would have liked but confident that this day was going to be memorable.

There was much crashing of branches as Bron, panicked beyond thinking of the need for silence, ran along a path in the woods. He had gone no further than about a quarter of a mile when, of a sudden, he skidded to a halt. On the path ahead of him stood the gatekeeper he had thought left far behind. Ralph had cut him off and now stood, arms akimbo, still and strong as a stone.

"There be no point in your going this way," said Ralph. "I know these woods. Wherever you run, I can catch you, so you might as well give up."

Like a caged animal, Bron swung from side to side, seeking a way out. Seeing only thick brush and large trees, and with nothing to lose, he launched himself at the man in front of him, throwing the sackcloth parcel he was carrying to the side.

Ralph had not expected such an assault and was caught by surprise. The two men crashed to the ground, the younger man on top of the gatekeeper, fists flying into the face of his would-be jailer and feet kicking at his legs. Ralph tried to fend him off, and, taking advantage of a slight pause as Bron tried to strike away his hand, the gatekeeper landed a good punch on Bron's jaw. Bron, now off balance, fell to the side as Ralph twisted out from under him.

Sergeant Ralph, a little dazed by the punches he had taken, tried to get on top of the other man, but Bron fended him off. The two men rolled around on the ground, swinging punches at each other. Some landed and some did not but, as both men began to gasp for air, the pace of the punches diminished.

Bron finally landed a heavy punch to Ralph's nose. Now I have the upper hand, thought Bron. Raising his fist to strike a last blow, Bron knew his opponent was finished.

Just as Ralph put up his hand in a weak attempt to fend off the swinging fist coming toward his face, the forest's waiting silence was interrupted by another sound.

In the heat of battle, neither man noticed the horse coming down the path until it reared up and snorted. The hounds following close behind the rider bayed and sprang forward.

"Whoa there," said the rider, pulling on the reins and trying to calm his skittish mount. "Stay!" he ordered the dogs. Then, as the two bloody and dirty men realized there was another in their midst, he looked at them and shouted: "Cease this immediately or I will set my dogs on you!"

CHAPTER TWENTY-TWO

Here the meat is being cooked and here the servants have served it

ILEEN HAD BEEN HAVING A BUSY DAY herself that Thursday. As soon as she had arrived for work that morning, Mistress Taylor had given her a new cope to border with fine gold thread. Knowing this was a testament to the robe-maker's trust in a relatively new member of her team of workers, Aileen focused on the work at hand without giving a thought to anything else until Mistress Taylor clapped her hands and told them all to take their midday break.

Now, sitting outside in the courtyard eating her food and basking in the rays of the sun that slanted down over the roofs of the abbey buildings, Aileen thought back to the night before.

The four friends had found Durand at home. If the reeve was surprised at being disturbed by such a motley group of young people, he did not show it. He invited them in and waved them to stools in front of the hearth. Seating himself where he could see all their faces in the warming light from the fire. the reeve asked how he could help them.

"Sir," said Aileen, unusually nervous. "You remember Ruth and Avraham, our friends, do you not?"

"How could I not?" Durand answered. "My memory is not so short that I cannot remember events that have occurred within the last year or two." His smile took away any perception of tartness in his words.

Robert cleared his throat. "Sir," he began, "there is something that we have to tell you." He fell silent.

Durand looked at the four faces in front of him. He was not used to seeing Aileen so nervous. Robert tended to be tongue-tied, but even for him, the young man seemed to be overly confused as to how to proceed. He scarce knew Avraham and Ruth, but he could see that the two of them were uncomfortable in his presence, shuffling their feet and looking down at the floor.

"You might as well come out with it," he said finally. "If you feel the need to visit me, I must assume you have been meddling in my business again and that you have discovered something that you believe may incur my wrath."

This is going to be worse than I expected, thought

Ruth miserably. Why did we not wait until we could think of a better plan?

Why did I allow that wicked man to escape us? thought Avraham unhappily. I should never have left Master Isaac alone with him.

He is going to be so angry with us, thought Robert wretchedly. Durand is usually very tolerant of our interference in his work, but this time he may believe we have gone too far.

The reeve sounds hard, thought Aileen, but I know him better than that. He has that twinkle in his eye that means he is well-prepared to hear what we have to say. I do not think this is going to be as bad as we had feared.

"I think Robert would be the best one of us to tell you about what we have discovered," she said. "He it was who first heard the tale from Avraham, and I know you like to hear things firsthand."

Robert wanted to sink into the ground, but he could not let his friend down. If Aileen thought it best he speak, then speak he would.

Taking a deep breath, Robert looked straight into Durand's eyes and began to explain their reason for coming. "It was like this," he said. "Avraham came to see me yesterday, and that was when I told him all about Bron and the tapestry. It was the first time Avi became aware of the theft of the tapestry and the disappearance of the serf. And of course had he and his friends been aware of all of this earlier, they would have done something sooner, but. . . "

"Stop," interrupted Durand, putting up his hand to halt the flow of words. "I can make neither heads nor tails of anything you are saying. Slow down and tell me what you are talking about."

Robert was so embarrassed he scarce knew how to proceed. Patting his friend on the shoulder, Avraham stepped forward.

"The explanation is mine to make," he said to the reeve. "My friends are simply worried that you will not receive it as well from someone with whom you have only slight acquaintance."

"I know you to be an honest young man," said Durand. "I hope I will always listen to truth and know it for what it is."

"Yes, sir," said Avraham.

Taking a deep breath, Avraham continued: "Ruth and I believe that we saw the man you have been looking for in the forest the other day."

Durand sat up straight but allowed Avraham to continue.

"We did not know who he was, of course. We come to St. Edmundsbury but rarely, and I am sure you know that few from the Liberty visit us in Fornham."

Avi looked at the reeve, who nodded and signed him to go on.

"The man we met told us he was an Irishman but recently come to this area," Avraham said carefully. "You understand we had no reason to doubt him?"

There is more to this story than these young people seem willing to say, Durand thought. Yet I believe that what the young man says is truth. I wonder what else there is that he does not want me to know.

"You know you should have reported this to me as soon as you had reason to believe this man was the escaped serf," he said bluntly. "You say you found out yesterday. Why did you wait until today to come to me? We have lost valuable time and wasted the effort of many men searching in the wrong places."

"Please do not be angry with us, master reeve," said Ruth hesitantly. "We did not mean to cause you so much trouble."

She looked so small and frightened, it would have taken a harder man than Durand to resist feeling sorry for her.

Sighing, Durand asked Ruth quite gently what it was she had to say.

"You know how the people of the Liberty feel about the Jews," she said, and Durand nodded. "It is not only in St. Edmundsbury that people feel this way about our people," she went on. "When nearly all the Jews were expelled from St. Edmundsbury over ten years ago, there were many within the country who felt that all Jews should be banished from England. At least, that is what my father has told us, and I know him to be a wise and truthful man."

"Your father did not lie," said Durand. "I did hear the same thing from many visitors to the town. I do not say that I did agree with that opinion, you understand, merely that it was one held by many at the time."

Ruth smiled at the reeve's words. "Knowing this, I am sure you will understand me when I say that our people have come to understand that it is not wise for us to interfere in the affairs of the town."

Durand was not sure where this was going, but he was content to let the girl speak. For Robert and Aileen, Ruth's sudden talkativeness was so unexpected as to be shocking. For Avraham, even in the midst of his surprise, he felt a sudden swell of pride in the girl he had known and, yes, loved his whole life.

"So you will recognize that, when Robert told Avraham the tale of the runaway serf and the missing embroidery, we were confused as to how to proceed," said Ruth, looking intently at the reeve.

Durand remained silent, but his expression was not forbidding, and Ruth, warming to her story, was encouraged to continue.

"We could not be sure that this man who claimed to be Irish was in fact the peasant Bron," she said earnestly. "Avraham was greatly disturbed when he returned from talking with Robert, and he felt that he had to talk to my father about this before any decision was made.

"After all," Ruth added simply, "my father is the leader of our community and the wisest amongst us. Both Avraham and I knew that he would know the right action to take."

As she spoke these last words, joining her fate with

her friends', Ruth reached out and took Avraham's hand.

"And what did your father tell you was the right thing to do?" Durand asked.

Ruth hesitated for a moment but then said that her father had said they must come and report to the reeve.

The four young people in front of him were very still, their faces expressionless. Ruth's choice of words in her last response did not escape Durand's attention, but he decided against pressing further. I do understand how the Jews might feel, he thought to himself, and it is clear they are trying to do the right thing. What the complete tale may be can wait for a little while.

"We will say no more about the timing of your report," he said and saw the four of them relax a little.

"For now..." he added. Four pairs of eyes looked quickly into his and then looked back down. All, that is, except for Avraham's, which remained fixed on Durand's face in something less than defiance but not quite compliance.

"Let us return to the subject of your meeting with the serf," Durand went on. "Where was it that you discovered him, and was he carrying anything with him at that time?"

Glad to have behind them the biggest obstacle the group had foreseen in coming to talk to the reeve, Avraham and Ruth readily opened up about their interaction with the serf. They told Durand Bron had carried only a small piece of sacking that probably contained mushrooms or something like that.

"Was there any sign that he had been doing anything other than running through the forest?" asked the reeve.

"I cannot say for certain, sir," said Ruth. "His hands were very dirty, as though he might perhaps have been digging in the earth beyond just picking mushrooms, but, since he did not appear to be one who kept himself very clean, I could not say if he had buried any stolen treasure."

Durand could not resist a slight smile at the gentle way in which Ruth described Bron's state of cleanliness. "Is there anything else you feel I should know at this time?" he asked, to be met with such stillness and quiet as he felt to be uncommon in the group.

Well, he said to himself, I know enough to be going on with for now. If there is a need for more questions later, I will ask them.

"Thank you for the information," he said to the group as a whole. "I must organize a search party now and see if we can find the man in the forest. Whether we can still find him there is not clear, but at least we have a starting point for the search now."

Durand gave the four people in front of him a stern look.

"If you think of anything else that may be important to our search for the serf or the tapestry, I expect you to come to me immediately," he said. "For now, you may go."

Greatly relieved at having survived the experience relatively unscathed, the four friends had departed the reeve's house and, after giving each other hugs and promises of a meeting on the morrow, gone their separate ways.

Now, a day later, Aileen turned over in her mind the reeve's reaction to what they had had to tell him. I am not certain he believed Avraham and Ruth that their time with Bron was so short, she said to herself. Durand looked skeptical more than once. But it seems as though Master Isaac had the right of it when he said the reeve was a good and fair man. Mayhap he really had deliberately refrained from asking too many awkward questions.

"Aileen," a voice called.

Shaken out of her revery, Aileen looked up to see Molly running toward her.

"Mistress Taylor sent me to find you," the girl said, reaching for Aileen's hand. "You are late returning from your noonday break."

Flustered, Aileen ran back to the linen room with Molly and offered apologies to the robemaker for her tardiness.

"We will let it be this time," said the woman magnanimously. "It is rare that you are not where you should be when you should be. See it does not happen again," she continued, wagging her finger severely at Aileen.

"No, Mistress Taylor," said Aileen. "I will not allow it to happen again."

Lucky I am that the robemaker is in such a good mood today, thought Aileen. I got off lightly this time.

Mistress Taylor seemed to spend more time than usual reviewing Aileen's work that afternoon. For a while, Aileen thought it was because she had been late back from lunch, but halfway through the afternoon, the robemaker came to stand beside the young woman and did not go away after a minute or two.

Aileen looked up, knowing that this delay often presaged what Mistress Taylor liked to call "a nice little chat."

"Your mother must be most distressed at the loss of the tapestry," the robemaker said sympathetically.

"I think that mother is most concerned about how the work is being treated, wherever it is," Aileen said.

Mistress Taylor nodded in a knowing manner.

"Yes, for those of us who value greatly the masterpieces of past embroiderers, it is like to break our hearts when such work is lost," she said. "Even those who know nothing about the skill it takes to create such a piece have been making comments about how valuable it must be and asking me whether I could say what exactly the work is."

Aileen's ears perked up. So that is why Mistress Taylor is hoping my mother has given me more information than is commonly known around town. But it is interesting that people have been asking questions of the robemaker. I wonder if it is possible that some of these people have tried plying mother with questions and have now turned to Mistress Taylor when they have failed to obtain satisfactory answers.

"Who has been asking you such questions?" she said.

Mistress Taylor looked a little taken aback at such a direct approach. "Oh, many people," she said vaguely. "Why, even the visiting cleric from Bayeux asked me questions the other day, and then only two days ago I was accosted in the market by the butcher, that impertinent young stable boy from the abbey stables, and even the chandler."

"They all know you are a skilled needlewoman, Mistress Taylor," Aileen said. "It is natural they would want to talk to an expert."

The robemaker beamed from ear to ear at Aileen's words, her rosy cheeks growing pinker than ever.

"Well, for all that that is true, it is a cheek to accost good people thus," she said. "I'm sure I don't know what the world is coming to!"

With such sage statement, the robemaker turned on her heel and went back to her work.

CHAPTER TWENTY-THREE

Here they made breakfast and here the bishop blesses the food and drink

ANNE HUSTLED OUT OF HER FRONT DOOR with a basket packed with coriander, mint, and lavender. Young John Miller had come running to ask her to visit his grandmother. Mother Miller and Anne were longtime friends, so, when the old woman woke up that morning feeling sick, the first person she wanted to see was Anne.

"Go fetch Mistress Arundel," Mother Miller instructed her grandson. "There be no one with a better garden filled with remedies for what ails 'ee."

So it was that Anne, instead of preparing dyes for some fine cloth that Thursday morning, was walking fast outside the abbey when she came face to face with the reeve.

"Good morrow, Mistress Arundel," said Durand, coming to a halt and doffing his cap to her.

Anne had perforce to stop herself or appear rude. "Good morrow, Master Durand," she said. "I trust that you are well today?"

"My health is excellent," said the reeve, recognizing the question for the courtesy commonly exchanged in brief meetings. "You and your family are all well?"

"We are so," said Anne, wondering if there was more to the reeve's interest than might appear.

"Young Aileen did seem in robust health last night," Durand said, watching the woman closely.

A quick smile crossed Anne's face. "Master Durand," she said. "Did you think that Aileen would not have told my husband and I what occurred last night?"

"Your pardon," the reeve said, abashed. "I know that you and your husband sometimes worry about the involvement of your daughter in my affairs. I merely wished to make sure that nothing I said or did would interfere with your will in these matters."

"And I thank you for that," said Anne. "We do indeed worry that Aileen become too entangled in your cases, as do Robert's parents. But we trust that you will ensure they come to no harm." She looked a question at him.

"I will always do my best in that regard," he said. "I do believe this time that there is little danger other than to their self-esteem should they fail to solve the mystery of your tapestry."

"My tapestry," Anne said. "Hardly that."

"The cloth may not belong to you," said Durand.

"You have been the person most linked with it since its arrival two weeks ago however. You have been working hard to bring the design back to life, and thus I have come to think of it as being associated with you."

"You do me too much honor," Anne said.

Durand paused.

Anne stood silent, knowing that the reeve's conversation was leading she knew not where.

"Mistress Arundel," he said at last. "I have heard much about the possible identity of this work, and I have heard as well that you have definite opinions on the matter. Is this more than idle gossip?"

"No, master reeve," said Anne. "You have not been misled. I have formed an opinion as to what this embroidery may be. I do not say that I am correct, merely that my experience has led me to believe this is a work not only of great skill but mayhap of great significance."

Anne explained to Durand how she had come to the conclusion that the tapestry could be a part of the commission of Bishop Odo. She went on to tell him about her great-grandmother's decision to leave the prow of one boat in the last panel empty.

"Had the panel not been stolen, I would perhaps have been able to confirm my suspicion the very next day," she said.

"You have not spoken of this opinion to the abbot," said Durand, looking quizzically at the woman.

"No," said Anne. "I do not believe in speaking

without evidence. Anything less would be, as you say, idle gossip."

"I understand," the reeve said. "I am sure that your principles have not prevented many in the town from asking you questions."

Anne laughed. "You are correct, Master Durand," she said. "Everyone within the Liberty seems to have known that I was cleaning and repairing the cloth. Even before it disappeared I was being pestered with questions as to its history. Once the serf and the tapestry were gone, I could scarce step out of my door without someone coming up and asking me questions I could not hope to answer."

"Rumors travel faster than a galloping horse," said Durand. "That is how the information as to your opinion arrived at my door, of course."

"It is a wonder that the tales that have been going around have not been more bizarre than they are," Anne said. "It would appear that what you have been told is close to the truth."

"It is sometimes said that truth is stranger than is falsehood," Durand said.

Anne was about to say her farewells to the reeve when he stopped her.

"Mistress Arundel, pray delay one more minute," he said. "You told me that many people had been asking you questions about the tapestry since its arrival."

"Yes," she said.

"Does any of the questioning stand out to you as being unusual?" Durand asked.

"In what way?" said Anne.

Durand rubbed his chin, a slight frown on his forehead.

"I mean, did anyone ask you questions that were different from those most commonly being asked," said the reeve. "I am not certain how to describe it. You would know better if, perhaps, someone wanted to know when you would be working on the embroidery, what kind of treatment would be needed to prevent damage, or whether you could guess its value."

Anne thought about it for a minute, and then shook her head.

"I think not," she said. "Of course, several people did ask about the value of the work, but I cannot think of any questions that I thought to be strange at the time."

"I had little hope of any other response," Durand said ruefully. "But you said some asked about the value of the tapestry. Can you remember who?"

"It is hard to be certain," said Anne. "There have been too many people stopping me in the street. It is hard to separate any one person or time."

"Well, then, may I ask who it is you can remember stopping you to make particular enquiry?" Durand said.

"Where to start?" Anne laughed. "Let me see," she continued. "Matilda Oliver cannot stop talking about the tapestry, Arlo the chandler was positively nosy about the work the abbot wished done, I could hardly get away from the miller when I purchased flour from him a week ago, and Aelred the butcher was concerned about the fate of the serf who stole it."

"I see how difficult it is for you to isolate any one person, Mistress Arundel," said Durand.

"If I had a penny for every person who has asked me about the embroidery in the last two weeks, I would be a rich woman," Anne said. "The fishmonger, the baker, vendors in the market, and even that visiting cleric from Bayeux have as good as chased me down to ask me what I know of the tapestry and how much I think it is worth!"

"Brother Lanfranc has sought you out?" asked Durand. "That is interesting, since he is in a better position than most to know about both the tapestry and the search for it."

"I got the impression he is a man who likes to gain knowledge for himself, rather than accept the word of another," said Anne.

"I think you have the right of it," Durand said, smiling. "But now that we are talking about visitors to the abbey, have you been approached by Sir Roger FitzGilbert, the serf's master? He of all people would seem to have the greatest interest in the tapestry and its recovery."

"No," said Anne. "Sir Roger is perhaps one of the few who has not talked to me about the tapestry. Mayhap he is one who, as you said, relies on the fact that he has been within the walls of St. Edmundsbury since the day the serf and the cloth disappeared and can be sure he will be one of the first people to know if there are any developments in the search."

"You may be right," said Durand hesitantly, but his brow was furrowed as he said the words.

"Master Durand, what is it that concerns you?" asked Anne.

"Your pardon, Mistress Arundel," the reeve said. "I cannot say what it is that troubles me. There is something I feel is important stuck in the back of my mind, but I cannot bring it forward. It is most vexing."

"I sympathize with you, master reeve," Anne said.

In her turn, she hesitated, looking at the ground. Then, raising her head and looking at Durand, she continued: "Now that you say that, I feel as though there is something that was said to me recently that may be of interest to you, but I cannot put my finger on it. How frustrating!"

"If we go over our conversation, do you think it might help you to remember?" Durand asked.

"I think I will just have to let it come back to me in its own good time," responded Anne. "Trying to force a memory rarely works, think you not?"

Durand sighed. "I think you are right, though I wish it were otherwise," said the reeve. "If you do remember what it is, please let me know as soon as possible."

"I will," said Anne. "Now I really must go on my way to Mistress Miller's, else she will be sending her grandson out again to find me."

"Of course," said Durand. "My pardon for delaying you so long."

With their farewells said and their thoughts turned toward their present tasks, each went their own way, subconsciously seeking out their respective elusive memories.

CHAPTER TWENTY-FOUR

He ordered that a motte should be dug at Hastings

HAD ROBERT KNOWN ALL THAT WAS happening that Thursday, he might have been frustrated at having to spend the day running errands for his father. At the time, however, he was glad of being able to leave the goldsmith's workshop because he really wanted to follow up on a couple of things Ruth had said down by the riverbank before the quartet had gone to see the reeve.

Ruth had told Aileen and Robert that Bron had seemed to want to talk to her more than any of the others after they had taken him to Fornham. Neither Robert nor Aileen was surprised to hear that piece of information. Ruth was as kind and gentle as her appearance suggested, and it would take a hard man indeed not to open up to her.

Thus it was that, while Ruth was bringing Bron some ale, the man had started chatting to her. Ruth had sat down to hear what he had to say and was a little surprised when he told her that merchants in St. Edmundsbury were much inclined to ask too many questions of strangers in town. Ruth had said that people were often interested in those who came from a long way away, to which Bron had replied that he wasn't from all that far away and the nosiness of the people of the Liberty was one reason why he had decided he should not stay there much longer.

"But I thought you left the shelter of the abbey because you saw people you recognized from Ireland," said Ruth.

"Oh, aye, I did," Bron said hurriedly. "But you must see that all those questions from people who should keep their own business made me wary, and so I kept a closer eye out for any visitors who might be dangerous to me."

Ruth nodded a little dubiously.

Bron tried again. "There was another reason I mentioned those rude people," he said. "I was worried that one of the people within the walls of the town might know people from Ireland, there being so many pilgrims clogging the taverns and crowding the markets. I was afeared that someone might send a message that would bring down on me the searchers."

That seemed a little more likely to Ruth, although she thought the man a little dramatic. Still, it was not her part to question the workings of any man's mind. At least, that was what she had thought at the time.

Aileen and Robert found Ruth's story interesting,

particularly the part where he had said he was not from so very far away from St. Edmundsbury. Ruth had not sought to question him on that statement, but Aileen had agreed that Robert should ask around town to see what connections the serf may have made in those days before the arrival of his lord.

So too had they thought it worth their while to enquire into another of Bron's conversations with Ruth.

According to their friend, during the Sabbath, when the people of Fornham were perforce more quietly occupied than the rest of the week, Bron had opened up to Ruth about another of his concerns. He told her that he had seen a priest or a monk in the abbey, although he was not dressed as an English cleric would be. He was clothed in rich garb, not at all as were most monks the serf had ever seen. Bron thought he was probably from France.

Ruth asked the serf why he was worried about a visiting priest. Surely there were many clerics who visited the shrine of the Christian saint?

Bron told Ruth that that was true and that he did not speak with the man at all. After all, men of high rank did not mix with the peasants, even if they were within the same walls. But Bron was convinced that the man had looked at him strangely on several occasions, as if he knew something about him that the peasant did not want known. Bron told Ruth he was worried the man might know he was a fugitive.

Quietly, Ruth told her friends she now realized

that the way Bron described his concerns was strange for a foreigner running from his victim's family. At the time, however, she had not really noticed it.

"That is not surprising, Ruth," said Aileen. "You had no reason to doubt his account, and you are ever one to believe the best of anyone you meet."

"That is why you doubted the account given to your father after the mushroom gathering, is it not?" A light had gone on in Avraham's head. "It was so unlike you to question a man's truthfulness, but you had remembered those conversations and now knew him to be a liar."

"Yes, Avi," said Ruth. "I remembered a little too late, I fear."

"No, Ruth," Robert said. "All will be well, I am sure of it. We will go and talk to the reeve. He will find the serf and the tapestry. . ."

"With our help," interposed Aileen, smiling.

"With our help," Robert repeated. "Once the serf is found, Sir Roger will take him back to his estate, and no one in St. Edmundsbury will even know that the good people of Fornham were ever involved."

Now, the first part of their plan having been set in motion, Robert had been tasked with seeing what the townsfolk had to say about alltheir chief suspects in the theft of the tapestry.

I know William will do a good job of talking to that French cleric, Robert allowed grudgingly. But if the man has been seen around town, he may have let drop something that could be of interest to us. And while I am at it, I might as well see what the townsfolk think of Sir Roger FitzGilbert.

Robert strolled up Abbeygate Street and down Churchgate Street, doing the errands given him by his father and stopping to chat with merchants and townsfolk running their own errands on this sunny day. He was a little frustrated to find that they rarely had anything to contribute to his store of knowledge other than the general gossip. No one had anything to say about Bron that had not already been passed around the entire Liberty. If he was from anywhere around St. Edmundsbury none knew it to be so or cared if it was truth.

When it came to Sir Roger FitzGilbert and Lanfranc of Bayeux only small snippets of information could be gleaned, and that related mostly to the differing temperaments of the two men.

Mistress Fitchett, swatting at her brood of small children running around and pulling on her skirts, did say that she had seen both Bron and the cleric from across the South Sea, she thought at the Tuesday market by the south gate. To her, they appeared to be as disagreeable as each other, the one so superior in his manner that he looked as though he was surrounded by a bad smell, the other shifty-looking, as though he was looking around to see if anyone would notice if he picked up a pie without paying for it.

I wonder if they met each other, thought Robert as he walked on. Mayhap that is one of those occasions when Lanfranc gave Bron a "strange" look. I am not sure this greatly helps us though.

Old Robin, the thatcher, said he thought he remembered seeing that "French cockalorum" looking down his nose at the goods in the shops a few days since, but as far as he could tell, he spoke to no one. "Nay, I doubt he thinks any of us are worth his time," was Old Robin's judgment. Robert thought that, as far as he could tell, that was a common opinion of the cleric in town.

Dispirited, Robert turned the corner into Churchgate Street and almost ran into the chandler and Mistress Oliver who were having a lively, if one-sided conversation. Mistress Oliver gave a little shriek as Robert almost ran into her and then gave him a great smile.

"Master Robert Palgrave, as I live and breathe," she said happily. "I have not seen my favorite strong young man in a month of Sundays. How fare you and that lovely family of yours?"

Robert blushed but greeted her politely enough and informed her that his family was in very good health.

"Good morrow, master chandler," Robert continued. "I am sorry to have interrupted your discussion."

Arlo's response was gruff, but Robert had expected nothing more. He was more interested in their discussion, given that he had heard the words "cloth" and "missing" as he approached.

"The town is still full of talk about the serf and the

tapestry," he said. "Have either of you heard anything further about the search for them?"

"Nay," said Mistress Oliver. "That is what we were talking about. It is so frustrating not knowing what is happened in the search. How can that man have gone missing so long without anyone seeing him? For sure he has the tapestry with him, and I just cannot bear to think of what condition it is in by now. Poor Mistress Arundel. She must be so distressed at the thought of all that hard work of hers being for nought."

I am certain sure she took no breath the whole time she spoke, thought Robert. She is a rare woman indeed.

Arlo looked as though he was thinking of a way to escape but could find no way of doing so without seriously offending a good customer.

"The serf's lord must be distressed as well," said Robert, hoping to open up a new opportunity to gather information. "And, from all I hear, the man from Bayeux is more disturbed than even Sir Roger FitzGilbert."

Matilda burst out laughing. "That cleric," she said. "I've seen neither hide nor hair of him the past few days, but that causes me no grief."

"You have not found him congenial on those occasions when you have seen him?" asked Robert.

"A man whose nose is so far in the air, it is a wonder he does not hurt his neck," Mistress Oliver said dismissively. "He visited our tavern but one time and acted as though he was far too good for the likes of us. I will shed no tears if he is fuddled."

Matilda flicked her hand in the air as if to swat a fly.

"What about Sir Roger?" Robert put in quickly, hoping to divert the good woman's focus.

"Aye, I have seen him," Matilda said. "He is not at all like that so-called Man of God from Bayeux."

Arlo could be heard muttering under his breath, but Mistress Oliver ignored him and went on with what she had to say about the lord of Fitching.

"He was in our tavern when he first arrived in town, asking anyone who would listen for news of his serf. He was most gracious about the quality of our food and ale, although I think he must have been tired from his journey."

Matilda beamed her approval of the knight's discernment, but Robert was more interested in another part of her assessment of the man.

"Why do you say he must have been tired?" he asked.

"Well, it stands to reason, does it not?" said the woman. "His manners were gentle, but he was clearly tired and angry at having to chase down that serf of his. His voice was sharp, but he was not roaring like a lion, cursing and threatening what he would do when his serf was captured."

"You like Sir Roger," Robert stated.

"As much as anyone can like a Norman lord who is a stranger to our town," Matilda said firmly.

Arlo muttered something that sounded like "a pox on all Normans," giving Robert the chance to ask him if he had seen either the cleric or the knight.

"Praise be, neither one of them has cast their shadow over my threshold," said Arlo. "It may be that I have seen one or other of them walking in the town or within the walls of the abbey but that would be a dark enough day for me."

"You seem to have a strong dislike for two men you have never seen," said Robert.

Arlo spat on the ground. "And why should I think anything else?" the chandler said. "All the people of the Liberty know what will happen once that Norman knight has hold of his property again, and I am not talking about the tapestry."

Once he had started speaking, Arlo seemed unable to stop.

"The Normans take what they want and brook no interference," he said. "They have no mercy and care nothing for simple folk. That serf is nothing but a speck of dust to his master. All he wants is to teach his other serfs a lesson. Bron will be dead before he can pray to God for mercy on his soul."

Robert and Matilda were staring at Arlo, surprised by the vehemence of his speech. Matilda thought the man needed a good tankard of ale to cool down. Robert thought he needed to dig deeper into the reason for the flood of words from a man who was rarely known to utter more than one or two in succession.

Robert opened his mouth to continue the conversation, but at that moment, a young boy came running up the street waving his arms and shouting: "They've got him!"

"Got who?" called Robert.

"They've caught the runaway serf," yelled the boy. "They are bringing him in to town now."

All those within earshot took to their feet, running down the hill to see for themselves this exciting event. Robert and the others joined the throng, Robert moving easily, Matilda puffing to keep up the pace, and Arlo, initially startled by the news and then frowning in deep thought, following close behind.

CHAPTER TWENTY-FIVE

Here it was announced to William concerning Harold
and here a house is burned

THAT EVENING, AILEEN BROUGHT William with her to the riverbank. Robert had half-expected her to do so, given how excited the young lord was about being a part of their investigation, so he rallied quickly enough from his disappointment at seeing him.

William had been at the forefront of those who saw the procession of men coming through the south gate that afternoon. Robert had not arrived soon enough in the process to see and hear everything that went on, and Aileen had not even known about it until Mistress Taylor came bustling in with the news.

"Tell us all," instructed Aileen. "I am quite disappointed to have missed it all."

William said it certainly had been one of the most lively scenes he had ever seen played out before him.

"Bron was brought through the gates by the lord of Cattishall, a little the worse for wear and definitely in fear of what is to come," said William. "He was shaking like a leaf and casting his gaze all around, searching for some way to escape and despairing at finding none."

"The poor man," Aileen said. She thought he sounded like a trapped animal, and her natural compassion came to the fore.

"Poor thief, more like," said Robert with a snort. Aileen frowned at him, and he subsided.

"Pray continue," said Aileen to William.

"It really did seem as though the whole of St. Edmundsbury had turned out to see the end of the search," the lord de Vere said. "But strangely enough, the crowd was very quiet and there was little comment among the folk standing there as Durand took charge of the rope by which John of Cattishall was leading the serf."

"Then what happened?" Aileen breathed, leaning forward to catch every word and nuance uttered by William. Even Robert was paying close attention to the narrative.

"Durand asked John how he had caught the serf," said William. "Sir John said he found him in the forest. He had been hunting with his hounds and heard the sounds of fighting through the trees.

"Sir John followed the sounds and found Bron fighting with another man," William went on. "The lord of Cattishall indicated that the other man was standing at the back of the procession that had come through the gate. He was limping and bruised, but when I saw who it was, I realized he was the gatekeeper of the abbey."

"Sergeant Ralph," exclaimed Robert. "Now that I did not expect."

"I did not either," added Aileen. "He has never seemed to be so. . . active a man."

William smiled. "I can see why you would say that," he said. "When Sir John brought attention to him, he was trying to get to through the courtyard gate without being noticed. Failing that, he stood still and mumbled something that few heard."

"Did you hear him?" asked Aileen.

"I was standing close by him," said William. "I think he said 'I thought to catch him, but he was quick'."

"That sounds like Ralph," laughed Robert and all three of them took a moment to chuckle.

"Go on," said Aileen. "What happened next?"

"Sir Roger FitzGilbert came out of the courtyard gate," William said. "Apparently, he had asked one of the lay servants of the abbey what the hubbub was, and, on being told, he obviously wanted to come outside immediately to see for himself."

"Was he angry or pleased?" asked Aileen.

"It was hard to tell what he was thinking," William said. "His face gave away nothing."

"What did he say?" Robert said.

"He said nothing at first," said William. "But Bron,

seeing him come to the front of the throng, dropped to his knees, blubbering with fear and begging mercy of his lord."

Aileen's expression showed her distress, but this time she said nothing.

"Still Roger said nothing," William said. "He stood with his hands on his hips and just looked at the man who had led him on such a chase. Then, turning to the reeve, he said that Durand should take him into custody and that he would take the serf back with him when he left."

"And then?" Robert could not stand the pause that followed William's last statement.

"Then Sir Roger turned to leave," said William. "Durand stopped him."

"What?" two voices said at once. "Why?"

William could not have wished for a better audience. I am so glad I decided to come to St. Edmundsbury, he thought. I would not have missed this for the world.

"Durand said that there was still the matter of the missing cloth," he said. "His tone was such that Sir Roger stopped and turned around, his eyes boring into those of the reeve. He shook his head slightly and then looked at the serf who had been hauled to his feet by Durand and now stood beside that officer, head down and eyes filled with tears."

William stopped for a moment, remembering how it seemed as though the whole throng, himself included, was holding its breath, waiting to see what the knight would do.

"The knight bent toward the serf," said William. "'Indeed,' he said, and then his tone hardened.

"'Bron, where is the cloth?'" William's voice was sharper, almost as if he was mimicking the tone of the serf's master.

"Bron raised his head and looked at Sir Roger blankly," William went on. "'I know not,' he said. 'Last I knew, it was here in the abbey.'"

Aileen looked a little startled at hearing this.

"To me it sounded as though a sigh of wind went through the crowd," said William. Turning to Robert, he said: "Did you not feel that also? You must have been there by then."

"I heard people hiss," replied Robert. "I had not heard what it was that Sir Roger had said though, so I was unaware of the reason for the sound.

"It was very frustrating to be so near and yet not be able to see or hear much," Robert went on a little resentfully.

"I can imagine," William said in a flat tone.

Robert looked at him suspiciously, but William's bland expression gave no hint of laughter.

"Go on, William," urged Aileen. "You know we want to hear the whole story."

"Durand looked at Bron in a way that made me think he might believe the serf," said the young lord. "He could hardly leave it there with such a large crowd in attendance though.

"'It is hard to believe you know nothing of the disappearance of the very fabric for which you risked so much,' the reeve said. Bron's eyes shifted, and he finally muttered that he might have heard the cloth was missing."

William's telling of events was speeding up, and his voice was all but taking on the accents of the participants in the drama.

"'From whom did you hear this?' asked the reeve.

"'From the Jews,' came the reply.'

Aileen and Robert gasped at hearing this.

"Do not be concerned," William said hurriedly. "The man did not say anything about hiding in the homes of the Jews in Fornham."

The friends let the air out of their lungs in a relieved whoosh.

"I do believe that the reeve failed to press the matter deliberately," said William. "It is gratifying to know that our assessment of the man was accurate."

"What happened then?" asked Robert.

William smiled. "That was the point at which Arlo stepped forward," he said. "Mayhap you can take the tale forward from here?"

"I can," said Robert, relieved to know he had not missed the whole drama and could now gratify Aileen's curiosity himself. "I had reached the front of the crowd in time to hear the word 'Jews.' Since I did not hear the rest of the sentence, I was worried that Bron had betrayed our friends."

"I would have been afraid of that as well," said Aileen.

"Then Arlo began to speak and changed the subject completely," Robert went on.

"What did the chandler have to do with all of this?" Aileen said.

"He was in a fine temper," said Robert. "He pushed his way to the front of the crowd and demanded to know why the serf was being persecuted."

"Truly?" said Aileen.

"Truly," said Robert. "He said the man's words had the ring of truth to them, and just because he was a lowly serf did not mean his account could not be believed."

"What did the reeve answer to that?" asked Aileen.

"Before he could really say anything," said Robert, "Arlo seemed to realize that everyone around him was staring at him, and he subsided a little, mumbling something about lords and their manners. Then he backed away in the same way in which he had pushed forward."

"Sir Roger must have been disturbed by such a reaction," Aileen said. "Did he say anything?"

"No," said Robert. "He kept his eyes on Arlo as he moved to the back of the crowd. I think he did not see what happened next. I only saw it because I was at the back of the throng myself and thus no one was blocking my view."

"What was it that he did not see?" William was

interested to hear that there was something that had gone on out of his own sight.

Delighted to see that he was now the one who could provide new information, Robert picked up his account. "Arlo stood alone at the back of the crowd," he said. "He looked as though he was cross with himself for having lost his self-control in front of so many people."

"I can understand how it would be embarrassing," Aileen said.

"I would have wanted to hide my head in the dirt for shame," Robert agreed. "At any rate, before even a minute had passed, the butcher came over to talk to Arlo."

"Aelred?" Aileen said. "I did not know they were friends. Neither man often seems of a cordial nature."

"I know what you mean," laughed Robert.

"Could you hear what they said to each other?" asked William.

Robert shook his head. "I fear not. But Aelred obviously said something that made the chandler feel better. Arlo raised his head and looked at the butcher. Then he nodded his head, and the men exchanged some words. Arlo then put his hand on Aelred's shoulder and they parted ways."

"Interesting," said Aileen. "A pity it is that we do not know what was said."

"I am sorry, Aileen," said Robert miserably.

"I did not mean that as criticism, Robert," Aileen

said fondly and touched the back of his hand. "It was a mere comment."

William thought it was about time they got back to the matter of the serf and the tapestry. "Are you able to tell Mistress Aileen what happened next?"

"Yes," said Robert. "I worked my way toward the front of the crowd after Arlo had said his piece and was in time to hear Durand asking Sergeant Ralph about the chase."

"The gatekeeper did appear to have recovered from his embarrassment by this time," said William. "He was quite ready to let everyone know how brave and strong he was."

"Poor Ralph," said Aileen. "I believe he does feel quite as though he is not appreciated most of the time. Mayhap that is why he found it quite pleasant to be the center of attention for once."

"You are probably right, Aileen," said Robert. "When Durand asked him about the chase, Sergeant Ralph stepped forward quite willingly and told the reeve how it came about that he chased Bron. He said he was taken by surprise when, after he was cornered, the serf threw his parcel hard into the brush and launched himself at Ralph."

"I would have been surprised as well," said Aileen. "Nothing that I have seen of the serf has made me think him a violent man."

"Perhaps not," said William. "But desperation will drive a man to do many things he would not otherwise consider." He sounded sad, as though he was remembering his past missteps.

Aileen gave him an encouraging smile, and Robert, for once in sympathy with the young lord, suggested that William pick up the tale once again.

"I do remember the gatekeeper saying that he was sure he would have prevailed in the fight," said William. "He then went on to say that he was of course grateful to the lord of Cattishall for coming upon the scene and helping him capture the serf."

"And how did the lord of Cattishall feel about Ralph's version of events?" Aileen said, laughing.

"I did see his eyebrows rise," responded William. "The man is tall and swarthy, strong as a bull. His brows almost disappeared into his black hair at Ralph's statement."

"The sergeant's next comment, I fear, made it clear that public service was not necessarily at the forefront of his mind," Robert said.

"Just so, Robert," said William.

"Ralph turned to Sir Roger FitzGilbert and asked about the reward," said Robert. "He said he had been told there was a reward of three silver pennies for the capture of the serf, and he wanted to know if the knight was willing to pay it."

"He certainly seems to have got over his embarrassment, does he not?" said Aileen, a little shocked at the blunt words Sergeant Ralph had used in talking to the knight.

"I would say so," Robert said. "Whether that be

the case or not, Sir Roger said immediately he would pay it but asked to whom it should be paid. He said, as far as he could see, there were two claimants to the reward: Sergeant Ralph and the lord of Cattishall. Should he give half to one and half to the other?"

"Ralph scowled at this." William picked up the story. "He said nothing, but you could see what he was thinking. But then Sir John spoke up and said he would take no share. As far as he could see, Ralph had caught the man first, and it was only due to the gate-keeper's quick thinking in cornering Bron that there had been any fight for him to break up."

"That was nice of him," Aileen said.

"It was truth, but not every man would see it so," agreed William. "Sergeant Ralph was obviously surprised at his words too."

"So Sir Roger has agreed to give the silver pennies to Sergeant Ralph?" asked Aileen.

"He has so," responded William. "He said that he would ensure Ralph had his reward in good time for the next market day. Ralph looked very happy at the prospect of having money to spend for a change."

"I think that that comment may be what led to the next thing that happened," Robert said slowly. "I had not thought about it at the time but it would make sense."

"What happened?" asked Aileen, feeling even more that she had missed the most important thing to happen since the disappearance of the tapestry.

"Well," said William, "Durand asked Sir Roger if

he believed his serf when he said he did not take the cloth. Roger responded that he did not know who else could have stolen the tapestry if Bron had not done so, and, given his history with the man, he might not be the best person for the reeve to ask."

"There was this big pause after the knight had spoken," said Robert. He was not going to let William have the credit for working out this bit of the puzzle. "Durand had been standing there with his brow furrowed ever since the conversation between Ralph and Sir Roger about the reward. Then, of a sudden, his brow cleared, and he said out loud, 'Of course, market day. I knew something did not sound right.'"

"I do not understand," said Aileen. "What did market days have to do with the disappearance of the tapestry?"

For once I know something before Aileen, thought Robert and then was immediately ashamed of himself for being so prideful.

"I thought the same thing myself," he admitted. "By that time, I was close enough to hear the conversation between the knight and the reeve. Most of the people that had come to see the captured serf were leaving by that time, thinking that all the excitement was over. There was a lot of chatter as they walked back to their homes, and thus only those of us really close in could hear what was said."

"They spoke so softly I could not hear the words myself," said William a little ruefully. "I saw that there was some kind of disagreement between the two men, but I could not tell what it was about."

"Do not tease us so, Robert," said Aileen. "What did they say to each other?"

"I was merely setting the scene," Robert said. "I was not teasing you."

Aileen threw a clump of grass at him, and Robert put up his hands in mock surrender.

"Durand reminded Sir Roger that, at the time the knight had offered the reward, Sir Roger had commented on the price of goods at the market that was taking place outside the south gate when he arrived.

"'That is so,' the knight said. 'I am not sure I understand why you find that so significant.'"

"Why did he?" Aileen asked simply.

Robert beamed from ear to ear. "Sir Roger said he arrived in St. Edmundsbury on Wednesday, eight days ago."

Aileen's face lit up.

"That market is on Tuesday, not Wednesday."

"Exactly," Robert said.

"That does put a different light on things, does it not?" said William.

"What did the knight reply?" Aileen asked, wanting to know more.

"He told the reeve that he did not see any need to say he had arrived the day before they met," Robert said. "He told Durand that he had indeed arrived on Tuesday and had asked questions of some of the townsfolk. Following a comment made by one of them, he rode out to Bertuna to see if a stranger noted there could have been Bron. Finding out that it was not, he made camp for the night and rode back to St. Edmundsbury on Wednesday."

"Did Sir Roger seem honest in his response?" asked Aileen.

"He spoke up most easily and looked Durand in the eye as he spoke," Robert said. "When he had explained himself, he told Durand that he resented the implication in the reeve's line of thought."

"That was awkward," said Aileen.

"That certainly explains why they had the appearance of disagreeing about something," said William.

"What did Durand say to all of this?" asked Aileen.

"He apologized to the knight and thanked him for explaining how it was that the wrong impression had been gained," Robert said. "I thought that was a nice way of apologizing without saying he regretted his words."

"It was indeed," said William. "Altogether, I am most impressed by the intelligence of your reeve. The abbot chose well when he appointed Durand."

"What did you think of the knight's explanation, Robert?" Aileen asked. "Do you think it changes anything?"

"Sir Roger did seem to be truthful," Robert said a little reluctantly, "But I think we should put this information together with all the rest we have gathered and see if that helps us in our search for the tapestry."

"That is a good idea," said Aileen.

The trio sat on the riverbank for quite a long time that evening discussing the latest developments, from the confrontation in the courtyard between Durand and Roger to the discussion William had with Roger and Lanfranc, and from Robert's conversation with Matilda and Arlo to the gleanings Aileen had gained from her mother and Mistress Taylor.

"Is this not exciting?" said William after they had finished exchanging all their information. "But I am not clear. Has all this knowledge solved the mystery yet?"

Robert scowled at William, and Aileen giggled a little.

"I think we should mull it all over in our minds tonight, sir," she said. "Who knows, we may find we have indeed solved the mystery but that we have yet to pull it out of all the tangled threads of gossip and guesswork."

With this comforting thought, the trio stood up stiffly from their grassy seats and headed homeward.

CHAPTER TWENTY-SIX

*Here the knights have left Hastings and have come to the
battle against King Harold*

"OUCH!" SAID AILEEN. Sucking her pricked finger, she hastily checked the cope she was working on that Friday morning to make sure no blood had stained the fabric. Relieved to see nothing, she checked her finger and found that the needle had not penetrated far enough to cause it to bleed.

"I really must concentrate on what I am doing," Aileen said to herself. Mistress Taylor would never forgive me if I damaged the cope in any way.

Bending determinedly over her work, Aileen was able to put aside all thoughts of the missing tapestry for a good while. It was impossible for that state of disengagement to last forever, though. As soon as Aileen had completed a particularly difficult piece of gold thread stitching, her mind started to wander back again to the puzzle of the embroidery.

The whole subject of displaced Saxons has become a talking point in the town, she mused. Always it has been under the surface. I have heard my father and mother talk of the conditions of the native English people after William slew King Harold, and I know that their discussions were mirrored in many homes within the Liberty.

Why have these hard feelings risen to the surface now, she wondered. Aelred and Arlo have spoken openly about the loss of their lands after the arrival of the Normans, and they are not alone. I am sure there are many citizens of St. Edmundsbury who could tell a similar tale.

Has this become such a topic of conversation because of people like Aelred and Arlo who have so passionately argued for the serf? Judging from what I have heard, there are more than a few people in town who are sympathetic toward his plight. There is strong feeling amongst many that, although he did wrong, the Normans are an unmerciful people and Bron is likely to suffer greatly because of that wrong. On the other hand, some are saying that Sir Roger does not seem to be a bad man and mayhap he will not put Bron to death. Mayhap he will only cut off a hand.

Aileen shivered. The loss of a hand for many would be very nearly the loss of their life. Even were they to survive the injury itself, there were many who died of the infection that so often came after.

Aileen mentally set aside this problem for the moment and went on to consider the man from Bayeux. It seems as though he could have a motive for taking the tapestry, she said to herself. He is very proud, and it is clear he believes that Bayeux is where the work belongs, assuming that it is indeed part of the work commissioned by Bishop Odo.

Aileen put down her needle, her brow creasing in concentration.

Would a man of the church steal this embroidery, knowing its origins not certain, and then lie so blatantly? I know not all churchmen are holy in their conduct, she thought, and of course all men are sinners. Just because they have taken holy vows does not mean they will be free of wrongdoing from then on.

Even if Lanfranc intended to steal the tapestry, Aileen reflected, the timing of the deed was not easy to establish. The tapestry had to have been taken around the time Bron ran away. How would Lanfranc have known that was happening, and, even if he saw the man leave, would he have been able to take advantage of that event to carry out the theft?

Aileen sighed in frustration, only to hear the sound echoed beside her. Turning her head, she saw Mistress Taylor standing there, frown on her face and hands on her hips.

"I take my oath you are the most daydreaming girl I have ever known," said the robemaker. "You have your mother's talent with the needle, but sometimes you are enough to frustrate a saint with your stargazey eyes and your idle hands."

"Your pardon, Mistress Taylor," Aileen said remorsefully. "I did not mean to neglect my work. It is just that so much has happened in the past week, and it is hard to stop your mind from dwelling on it."

Mistress Taylor's expression softened a little. She leaned in to Aileen and, so softly that others could not hear, said, "I cannot deny what you say. I scarce slept last night for all the excitement."

The robemaker straightened and continued in a louder voice.

"Howsoever that may be," she opined, "I will not have my women ignoring their duty. Set all thought of anything other than that cope out of your mind and get to work."

"Yes, Mistress Taylor," Aileen said meekly and immediately picked up her needle.

Aileen did her best to focus on her work, and, for the most part, she succeeded. It was hard to completely leave aside all thoughts of the mystery though, however hard she tried.

Surely the man from Bayeux would not have stolen something which he may have been considering purchasing, Aileen thought to herself. There would be no need to steal it.

But what if Lanfranc did not have the funds to purchase the tapestry? Mayhap he did not think he had time to send to Bayeux and possibly get the money from the bishop there. Would he really have wanted it badly enough to steal it from under the noses of the monks?

We come back to the timing, Aileen went on. Why would the cleric have stolen the tapestry at that particular time, rather than wait until closer to the time he was planning to leave? It would not be easy for a stranger to hide such an object.

Altogether, none of this makes any sense, Aileen almost said out loud. She bent back over her work, realizing her thoughts had once again strayed from the task at hand.

It was almost the noon hour when Aileen started thinking about Sir Roger FitzGilbert. She was hemming the cope by now, and mechanical work was boring enough that it was hard to prevent her mind from wandering.

Surely, he cannot be a true suspect, she thought. We know now that it would have been physically possible for him to have taken the tapestry from the linen room since he had arrived in St. Edmundsbury the day before it was thought he had ridden through the gates. But why would he do so? He has the best claim to the tapestry.

Did the knight fear that another, mayhap Lanfranc, would lay claim to the work? To suspect that Sir Roger would have had to have known there was another potential claimant to an as yet unidentified tapestry. How could that be?

Even had the knight known about the risk of losing the work to another, there is still the question of why he should want to steal it, Aileen mused. He is not a poor man. He did not need to sell it to maintain his estates. Or did he?

No, Aileen said to herself firmly. He put up a reward of three silver pennies for the capture of Bron. No man worried about his money would do something like that. On top of that, William has commented on the man's rich garb. According to William, it was not old and worn, and, if there was one man who could be trusted to properly judge fine clothes, it was William de Vere.

So we come back to Bron. He says he did not steal the tapestry. . . for a second time. The problem is he is obviously not trustworthy. After all, Ruth thinks only the best of everyone, and even she doubted the man's word.

The serf's motive is obvious, Aileen thought. He it was who stole it in the first place, hoping to have a better life away from his feudal lord. He was terrified of what Sir Roger was going to do with him, so, when he saw the knight arrive, he grabbed the tapestry and ran. That is what everyone thinks happened and, his denial notwithstanding, that is what makes the most sense.

Why am I not satisfied with that solution? Aileen shook her head in frustration. What more do I need to accept the most logical explanation?

Is there anything else that I need to take into account when looking at Bron's actions? she considered. Well, Ruth and Avraham did talk about the dirt on his clothes and hands and said he had a torn piece of sacking when they found him. Does that amount to anything?

Aileen stopped short as she contemplated this piece of information. According to the account William and Robert gave, Ralph said something about Bron carrying a parcel. He said the serf had thrown it hard into the brush before he attacked the gatekeeper.

Has no one gone into the forest to see if they can find this parcel? Could it be that the tapestry is lying on the damp forest floor covered only by a piece of sacking?

Aileen started to her feet at the thought, and Mistress Taylor was forced to say sharply that it was not yet the hour for her midday break. Aileen started to say something but thought better of it. She sat back down and dutifully picked up her needle.

I must find Sergeant Ralph during the lunch hour, she thought. I need to find out where the fight between him and Bron took place. Robert and I can go there before the light fades this evening and search for the sackcloth.

As soon as Mistress Taylor told her women they could take their break, Aileen ran from the linen room and across the courtyard, intent on finding the gatekeeper. Before she could reach the man's guard post, however, she saw William running toward her, face flushed and hands hanging on tight to something bulky and dirty.

"Mistress Aileen," the young lord said, skidding to a halt in front of her. "Look what I found!"

William opened his armss to reveal a bundle of sackcloth. As he unwrapped it, Aileen bent over to see what was inside and gasped.

CHAPTER TWENTY-SEVEN

Here Duke William asks Vitalis if he has seen Harold's army and here this man tells King Harold about Duke William's army

"MASTER REEVE," SAID THE ABBOT softly. "Methinks you are not satisfied that we have found the entire solution to our mystery."

Durand was sitting in the abbot's chambers, drinking ale and staring moodily into the fire. When the abbot spoke, the reeve jumped, and a little ale spilled over the top of the tankard.

"Your pardon, father abbot," Durand said guiltily, swiping at his tunic. "I was sunk too deep in my own thoughts."

"Clearly," the abbot said wryly. "But my question was regarding the apparent solution to this crime. You do not believe that Sir Roger's serf is responsible for the disappearance of the tapestry?"

"I am not sure, father," said Durand. "The man is a liar. Of that there is no doubt. Yet his reaction to the suggestion that he had taken the tapestry from the abbey seemed genuine. It is hard to feign real surprise. It may be that he is actually telling the truth on this occasion."

Abbot Samson looked inquiringly at the reeve. "There must be more to make you study the flames of the fire so intently." he said.

Durand admitted as much, put down his tankard, and turned to faced the abbot. "The revelations yesterday were not confined to those regarding the serf," he said. "It would appear that Sir Roger Fitz-Gilbert has not been as forthcoming as we might have hoped."

"Truly?" The abbot was surprised. "In what way?"

"It has come to light that the knight in fact arrived in St. Edmundsbury the day before we had believed," said Durand. "He had an explanation for why he had not revealed that information, but the fact remains that Sir Roger had time to find the lay of the land and conceive a plan to deceive before the embroidery was taken."

The abbot's eyebrows rose. "Is it your opinion that the knight stole his own property?"

"No, father abbot," Durand said. "I think it unlikely. He is a wealthy man, and his personality does not seem especially proud or vengeful."

"Then what is it that concerns you in particular?" enquired the abbot.

"Sir Roger did not have any reason to lie to me regarding his whereabouts," replied the reeve. "It worries me that he did so."

"I can understand that," said the abbot. "I share your concern. However, I cannot see a reason for him to steal the tapestry. On balance, I must still believe the man to be genuine."

Durand sighed. "As must I," he said.

Abbot Samson remained silent, knowing that more was to come.

"Father, I am beginning to wonder who would have had motive to steal this tapestry other than Bron," Durand blurted out. "The story just does not seem complete, and if there is one thing that I cannot stand, it is an unsatisfactory end to a mystery."

"Then let us discuss who else it could be who might have done this deed," the abbot said. "And why."

Samson paused. Then, with a tone of determination, went on: "It is difficult to say this, but have you considered Brother Lanfranc?"

It must have cost the abbot something to put forward this cleric as his first suspect, thought Durand, even if the man be from Bayeux.

"I have considered the possibility," he said carefully. "I first gave it thought after you told me of his family history."

Samson nodded. "I confess I was reluctant to talk about that, but I knew that it was something of which you had to be aware," he said. "His pride leaves him little option but to desire possession of what he believes to be part of a treasure that belongs to the cathedral in Bayeux."

"Brother Lanfranc is a man full of self-esteem and ambition," Durand said.

The abbot laughed. "A very diplomatic way of saying it, master reeve," he said. Then he became serious. "I do wonder, you see, if the return of such a treasure might offer Brother Lanfranc future preferment."

"You mean that he might have hopes of becoming bishop or even a counselor to the King?" Durand asked.

"Brother Lanfranc is an ambitious man," the abbot said. "Ambition can sometimes blind a man to the rightness of his actions, or indeed, to their consequences."

"I wonder if Sir Roger sees him in the same light?" mused the reeve.

"I think it likely that the two men may disagree as to the fate of the tapestry," said the abbot. "However, I imagine that such a disagreement cannot have come to pass before the day on which the tapestry was taken from the abbey."

"I agree," said Durand. "I cannot believe that any such argument over ownership would have had any impact on what occurred on the night of the theft. It has always seemed to me a crime of opportunity, not one carefully planned and carried out."

"That is a good point, master reeve," said the

abbot. "I suggest that we consider all possible suspects in that light."

The men sat and talked a little while longer, and then the abbot said he must attend to chapter business.

"I will have more discussion with Brother Lanfranc," he told the reeve. "Mayhap he will say something that will enlighten us further."

"And I will send a man to Bertuna," said Durand. "It is, I believe, advisable to check Sir Roger's story and see if he was in fact there the day before the theft."

Unaware that he and the reeve were thinking along the same lines, Robert had begged the horse and cart of his father that Friday morning and asked if he could be excused for the afternoon.

Once on the road to Bertuna, Robert's thoughts turned to more personal matters.

Father says that my skills are developing well, he thought to himself. The other day, he talked about sending me to London in a year if things continue to progress as they do now. He says that I could learn even more from the goldsmith who taught him and that I would then return to the Liberty an even greater craftsman than my father is now.

Father is proud of me, I know. I am happy that I am able to make him proud, and it is certainly true that all I have ever thought of is to carry on the gold-smithing tradition within our family. If father thinks it is best I travel away from home to gain more skills, Robert sighed, then I must do as he wills.

Absentmindedly, Robert steered the horse to the left at the fork in the road and cast an eye at the sky to check that the weather continued to promise a warm, sunny day.

I do not know how I feel about this idea of going to London to learn more, Robert mused. My home is here and London is so far away. I have never been further than Sudbury in my whole life. I cannot even think about living in a place where there are more than 20,000 people.

Robert's face scrunched up as he tried to get his mind around that many people in one city. Why, I thought St. Edmundsbury was huge with a quarter of the people, and even then, that is the number of folk who come on a feast day for St. Edmund. I would never be able to find my way around in a place that large.

I need to stop thinking this way, Robert said, taking himself to task. Aileen would tell me not to borrow trouble. Who knows what may happen in a year. My father may change his mind or mayhap I will decide I would like the adventure of staying in London for a while. Unlikely, but one should never say never.

Still, his mind went on relentlessly, going to London would mean leaving behind all those I care about: My family, my friends, Aileen. . .

Robert's rogue thoughts could continue no longer. Bertuna was just ahead, and he had work to do.

"God save you, young master," said a charcoal burner walking toward him from the village.

"Good morrow, sir," replied Robert.

"A fair day for business, is it not?" The charcoal burner was looking at Robert inquisitively, and Robert realized that it must be rare for strangers to ride to the village without there being some good reason.

"Yes, it is," said Robert, thinking that he might as well take advantage of the curiosity of the man. "I am come in search of some information."

The charcoal burner's open expression closed down a little at Robert's words. You fool, Robert admonished himself. Could you have thought of a more unlikely opening to draw information out of anyone? How I wish Aileen were here. She is so much better at this sort of thing than I am.

"What kind of information?" the charcoal burner asked suspiciously.

Robert took a deep breath and tried again. "You see, a friend of mine and I have a wager on a small matter," he whispered as though he was afraid someone might overhear him telling the man a secret. "It is not a large wager, for neither of us is weighed down with coin." Robert forced a laugh as if he had made a great joke.

The man's face lost some of its wariness. "What kind of wager would have a young man like you ride to a poor village such as Bertuna to settle it?"

Good question, thought Robert. I would have better thought out what I was going to say ahead of time.

He laughed again. "It is foolish, really," he said. "William, for that is the name of my friend, said that another friend of ours, Roger, had found a great number of sturgeon in a river close by Bertuna."

"I have never heard so," said the puzzled charcoal burner.

"That is what I said." Robert slapped his knee as though he had already won the bet. "William would not have it that Roger was mistaken, but I know that Roger is as short-sighted as a drunken flea, so I wagered William that I could prove him wrong."

The charcoal burner's face by now was wreathed in smiles. "I think you will have no problem winning your wager, young sir," said the man. "I fancy none around here have ever seen such a fish in our waters, let alone eaten one."

"Thank you kindly," said Robert sincerely. At least now he knew how to approach the people in the village.

The two men parted the best of friends, and Robert proceeded on his way to Bertuna, whistling as he went.

Unfortunately, Robert gained little information from the good people of the village that day. By the time he turned his cart back to St. Edmundsbury, he had confirmed that Sir Roger FitzGilbert, or at least someone very like him, had indeed visited Bertuna the day before the tapestry was taken from the abbey. The good people of the village were certain sure it was that day because one of their own had been in St. Edmundsbury the day of the theft and it was all the villagers could talk about after he got home that night.

Other than that, there was little to be discovered. The man had been asking questions, just as Robert was, but his questions had nothing to do with winning a silly wager about fish. No, he was looking for a small dark man with dirty clothes and an old cedar chest.

The only new information that Robert was able to glean was that the knight never told any in the village who he was or that Bron was a runaway serf. I am not sure I would have told them that either, thought Robert. Country folk are not likely to tell a Norman lord anything that might cause trouble for one of their own. Sir Roger was wise enough to know that.

Other than this meager piece of information, the only good thing was that Robert would now be able to confirm to Aileen and William that Sir Roger had ridden to Bertuna that day and, as far as the villagers knew, left to return to St. Edmundsbury late in the afternoon.

As he rode back, Robert looked around more carefully than when he had driven the road that morning. He was looking for any site that seemed a likely spot to make camp for the night. One last confirmation of Sir Roger's story would be a good thing, thought Robert.

It really was not easy to identify disturbances off the road that might be a sign of a recent campfire. I remember how hard it was to find the place where a rider had left the road when we were trying to find the holy relic, thought Robert. I stuck with it that time because it was really important. This time, it is not such a big thing and I am not going to search until dark.

In spite of the lack of urgency in his mind, Robert was delighted to find a place showing clear signs of a recent campfire about halfway along the route to St. Edmundsbury. I cannot tell if this is the camp of Sir Roger, of course, but it is what I was looking for, and thus I am content.

Having thus been relieved of the responsibility to make any further investigative efforts, Robert spent the rest of the ride home thinking about his future and the people he hoped would share it with him.

CHAPTER TWENTY-EIGHT

Here Duke William speaks to his knights to prepare themselves manfully and wisely for the battle against the army of the English

B RON WAS SITTING ON THE FLOOR OF HIS cell, disconsolate. All my plans have come to nought, he sniffed, and now I am going to die.

Tears welled up in Bron's eyes as he thought of the injustice of it all. They were tears of frustration and fear, not of remorse.

The serf wiped his arm across his eyes as he heard the sound of a key turning in the lock of his cell. Looking up, he saw Durand stride in, a dirty piece of sackcloth in his hands. The reeve stood for a moment, watching the start of surprise as Bron saw the parcel. He knows what it is I hold, thought Durand. I expected as much, but it is always good to have confirmation.

Unwrapping the package, Durand thrust it in front of the serf's face.

Dust motes swirling in the rays from the sparse light that entered the small window of the cell highlighted what it was that Durand was holding: A skinner knife with its long handle curved back on itself, two quarter pennies, and the missing silver candlestick from the abbey.

"Where did you get these?" he demanded.

Bron's eyes shifted. Durand allowed the silence to stretch out between them until Bron could stand it no longer.

"I brought the abbey a rich tapestry worth many silver pennies," he burst out. "I only took what I was due for such a gift, and probably not even that."

"Theft is still theft," Durand said sternly.

Did the man really think his explanation would save him? thought the reeve. I am not sure he even has the wits to think his actions through. From all that I have heard, it would not seem that he has many wits about him at all.

Bron, curled up on his knees with his nose all but touching the cold stone floor of the cell, sniveled and begged for mercy.

"Mercy is not mine to grant," Durand said. "But it may go a long way toward dulling the sharpness of your master's anger if you tell me the truth. Nothing less will serve."

Bron did not move, but the sniveling and wringing of hands quieted.

"Did you take the tapestry from the abbey?" the reeve said.

"Nay, my lord," the serf said. "On my oath, I never did."

Durand looked skeptical. Hearing no answer, the serf looked up and, seeing the reeve's doubt writ large in his eyes, crawled forward and grasped the hem of Durand's tunic.

"I saw my master ride through the gate of the abbey and knew I had to run away as fast as I could," the man continued desperately. "There was no chance to run all the way to the linen room to take my tapestry."

Durand stepped back, pulling the serf's hand off his tunic. He noted the wording of the reply but was inclined to believe the serf had panicked. There was still the matter of the items in the sackcloth however.

"How then did the candlestick come to be within your pack if you had no time to take the tapestry?" Durand was testing the man, but Bron was too far gone in his panic to notice the piercing gaze of the reeve's eyes.

"I was near by the church when I saw my lord," replied the serf. "I thought to recover some value for a tapestry I now knew was lost, so I ran in and took the candlestick before I escaped the abbey's walls."

"And what about the knife and the pennies," said Durand mercilessly.

"I. . . I found them." Bron's reply was hesitant and unconvincing.

"Bron, let me remind you that your life is forfeit unless your master shows you some portion of mercy," said Durand. "If you wish to save your immortal soul, you will confess the truth."

Durand stood straight and tall, hand stretched out toward the serf. To Bron, it seemed as though the words, deep and sonorous, rang out from the final judgment seat of God.

Terrified, his face once again pointing to the floor, Bron could be heard to mumble something.

"What is that you say?" the reeve said.

"I do not want to cause another to be punished for helping me," said Bron a little more clearly.

If that is so, thought Durand, it may be the first time in his life that this serf has given consideration to any other than himself.

"It is too late to hide what has been done and who else may be involved in any part of this," said Durand. "But I am neither vengeful nor cruel. If someone gave you succor without realizing that you were a fugitive, it will not go too hard on them. That is all I can promise."

He will tell me now, thought Durand. I will have to consider how to respond when he tells me there was more to his meeting with Avraham and Ruth than they revealed.

Bron hesitated only a moment and then raised his head. "It be a Saxon who gave me the knife," he said.

Durand had not expected that.

"Who?" he said sharply.

Friday evening, and the family was enjoying their usual meal of fish with their bread.

"Mother," said Aileen, "the lord de Vere met me at the abbey gates after I had finished work this evening."

Mabel looked up from her trencher. "Aileen is sweet on the Norman lord," she taunted in her shrill, sing-song voice.

Aileen blushed. "I am not," she said angrily. "You do not know what you are talking about."

"Peace," their father said. "You are both too old to behave like small children."

"Yes, father," they both chimed.

Anne smiled to herself. If Aileen is sweet on anyone, I doubt it be the lord de Vere, she thought. But time will tell.

"What was it that the lord de Vere had to say, Aileen?" Anne said.

"He told me that he had just met Durand coming from the abbot's chambers," said Aileen. "Apparently, Bron told Durand that the knife in the sackcloth found in the forest was given to him by Aelred."

"The butcher?" Jude said in surprise.

"Yes," Aileen said. "Bron told Durand that he had

almost run into Aelred just outside the abbey wall when he was running from Sir Roger. The serf was so terrified of capture, even a blind man could have seen that something was badly wrong."

"So Aelred asked Bron what he was doing, I suppose," said Jude.

"Yes, and I think Bron must have given away some of the truth," said Aileen.

"What amazes me is that Aelred helped him," said Jude. "The butcher is not one I would expect to do anything other than walk away. I would not have expected him to volunteer any information to the reeve, but to get involved by aiding a runaway serf? That is a surprise."

Anne was quiet, obviously thinking about something of concern to her.

"What is it, my dear?" said Jude, who knew his wife's moods very well.

"I was remembering conversations that I had in the past few days," said Anne.

"With whom?" Jude asked.

"I think I have mentioned before that I had talked with Arlo and with Aelred," said Anne. "But I did not give you much detail about the actual conversations."

Anne collected her thoughts.

"At the time, I was struck by how strong both men's feelings were," she said. "I did think it was unlike either of them to be so free with their opinions, and thus I felt almost as though their words were a confidence that I should not reveal to others."

Aileen was sitting up straight now, a tingling in her body hinting at something important to come. Has my mother had the solution to this mystery all the time? she thought. How strange if that be the case.

"What was it that the chandler and the butcher had such strong opinions about, mother?" she asked.

So Anne told them about Arlo and his anger at the Normans taking over his family's lands. "It was as though he was seeing the terror of his own ancestors running from the invaders. His family owned land not that far from the manor of Sir Roger, apparently."

"That explains his conduct when Bron was brought back to St. Edmundsbury," said Aileen. "It is probably also why Aelred went over to speak to him afterwards."

"Did he?" asked her mother. "I did not know that."

"Robert saw them together," said Aileen. "He could not hear what was said, but it must have been something about the Normans taking Saxon land."

"I would believe it," Anne said. "Aelred also became very angry at the thought of a Norman taking possession of the tapestry. He talked about Saxons burying their wealth before they fled from the invaders, hoping that one day they would be able to retrieve it."

"Burying their wealth," Aileen repeated.

"What is it, Aileen?" asked her mother. "What did I say?"

"Nothing, mother," Aileen said. "You just made

me realize I may have been thinking about this all wrong."

"Thinking about what all wrong?" Aileen's father said.

"Sir Roger and that man from Bayeux," replied Aileen. "I was looking at Bron and the tapestry and trying to put things together in a certain way, but it was all wrong."

For a moment Aileen sat in silence, thinking furiously.

Mabel giggled. "Your face is all screwed up like a walnut," she said.

Aileen was too deep in thought to notice, but her mother shushed her younger daughter and waited patiently.

"Please may I be excused," Aileen said suddenly. "I really do need to ask Robert a question. It cannot wait."

Jude was a little put out. "It is too late for running around town," he said. "And in any case, what would Robert's parents think if you show up at their door at this hour."

"Please, father," said Aileen.

"Let her go, Jude," said Anne quietly. "If I am not mistaken, our daughter has once again put her finger on the solution to a mystery. I think we should not hinder the course of justice."

Jude looked at Aileen sternly. "Very well," he said. "You may go. But see that you apologize to Master

Palgrave for interrupting their evening, and, if they are unwilling to permit you to talk with Robert at this time, you must promise me you will not press the matter."

"I promise, father," said Aileen.

So it was that Aileen ran all the way to Robert's house, arriving out of breath and a bit disheveled. If Master Palgrave was surprised to see the young woman at his door at such an hour, he managed to hide it very well. Good temperedly, he called to Robert and told him he had a visitor.

"Aileen," said Robert. "I did not expect to see you. Is everything well?" He was obviously worried that there was some dire reason for her visit, and Aileen hastened to put him at his ease.

"Robert," she said. "I am well. Father gave me permission to come when I told him that it was urgent that I ask you a very important question."

Robert was not as skilled at hiding his emotions as was his father. His eyebrows danced above his eyes and his eyes opened wide. "A question?" he said. "Now?"

"Yes," Aileen said. "I should have asked for more details when you first mentioned this, but it only occurred to me this evening that it was mayhap the last clue we need to solve this mystery."

"Ask your question," Robert said eagerly.

She has done it again, he thought to himself. She has solved the puzzle. But Aileen seems to think that I hold the key. A pity it is that I did not realize that.

In the second before Aileen asked what she needed to know, a vision flashed through Robert's mind of William de Vere slapping him on the back and telling him how brilliant he was while Aileen held his hand, admiration shimmering in her eyes.

CHAPTER TWENTY-NINE

Here have fallen dead Leofwine and Gyrth, brothers of King Harold and here English and French fell at the same time in battle

"YOUR PARDON FOR INTERRUPTING your studies, father abbot," said Durand from the doorway.

"I know you never disturb me without good cause," responded the abbot, waving Durand into the room.

Abbot Samson was slightly surprised to see Aileen following the reeve. "I perceive that there have been developments," he said dryly.

Durand would have smiled had he not been so intent on his errand. "Father abbot," he said. "I have learned much in the last twenty-four hours, much of it from Aileen here. I believe I know who took the tapestry from your abbey."

"That is excellent news, master reeve," said the abbot.

"Yes, father," said Durand. "However, there is little evidence to prove the case."

The reeve hesitated a moment before going on.

"In speaking to Mistress Aileen, we have come up with an idea that we believe may bring the thief out into the open."

"And you need my help to put this idea into motion." This time, the abbot could not restrain the smile that came to his lips.

"We do, father," said Durand.

"What is it that you wish me to do?" asked the abbot.

"Tomorrow is Sunday," the reeve said. "We did think that mayhap it would be a good time to have a celebration during the mass for the return of the tapestry."

The abbot's brow furrowed. "But the tapestry has not been returned."

"No, it has not," Durand said. "But if Mistress Aileen's idea works, then I believe the thief will make himself known."

"I see," said the abbot. "Pray tell me more."

Durand turned to Aileen. "Yours was the initial plan. You should be the one to tell the abbot about it."

Aileen was surprised to be asked but moved forward willingly enough. "Father abbot," she said. "We did wonder if you would agree to a solemn play being performed during the mass tomorrow morning.

We could send word to all within the Liberty and mayhap those in hamlets close by, letting them know there will be a play of celebration and inviting all who will to come."

The abbot thought about it for a moment. "I would that I could approve this plan," he said. "It has the air of creativity I expect from our young investigator. But I cannot hold a sacred service based on a lie."

Aileen had been so excited about the idea that she could not fail to be disappointed by the abbot's response. Durand, however, had been afraid the abbot would be of this opinion and had an alternative plan ready to present.

"Father abbot," he said. "I do believe there is another way in which this scheme could be put into effect without the risk of any falsehood or disrespect to our God."

Abbot Samson inclined his head as indication that Durand should continue.

"Mayhap it would be possible to send word that the play will be performed after the conclusion of the mass," he said. "We could let it be known that the Sabbath was chosen as being the perfect time to ask our Lord to aid us in discovering the whereabouts of the tapestry. We can also let it be known that the actors intend to offer up prayers of thanksgiving for our Lord's intervention in its safe return."

The abbot thought about it for a moment while Aileen and Durand waited in respectful silence.

"I see no problem with this plan," Abbot Samson

said eventually. "No untruth would be told, and thus no commandment would be broken."

Aileen was impressed by Durand's quick response to the abbot's refusal to go along with their plan. I have always known he was a good ally to have, she thought. Every time we have had need of him, he has proven to be so.

The abbot, in spite of his agreement to follow their plan, was still unsure.

"Forgive my doubts," he said to the pair. "I am sure you have thought this through, but I can think of no play I have seen that would be likely to achieve the result you hope for. More than that, how can you put together the actors and have them ready to perform in only one day?"

Durand smiled. "Father abbot," he said. "Your words mirror my own when Mistress Aileen put the scheme to me last night. I will let her respond to your question."

Once again, Aileen stepped forward. "Father abbot," she said, "I have seen but one or two plays in my life, and those were performed on feast days. As you say, none of those seemed to be fitting for our purpose. Thus I have worked with my friends to prepare a simple play of our own."

The abbot's eyebrows rose. "You have written a play?"

Aileen blushed. "It contains not many words, and it is not long," she said, not wishing to appear prideful.

"Robert and Avraham and Ruth and I will play the

parts, and I believe we can be ready by tomorrow morning. If we have need of more players, there will not be much for them to learn."

"Avraham and Ruth," mused the abbot. "So your friends from Fornham are a part of this as well?"

Oh dear, thought Aileen. Surely such a simple thing will not be the downfall of my friends. I would never forgive myself if such a thing should happen.

There has always been the risk of discovery for the young Jews, Durand thought. I am certain sure all along they have known more than they have revealed to me.

"Father abbot," said the reeve, "You will remember that Isaac of Cordoba was of assistance to us in the past. It is our hope that Aileen's friends will be of help once again."

Abbot Samson looked long and hard at the pair before him. "I expect it would be hard to find sufficient players before tomorrow," he said.

Aileen let out the breath she had not realized she was holding.

"Thank you, father abbot," she said sincerely.

"Master reeve," said the abbot, "you make an excellent case for this unusual course of action. While I admit to some doubts as to whether it will prove successful in drawing out the thief, I am willing to permit the performance of this play for the sake of the soul of whoever it was who stole the tapestry. You may proceed."

"Mistress Aileen, there are other matters that I

have need of discussing with the abbot," said the reeve. "If you will forgive me, I will not accompany you from the abbey."

Throwing a grateful glance at Durand, Aileen curtseyed to the abbot and made her farewells.

Fairly skipping across the courtyard, Aileen started making plans for everything that needed to be done before the morrow. First of all, she thought, I must tell Robert that the abbot has given us permission to move forward with the play. Then I will have to ask mother for something that can take the place of the tapestry.

Arriving at the goldsmith's shop, Aileen found Robert spending his Saturday morning practicing his scrollwork. As expected, he was both excited and nervous when Aileen told him the news.

"Shall we go to Fornham now to tell Avi and Ruth?" he asked.

"We should not disturb their Sabbath," Aileen responded. "I suggested we spend the afternoon making all necessary arrangements and then take the road to Fornham after dusk. I am sure mother and father will not worry if I am with you at that time."

"You know we will have to ask permission of Ruth's father if Avi and Ruth are to take part in our little play," said Robert.

"Yes, I know," said Aileen. "It would be hard for us to carry out the plan without the two of them, but I realize Isaac of Cordoba might be unwilling to go along with it."

She paused for a moment.

"Without Ruth's father, we might never have solved the mystery of who stole the holy relic," she said. "I do believe that he will not let us down now."

CHAPTER THIRTY

*Here Bishop Odo, holding a club, gave strength to
the boys*

I T SEEMED THAT ALL THE PEOPLE OF THE
Liberty flocked to the abbey church that Sunday
morning. Before the processional, there was a lot
of whispering, everyone being curious about what had
happened. Many had heard a rumor that the tapestry
had been recovered, although they had to admit that
such a result had not been a part of the announcement
of the play.

Once the mass had been said and the service was
over, there was none of the usual movement toward
the door. Indeed, more people began to flood in until
there was scarce room to stand. Some moved into the
Lady Chapel, and there were even some people occu-
pying the family vaults along the side of the church.

Aileen's family stood with Robert's. Jude and

Anne had saved some room, knowing that John Palgrave and his family would want to come to see the play after the service at their church. Aileen had had the foresight to tell Robert where her parents usually stood, otherwise the Palgrave's would never have been able to see through the throng to spot Jude.

"God save you," John Palgrave said in greeting.

"Good morrow to you too,' responded Jude.

Anne and Jane Palgrave gathered their smaller children around them and softly talked about the play.

"Aileen and Robert have high hopes for this drama," said Jane. "I worry lest they be disappointed."

"I share your concern," said Anne. "Yet I am confident in their belief, and I trust that the good Lord will grant them success."

Anne might have expressed confidence, but her shadowed eyes showed her anxiety. Once again, Aileen had involved herself in the business of more experienced adults and brought her friends along with her. Now that she is grown into a woman, Anne thought to herself, she must cast aside childish notions. What will her father say if she does not change her ways soon?

Anne's thoughts moved on to visualize the discussion that might take place if her husband felt it necessary to have a talk to Aileen about her responsibilities as an adult. In spite of herself, Anne's lips twitched as she envisioned that occasion.

Across the church, Lanfranc and Roger, honored guests of the abbey as they were, stood near the front of the church, close by the chancel. They gazed across the throng of people gathering inside the church, but neither man had a word to say to the other.

Aileen, nervously watching for all her players to arrive, stood outside the sanctuary door. William was nowhere to be seen, but she had spotted Ruth's father outside the abbey walls earlier. She had moved forward to greet him, but he put his finger to his lips and said softly that he was just there to make sure his child was safe.

"I do not wish my presence to be noted," he said, and Aileen had nodded and then made her way inside.

The babble of voices both inside and outside the church had risen to such a pitch that it was hard to discern any distinct words. Tradesmen, craftsman, and farmers all stood together in the body of the church, jostling for position so that they would be able to see the play. Children, stuck behind adults blocking their way, were jumping up and down trying to see anything.

Mistress Oliver, who stood next to Mistress Palmer as close to the front of the church as possible, could scarce control her desire to guess who might be behind the theft. Mistress Palmer was a quiet woman who rarely spoke and had the hunched back of someone who constantly bent over tables in poor light in order to do her work. She merely nodded her head at the stream of words uttered by the garrulous tavern-keeper's wife.

Arlo was almost hidden from view, standing as he

was in the middle of the crowd. He looked as sour as ever and talked to no one.

Aelred the butcher came as well, his face pale with worry. As he had approached the door to the church, he had seen Durand standing there and was unable to repress the shiver that ran through him. Durand slightly shook his head at the man and gestured for him to enter. Aelred scuttled through the door into the dark echoing church, relieved not to have been taken into custody.

Anne saw him standing not far from her, fidgeting and avoiding the eyes of any who might look at him. If Aileen has the right of it, thought Anne, he must be worried that he will be thought to have aided a fugitive and be made to suffer the consequences.

Soon all the players were gathered together in the sanctuary for a blessing from the abbot. Raising his hand in the sign of the cross, the abbot prayed over them.

"May the grace of God be with you," he said. "May He guide you in your endeavor and may He work within the heart of the evildoer to save his very soul."

"Amen," was heard in unison from those who knelt in front of Samson.

A hush came over the crowd of people as the celebrants of the mass walked back into the body of the church from the sanctuary.

Waiting for the last of the noise to die down, the priest welcomed all to this mysterious drama that was to be offered up to the Lord. He gestured to the makeshift stage that had been set up to his right.

"Let the play begin," he intoned. Anne smiled at the dramatic way in which the parish priest spoke. The atmosphere of anticipation was contagious.

The curtain hung at the front of the stage was drawn aside to display a tableau. A cloth painted as a stone wall with turrets above, which many recognized as being from the last play to have been presented, hung at the back behind two men holding spears and with helms on their heads.

The helmets seemed a little large, and Anne smiled as she recognized Robert as one of the men. Then, with a shock, she realized that the other guard must be Avraham. She cast her eyes around to see if anyone else had realized a Jew was playing a part in a Christian miracle play, but no one seemed to be paying any attention to the man whose helm obscured his face.

Before the two young men lay a chest covered by a rich cloth. The cloth was in fact a small tapestry with gold threads running through it that hung in the abbot's chambers, but, since almost no one present had ever stood within that room, the congregation as a whole did not know it for what it was.

Taking in the scene and seeing the light of candles burning close by glinting off the tapestry, most of the audience initially believed the tapestry to be the one taken from the abbey. A gasp went around the church before they realized that this fabric looked too new to be the missing treasure.

The people turned their attention back to the stage and saw that there was a man kneeling in front of the chest, hands reaching out to it. The man was William de Vere. He was having a hard time concealing a smile, but probably there were few in the congregation who knew him well enough to realize that.

Looking around surreptitiously William took the cloth off the chest, folded it, and put it inside his jerkin. Then he opened the chest and reached in, pulling out some gold plates and a goblet.

Behind the scenes came a voice, deep and commanding: "He who disobeys the word of the Lord and all those who permit the sin shall suffer the same punishment."

With a shock, the audience realized that the voice was that of the abbot.

The two guards stepped forward, spears pointed at the kneeling man. William stood up, still holding the plates, and looked around as though seeking the source of the voice.

"Achan," said the voice, "you have turned from the order I gave Joshua before the walls of Jericho fell. The gold and fine cloth were Mine by divine right and you have made it profane."

A sigh went round the audience. All present knew the story of Achan's disobedience, and they could sense what was to come.

For a moment after the condemning words, William thoroughly incorporated the role he was playing, knees shaking, eyes wide and mouth hanging open in abject terror. He was hardly even aware of the intense attention of the congregation.

Achan stood up straight, and his voice hardened. "But we conquered the city. We should be rewarded," he said.

The sound of thunder came from behind the scenes, and two young women ran forward from the side of the stage, falling to their knees and taking hold of Achan's hands. The two actors were Aileen and Ruth.

"Father, please," said Aileen. "Repent of your sins lest we all die."

But Achan was not to be turned. He snatched his hands out of those of the two weeping women and turned toward the audience.

"Is it not so?" he cajoled. "We have conquered these miserable people and have the right to take their treasures. Who among you can doubt that?"

There was a murmuring among the congregation.

Achan turned back to the women. "Can you doubt that?" he demanded of them.

Aileen rose and stepped softly to him, again taking his hand.

"Our God is mighty," she said. "Your sin will condemn us all to eternal perdition. Yet, if you beg for mercy and repent of your actions, we may yet escape that dread punishment."

Achan snorted and turned back to the audience. "We crossed the sea and spent many years in the desert," he said. "We have fought bravely and won the victory."

Shaking off Aileen's hand and striding to the front of the stage, Achan pulled the cloth out of his jerkin and held it aloft. "The spoils of war are ours!" he shouted.

"No, they are not," a voice from the spectators in the body of the church shouted in return. "Foul murderers and usurpers have no right to take what is not theirs."

CHAPTER THIRTY-ONE

Here the French are fighting and have killed those who
were with Harold

A S THE ECHOES OF THE
CONDEMNATION died away, people
around the church were craning their necks
to see who it was who had interrupted the fascinating
drama playing out before them. Durand, who had
moved slowly toward the front of the church during
the play, also peered through the throng to try and
identify who it was who had spoken. William stopped
in his tracks and stared into the crowd as the abbot and
the other players came out from behind the stage.

Gradually, the throng parted as a path appeared
down the center of the nave. Down the avenue strode
Arlo, face like thunder and fists clenched. Almost it
seemed as though there was no one within the walls
beside the chandler and the actors on the stage, so
focused was Arlo's gaze.

"You are a Norman yourself," Arlo said to William disgustedly. "From your mouth I could expect nothing more."

Turning to the abbot, he continued: "But that you, the spiritual leader of all within the Liberty, and all you who know me and talk with me every day should let such a tale be told within the walls of our great abbey is more than I can bear."

"The tale of Achan is told in the Bible," said the abbot gently. "It is a warning to us all that we should not covet that which is not ours and that God's commandments are to be obeyed, lest we fall so far from grace that we cannot return."

"But that is the point," said Arlo fiercely. "The invaders took all that we cared about and worked so hard to keep. They threw us off our lands and made of us beggars. Where was God then?"

"Be still, my son," commanded the abbot. "You risk the wrath of God in the same way as did Achan. God is not to be trifled with. He is a fierce and wrathful God and will surely punish evildoers."

Ruth, standing quietly in the background, looked at the abbot in surprise. He had always seemed to be a gentle man to her, in many ways much like her father. Aileen was always talking about her God as loving, but in this moment, Ruth saw a side of the abbot and heard about a different side of the Christian God. This God sounded more like the God of the Hebrew Bible, not the Christian testament of the Galilean and his followers.

Arlo was standing before the abbot by this time, fists clenched in red bunches matching the shade of his face. Durand came up to stand by the side of Abbot Samson.

Not a sound disturbed the silence of the church. Dust motes danced in the colored rays of the sun that worked their way through the stained glass of the windows.

The abbot drew a deep breath.

"My son," he said, "it is long years since our country came under the rule of the Conqueror. Time enough to heal the wounds of loss and sorrow. You cannot allow your soul to be destroyed by anger and hatred. God has not forsaken us, nor will He do so in times to come."

"I say again," hissed Arlo, "where was God when my grandfather's father was thrown off his land? What sin had Aelred's ancestors committed to be beggared by a man who had sworn to the Confessor that he would not dispossess our people?"

The chandler waved his hand toward the congregation who stood still as statues, held in thrall by the real-life drama before them.

"Christians we are now," the chandler said. "Christians we were then. Yet our prayers went unanswered and many good men and women died."

"No prayers go unanswered," said the abbot sharply. "The answer may not be what we wish to hear, but God's will be done. His knowledge far outstrips ours."

Samson had been speaking directly to Arlo, but now he turned and faced the congregation. His voice rose to a passionate plea.

"While we may not understand why He allows suffering, we can only follow Him and remember that God Himself did not forbear to feel the pain of suffering. For you and I He bore the weight of our sin, dying a brutal death."

Still his audience remained unmoving, not a sound to be heard beyond that of the skittering of mice.

"We are all sinners who deserve no better," the abbot continued earnestly. "Yet, by His grace and mercy, He has spared us and offered us life eternal."

"That may be," said Arlo angrily. "But just as what was justly ours was taken from us, why should we not be given grace to reclaim a part of it from those who neither knew nor cared for its existence?"

A shift in the mood of the congregation was becoming apparent in a low murmur of voices. Best to bring this to a close, thought Durand, before the townsfolk express their sympathy with Arlo's point of view. There is enough strife between abbey and town over taxes and rights without this making it worse.

Stepping forward, Durand faced the Saxon. Not unkindly he said, "Where is it, Master Arlo?"

The murmuring stopped. The players standing at the front of the stage could see surprise written all over the faces of those who stood within the glow of the candles near them.

Arlo turned to look at the reeve. Slowly, the color

faded from his face, and his fists unclenched, the sharp stains from his fingers showing blanched white on his palms.

"You set a trap for me," Arlo said, sighing. The reeve gave no answer.

For a moment, Arlo did not move, his head drooping in defeat. Then he straightened his shoulders and raised his head to look at the reeve.

As he opened his mouth to speak, a cry rang out from the dim church. "Nay," said the voice. "The chandler speaks truth. Why should this stranger, who never worked for the prize nor cared for the makers, take possession of it? It belongs to he who buried it or his descendants."

Turning and pointing straight at Sir Roger, who had remained quiet and unnoticed by most standing outside the light cast by the dying candles, Aelred shouted words of triumph for all within the church to hear.

"You claim the tapestry by right, but I say that the ancient law of treasure trove gives that right to the heirs of he who buried it."

A stunned silence greeted the butcher's announcement. Sir Roger's expression as he gazed at Aelred was composed of pity and surprise, Lanfranc's face ran the gamut of consternation, contempt, and finally calculation. The abbot and the players stared at Aelred for a moment and then turned to Durand, waiting for him to speak.

Arlo looked as shocked as everyone else, but in his

eyes awoke hope. Mayhap there will be justice in some measure after all, he thought.

Durand stepped toward the butcher, but before he could speak, the cleric from Bayeux stepped forward. Pride and victory seemed equally present in his stance and visage.

"I am not of this land," he said. "But I am content to be held to its laws as, I would expect, would Sir Roger FitzGilbert." He turned to look at the knight and smiled.

Robert, standing where he could see the face of the cleric, thought that the man's smiling face resembled that of a fox more than anything else. He makes me want to shiver, Robert said to himself. He is not a man I would trust.

Sir Roger smiled in his turn, but even his usually amiable expression was more calculated than usual.

Lanfranc, seeing this, faltered a moment before turning to the abbot. "Father abbot," he said, "yours is the word of law in this Liberty. I submit before you this claim to the tapestry found buried in land owned by this knight. I claim before this congregation the right to take ownership of a tapestry that was buried by order of the Bishop of Bayeux many long years ago. It rightfully belongs to the cathedral of Bayeux where can be found the entire remaining work commissioned by that same man, Bishop Odo of Bayeux."

A rumble of opposition rose from the mass of people in the church. Even more than their aversion to the idea of the embroidery being claimed by the

Norman knight did the good folk of St. Edmundsbury find the idea of the arrogant cleric taking possession of it distasteful.

Aelred became so red in the face that Aileen was concerned Isaac of Cordoba's skills would be called for. Arlo stared at the cleric, mouth agape and eyes filled with hatred.

The reeve stepped forward and held his hand high, calling in a loud voice for silence.

Most of those who were grumbling obeyed his command out of respect for a reeve that all there knew to be a fair and honest man, a man of their town.

"Father abbot," Durand said. "It is time, I believe, to bring this matter to a conclusion."

"I agree," said the abbot gravely. "Pray continue."

Durand turned back to those gathered in the church. "Be at peace," he said. "You know that I will see that all is done according to the will of our God and the law of this land."

Looking at the crowd, Durand saw that he was reaching the majority of them. I need to make sure there is no argument or, save God, rioting. I must tread carefully in what I say and do, he thought to himself.

"Will you now trust me to do what is right?" he said in a commanding voice.

There was some murmuring, but then the people fell silent. "We will," could be heard from a few places around the church.

Durand, satisfied, turned to Lanfranc. "Brother," he said. "you have stated that you are willing to abide by the law of England in this regard. Do you still maintain that confession?"

"I do." Lanfranc's words were solemn, but his face spoke of triumph.

"Then let me tell you what the law of treasure trove is in England," said Durand.

Raising his voice so that he could be heard from the corners of the church, Durand continued.

"It is true that the descendants of anyone who has hidden their property from others may claim that treasure once it is found. But our law defines treasure in such a way that a tapestry cannot be considered such property. To be claimed under our law, treasure must be of silver and gold. This embroidery cannot be claimed by the cathedral of Bayeux."

A cheer went up all around the church. Sir Roger looked thoughtful, the abbot inscrutable, and the players amazed.

Lanfranc, his expression thunderous, turned to the abbot and demanded of him whether this was truth.

"It is, my son," said the abbot mildly. "The tapestry is not yours to claim, even if it be a part of that great commission."

The cleric, unwilling to accept defeat, and yet aware that he had now shown his hand and lost, cast a venomous glance around and then stalked out of the church.

Aelred and Arlo looked at each other. It was a bitter pill to swallow that Aelred's clever strategy had failed, but they both knew now that the blow was fatal to their cause. Aelred faded back into the crowd, and Arlo stood there, still and miserable.

Durand turned back to the chandler. "I say again," he said, "where is the tapestry?"

After a moment, Arlo said so softly that he could be heard only by those standing close by: "It is at the bottom of the chest in my sleeping chamber."

Aileen and her friends exchanged glances. She was right, of course, said Robert to himself. She always is.

CHAPTER THIRTY-TWO

Here King Harold is slain and the English have turned in flight

"I understand why he did it," Ruth said as the group of five sat in the middle of a clearing in the forest the next evening. "I do not understand how he did it though."

"I think I may be able to guess," said Aileen to the surprise of none of her friends. "But I believe we may be able to hear precisely what happened from one who has been told by Sir Roger FitzGilbert in person. Is that not so, sir?"

William, who had been thrilled to be asked to join the quartet that evening, cleared his throat in embarrassment at having four pairs of eyes trained on him but spoke up happily enough.

"That is so," he said. "Sir Roger and I sat with the abbot last night and shared mulled wine. The abbot was as curious as I to know what happened after everyone left the church and the reeve took the chandler to recover the tapestry."

"Did Sir Roger then go with the reeve?" asked Robert.

"Yes," said William. "The tapestry was, after all, his to claim. Arlo did not seem eager to permit a Norman in his house, but there was little he could so about it so Roger went with them to open the chest in which Arlo had said the tapestry was to be found."

"And was it there?" Ruth asked.

"It was," said William. "It had been folded neatly and lain in the bottom of the chest. Your mother will be glad to know that, beyond a crease or two, there is no further damage to be seen."

"She will be very glad to hear that," said Aileen. "She has been waiting for the abbot to let her know she can resume work on the tapestry. When she heard nothing today, she became concerned that the work was either not where Arlo had said it was or that it was so badly damaged there was nothing that could be done to save it,"

"I am sure the abbot will be sending for her soon," said William.

"It will be good to relieve her anxiety," said Aileen. "Thank you."

William smiled at her and then, once again clearing his throat, picked up his tale. "Once the tapestry was safely in Durand's hands, he asked the chandler how it came about that he was able to take it from the abbey."

"That is what we all want to know," said Robert.

"The problem of timing has been one of our greatest concerns."

Aileen, Ruth, and Avraham all murmured their agreement. William took pity on them all.

"Well," he said, smiling, "it seems that Bron had come across Arlo during his first few days in St. Edmundsbury. It is apparent even to me that Arlo is not naturally a trusting kind of man."

"That is putting it mildly," Robert said. The others frowned at him.

"According to Sir Roger," said William, "the chandler was suspicious of Bron's claim to be a journeyman. He thought he had more the look of a rather unsuccessful pickpocket."

This time, Robert could not restrain his laughter, and the others could not stop themselves from joining in.

"Bron told Arlo about the cloth," William went on once the laughter had subsided. "Customers of the chandler also talked to him about the cloth and the man who had brought it to the Liberty. Arlo is no man's fool, and he began to think that Bron was what he in fact turned out to be, an escaped serf who had stolen the chest from his lord's land."

"Is that when he decided he was going to take the tapestry?" asked Ruth.

"Not quite," said William. "Arlo sympathized with Bron's situation to some extent but not to the point where he was going to actively help him."

"That does not surprise me," said Robert. "I do

not think he is the kind of man who would go out of his way to help another if it might mean getting into trouble himself."

"I doubt he would have done anything had not Sir Roger arrived," said Aileen.

"You are exactly right," said William approvingly. "Arlo told Durand that it was only when he realized that Bron's lord had arrived that he determined the cloth would not fall into Norman hands."

"But did he have time to steal the cloth between the time Sir Roger arrived and when they found it missing?" Ruth was confused.

"Remember, Ruth," said Aileen. "We thought at first that Sir Roger arrived on Wednesday, the day the tapestry was taken and Bron ran away. In fact, he had first arrived a day earlier, the day of the south gate market."

"That is so," agreed William. "And Arlo saw him on that Tuesday. Sir Roger walked through the streets asking questions, and the chandler was one of those he asked about Bron."

"So that was when Arlo not only knew for sure that Bron was a runaway serf but that the tapestry was going to be taken back to his estate by Sir Roger," Robert said eagerly.

"Yes," said William. "And that was when he decided upon quick action."

The others said nothing, but their faces spoke of how much they wanted to hear what happened next.

"Arlo knew that the tapestry was in the linen room

of the abbey," William said. "Late Tuesday afternoon, Arlo went to the abbey with candles for the guest hall."

"It was fortunate for Arlo that Brother Jocelyn had need of more candles at that time," said Aileen.

"It would appear that the good brother had not expected Arlo to bring him any candles that day, but he was glad of the unexpected bounty," William said.

"So that was his excuse for being within the abbey walls that day, should anyone ask," Aileen said.

"Yes," said William. "He told the reeve that, almost as soon as he had given the candles to the Guest Master, he saw Bron running for the gate out to the abbey vineyard. He realized that Sir Roger must be close by and understood well that he had little time to do anything about the tapestry."

"He is a man of quicker thought than I realized," said Avraham.

"I agree with you," William said. "He took great risk, but he seems to have been very calm and careful in his actions."

"So what did he do?" Ruth wished that William would approach his storytelling with greater urgency.

"Arlo knew that the workers in the linen room would have finished their day's labors by that time," said the young lord. "He strolled over to the linen room, wrapped up the cloth in the lining of his basket, and sauntered out of the courtyard gate."

"That took more nerve than I would have given Arlo credit for," Robert said.

But what was he going to do with the tapestry? Aileen asked herself.

"What was he going to do with the tapestry?" Robert asked. Aileen looked at him, a little startled at his seeming ability to read her thoughts.

"Sir Roger apparently asked the chandler that same question," said William. "Arlo told him reluctantly that, had Bron returned to St. Edmundsbury without being captured, he would have returned the tapestry to him. He added that he would never have allowed it to fall into the hands of Sir Roger, whatever happened."

"How did Sir Roger react to that?" Avraham asked.

"Quietly," said William. "I really do admire that man. He is, I think, a benevolent lord. There are many who would choose him as a master over those they have."

William seemed to be lost in thoughts of his own, so Aileen gently prompted him to answer Avraham's question.

"He told Arlo that, while he could not agree with the chandler's opinions regarding Normans, and certainly could not countenance his taking the tapestry, he did know how hard it was to let go of the anger of generations."

"That was an interesting statement," said Aileen. "I wonder why he put it that way?"

"I do not know," said William. "I did not ask him to explain."

"I would not have done so either," Aileen said. "It would have seemed rude."

William smiled. "Just as I thought," he said.

"What is going to happen to the chandler?" asked Ruth.

"I can answer that," said Aileen, surprising her friends. "I met Durand in the street this morning," she explained. "I asked him that very question, and he told me that Sir Roger had asked him not to pursue the chandler in court. He said the tapestry had been returned and that, in his opinion, the shame the chandler had suffered in public, exposed as he was as a vengeful liar, was sufficient punishment."

"A most unusual lord," William murmured.

"I think it was a good and generous decision," said Aileen. "I do not believe that Arlo is really a wicked man. He became caught up in his own anger and could not see that it was driving him in a direction he would not usually go."

"And the tapestry?" asked Robert. "Did Durand tell you also what is to become of that, once your good mother has completed her repairs?"

"Sir Roger has gifted it to the abbey," said Aileen. "He believes that the work has caused enough trouble, and he chooses not to hang it in any place where it would act as a reminder to some disgruntled servant of the attraction of running away."

"A man of good sense as well," William said under his breath.

"I am certain Abbot Samson is very pleased with that decision," said Robert.

"Durand smiled when I said the same thing," said Aileen. "It was nothing that he actually said, but I got the impression that quite possibly the abbot was undisturbed by the thought that Brother Lanfranc would not be taking the tapestry with him back to Bayeux."

The group laughed at the delicate way in which Aileen put the common opinion of the French cleric.

Of a sudden, Ruth became pensive.

"I wonder what will happen to that foolish serf," she said. "Sir Roger may be an unusual lord, but I doubt he will be as generous with Bron as he was with the tapestry."

Aileen reached over and took her hand. "Ruth, do not distress yourself," she said. "I asked Durand if he knew what Sir Roger's decision was about the punishment that Bron must bear. He said his curiosity had got the better of him and that he had asked the knight that very question."

"And what did he say?" Robert asked.

"Sir Roger said that for all the trouble Bron has caused he justly fears being put to death," said Aileen, and then put her hand up as Ruth began to say something. "But apparently the knight sees little reason to reduce his workforce by taking such an action, particularly as the man's brother is such a good and faithful worker. Sir Roger told Durand that he believed a lesser punishment would ensure the good will of his workers, all of whom know Bron's nature well. Putting the serf to death would more likely have the opposite effect."

"I am glad," said Ruth.

"So what is Sir Roger going to do with Bron?" asked Robert. "Will he cut off one of Bron's hands as a warning to others?"

"It seems not," said Aileen. "Sir Roger told Durand he will most likely have the man flogged and pilloried. He will also let Bron know that he will never be granted any part of Sir Roger's land to work, even should his brother die before Bron and leave no heir."

"A rare lord indeed," said William. "I think I would like to meet him again."

Twilight was setting in when Avraham and Ruth said they must return to their homes. The group stood up and said their farewells, waving to Ruth and Avi as they went on their way.

William turned to Robert and Aileen and gave them a sweeping bow. "I am so very glad I came to visit you," he said. "You made such a difference in my life when first we met, and I have wanted to come and thank you in person for some time."

Robert felt abashed. It was wrong of me to react to the man as I did, he thought.

Stepping forward, he slapped the young lord on the shoulder and said, "We are very glad you came. Mayhap you will be able to return again one day."

Aileen was not sure whether Robert or William was the more surprised at the exuberant response of the goldsmith's apprentice, but she was glad to see them friends.

"We have been honored to have you share some time with us, sir. . . William," she said.

"Mayhap I will be able to return one day," said William. "And mayhap I will be able to share another adventure with you when I do!"

Saying their farewells, William set off for the abbey guest hall, leaving Robert and Aileen to wend their way back to their homes.

"Aileen," said Robert as they walked. "Remember when you came to my house the other night late?"

"Yes," said Aileen. "I think your parents were a little surprised to see me then. I know my parents were quite unwilling to give me permission to come."

Robert smiled. "It was unusual," he said. "But I wanted to ask you about why it was important that you ask me your question that night. It seemed like such a small detail, but I could tell from your expression that it was crucial to your solution to the puzzle."

"It was, Robert," said Aileen. "It was only that night that I realized I had been thinking about the disappearance of the tapestry in the wrong way."

"I do not see how," Robert said, sounding rather frustrated.

Aileen turned to her friend and took his hand. "Without you, I would never have worked out the puzzle," she said. "Remember, you had told us some days ago about meeting a man days before the disappearance of the tapestry. You decided later that the man was Bron, and I asked you to tell me more about the conversation you had with him?"

"Yes," said Robert. "You asked me if Bron had given me the names of any of the people in the town who had refused to help him. I told you he did not say exactly but that he had mentioned Arlo, Mistress Oliver, and Aelred as people he had met."

"Exactly," said Aileen as though that explained everything.

"But how did that help you solve the puzzle?"

"I knew something of mother's conversations with the people in the town," said Aileen. "She talked about it in the evenings. But it was not until Friday night that she told us in detail about what Arlo and Aelred had said to her."

"I still do not understand," said Robert, his crinkled face demonstrating the truth of his statement.

"We had talked a lot about those likely to have stolen the tapestry, if it were not Bron," she went on. "We even said that some of the people of the town hated the Normans."

"Yes?" Robert's tone rose in query.

"We never thought of the possibility of the thief being someone in the town who hated the Normans most particularly for what they had done to his family and who might also have met Bron and guessed he was a runaway serf."

The light came on in Robert's eyes.

"I see," he said in delight. "We thought of all sorts of reasons for a stranger like Lanfranc or Bron, or even

Sir Roger, to take the tapestry. We did not think there was a strong enough reason for one of our own to take it."

"Exactly," Aileen said approvingly. "When mother told us more about Arlo's strong feelings and family history, I remembered what you had said. When you then told me that Bron had mentioned Arlo by name, I knew we had been thinking about the theft from the linen room in entirely the wrong way."

"Aileen, you are a wonder," said Robert.

Aileen blushed. She is even more pretty when she blushes like that, thought Robert, as the two of them said goodbye and ran towards their homes.

"Robert," called out John Palgrave as he entered his house. "I am glad you are home."

"Is something wrong, father?" Robert asked, the bubble of his happiness bursting in a moment.

"No, son, not at all," said his father. "We have received a handsome commission from Sir Roger Fitz-Gilbert. He told me he admires our work and that he would like us to design a ring he means to give to his betrothed."

"That is wonderful, father," said Robert, his joy returning just as quickly as it had fled.

Robert's exhilaration and satisfaction was mirrored by Aileen as she returned home.

"Aileen," called out her mother as she entered her house. "I am glad you are home."

"Mother, is all well?" responded her daughter.

"Yes, very well," said Anne. "The abbot sent word this afternoon that I am to return to my work on the tapestry tomorrow. Apparently, Sir Roger has gifted it to the abbey, and Abbot Samson means to hang it in the abbey church. He says it will hang there until the abbey is no more."

"Surely that will be when the Lord returns," said Aileen. "I cannot imagine the abbey falling before that."

"I know," said Anne, happy that her ancestor's work would be a permanent part of life in St. Edmundsbury. "We are indeed truly blessed."

Anne-Marie Amiel joined the Royal Navy straight from high school, after which she attended law school. In addition to her career in England, she has worked in France and as an attorney in several U.S. states.

In the course of her career, Ms. Amiel has won short-story competitions, been featured in several legal publications and has written for *Cobblestone* magazine and *Devotions for the Public Servant.* In her spare time, Ms. Amiel writes music and practices martial arts. Just like any self-respecting English woman, she also loves to drink hot tea and knit!

ALSO BY
ANNE-MARIE AMIEL

The St. Edmunsbury Mysteries Series

Crusader's Way (Book 1)

Penitent's Sword (Book 2)

Interconnected Trivia Book:

Road Trip Trivia: High Middle Ages